In the magic-laden levels of the keep...

Practor pulled aside a curtain to reveal a pile of old bones. "Whoever this was didn't find what he was looking for." He kicked at the pile.

Several of the bones went flying, bouncing off the wall. The single skull rolled over a few times, steadied itself, rose slowly into the air and stared straight back at Practor. He quickly drew his sword.

Maryld moved to stand next to him. "It's a litch," she told him. "A guard, a watch-thing."

"Guard for what?" Practor wondered. Maryld knelt and searched the bones which Practor's kick had failed to disturb. Sure enough, buried within the bone pile was a book bound in cream vellum.

"Maybe it's only designed to scare," Practor murmured as the skull watched his movements with empty sockets. "Maybe it's harmless."

His fingers were inches from the book when the empty eyes of the skull flared...

Published by
WARNER BOOKS

SHADOWKEEP™

ALAN DEAN FOSTER

WARNER BOOKS

A Warner Communications Company

Here's one for David Hagin,
who's likely to be designing the hardware
for some different fantasies one of these days.

SHADOWKEEP

Chapter I

Sasubree was the largest and most powerful city on the High Plains, alive with merchants and traders, farmers come in from far and near to market their produce, craftsmen, wandering soldiers-of-fortune, and all manner of adventurers of the several intelligent species. It was a thriving, impressive community. Exactly the kind of place one would go to find an impressive hero.

Locating one such individual was the reason for the stranger's visit to Sasubree. As his mount carried him down the narrow avenue back of the marketplace, the stranger knew he was the subject of many sideways stares from citizens and visitors alike. It did not bother him. He was used to being the focus of attention.

Or perhaps the curious who eyed his passage were merely intrigued by his peculiar mount. It was only a mule, though such a mule as had never been seen before in Sasubree. Its hindquarters were striped with white, and in color it was more maroon than brown. As was only natural, for what else could be expected to issue from a union between a jackass and an okapi?

The stranger was not nearly so colorful. All anyone could see of the rider was the heavy gray monkish robe which covered him from foot to crown. The hood formed a

1

cowl that shielded the rider's face from view. Despite this he had no trouble guiding his striped mount.

"Now, what do you make of that, ladies?" The fishmonger gazed out over his aromatic stock as the stranger passed his shop.

His two plump customers followed the peculiar visitor's passage with their eyes. "I certainly have never seen the like," the eldest commented softly. "Such an odd beast he rides."

"How do you know it's a he?" asked her friend. "There might be anything hiding beneath those robes. It might not even be human."

"No, it's human, and I'd bet by the way it rides that it is a man. Most unusual to ride so heavily veiled on such a warm day." She shuddered. "I am glad he did not stop here."

"I wonder what something like that wants here in Sasubree?"

The fishmonger stroked his short blond beard and leaned out to see as the stranger turned the far corner. "That, madam, is the interesting question. Perhaps I should run after him and ask him to join us so that we might question him at our leisure."

"No, no," said the elder woman hastily. As if aware of her unseemly panic, she added demurely, "That would not be polite. Anyone is free to come and go as they please in Sasubree, however peculiar their appearance or intentions."

"I'm sure if he had anything to say he would have stopped and asked," her companion added.

Actually the fishmonger was glad they had declined his offer; he'd made it only to tease them. He had no more desire to confront that monkish specter close up than did they. With luck they'd never set eyes on him again.

It was none of his business in any case. He had fish to

sell. Out of sight, out of mind, as his wife always said about the overdue bills.

But no matter how hard he tried to adhere to his wife's advice, the fishmonger could not dismiss the sight of the stranger from his thoughts all the remainder of that day.

Some boys were playing with a ball and several sticks in the middle of the next street when the stranger turned the corner. He was almost upon them before they became aware of his presence. Silently they stopped to stare. There were none of the usual casual boyish insults, none of the curious comments a typical stranger would provoke in passing.

The stranger searched their faces momentarily before leaning toward them. "You, boy." The voice was a distant whisper. It seemed to issue not from behind that concealing cowl but from somewhere unimaginably far away.

"Me?" The eldest among them struggled to affect an air of bravado, but confronted by that dark cowl it wasn't easy to appear confident.

"Yes, you. I am looking for the shop of a man called Shone Stelft."

"Stelft the Smithy he means," said one of the other boys.

The stranger nodded. "Yes. That is the one I seek. He is a great hero."

A couple of the boys laughed, but not as boisterously as usual.

"Maybe he used to be, sir," declared the eldest, "but he hasn't done anything much heroic lately."

"If you would be so kind as to direct me to his place of business?" There was no hint of menace, no threat in the stranger's voice. Neither was there kindness there.

The second boy, emboldened, stepped forward and pointed down the street. "Third shop on the right, sir. You can't miss it because there's usually smoke coming out of the

3

great chimney. The smithy has his forge going most of the time.''

"I thank you, boy.'' The stranger sat back in his saddle.

"Say, sir,'' the boy asked curiously, "are you come to buy crafts or arms from Stelft?''

"No. I do not come to buy. You might say that I am a trader of sorts. I deal in a bit of this and a smidgen of that.'' He rubbed the thumb and forefinger of his left hand together. "Small things, of no interest to little boys.'' Without urging, his mount resumed its walk down the street.

The players gathered in its wake. One spoke for the first time as he juggled the ball they'd been playing with. "*Farpal*, what a creepy one!''

"What do you suppose he is?'' asked a fourth.

"I don't know,'' said the eldest among them. "Maybe a weird, or a mage.''

"No, he isn't any of those things,'' the boy who'd provided directions declared confidently.

"Aw, how do you know?''

"Because I got a good look up under that hood he wears when I was giving him directions.''

"Yeah, and what did you see? Your crazy Uncle Gymoy?'' the bigger boy taunted him.

"No. I didn't see anybody who looked like Uncle Gymoy. I didn't see anything at all,'' he told them quietly. "There wasn't anything under the hood. No face at all. Just . . . black.''

Silently the little knot of boys turned to stare at the retreating rump of the stranger's mount. The tall sepulchral shape rode straight and stiff on its back. None of the boys ran after the whispery-voiced visitor to confirm the description.

There wasn't a coward among them, but they were not foolishly brave either. After all, even Shadowmages have faces.

4

The sign that hung over the wide entrance to the shop was large, straightforward, and forthright:

S. STELFT
WORKER IN METALS OF ALL KINDS

As the boy had predicted, a thick snake of black smoke was escaping from the heavy stone chimney that dominated the two-story structure. The huge double doors were swung wide.

The stranger dismounted, sniffing at the air. The smoke was thick with the aroma of charcoal and metal. Yes, this was surely the place. There was no hitching rail outside the building, but that did not matter. The striped mule stood motionless without being tied and cropped patiently at the sparse growth that poked green heads through the hardpack of the dirt street. It would not stir without word from its master.

Hiding his hands beneath his sleeves, the stranger entered the shop. Massive oak beams supported the high ceiling. Not one but two forges were raging beneath. There was another, smaller door set in the rear wall which doubtless led to living quarters beyond.

The man whom the stranger had come so far to find sat behind a heavy wooden table. Thick leather gloves protected his hands while glasses of mica shielded his eyes. Those big fingers moved with precision and unexpected delicacy as their owner employed them to add silver inlay to a finely tooled saddle. The half-finished seat was a work of high art, one of which any king would have been proud.

Those hands could wield a sword or longbow with equal fluidity and skill and had done so in the not-so-distant past.

The stranger stood and watched quietly, enjoying the display of skill. His gaze lifted to the shelves behind the table. These were filled with exquisite examples of the metalworker's art, some done in gold as well as silver, others fashioned of more prosaic metals.

There were knives designed to be worn for decoration as much as for protection, dirks with handles of rare horn, drinking goblets and engraved dinner plates for the very wealthy. There were even inlaid horseshoes, evidence that Stelft was as much a farrier as artisan.

The big man might have continued working for hours, but the stranger finally stepped forward. "You are the one they call Shone Stelft?"

Obviously startled, the smith almost dropped the tool in his right hand as he looked up. "By my soul, but you move quietly, visitor! I never heard nor saw you enter."

"I meant no subterfuge. It is my manner."

Stelft squinted as he tried to see beneath the gray cowl. The stranger maintained a monkish posture, head down, hands together, concealing his face from view. Stelft finally gave up lest he appear impolite.

"Well, I'm him. What can I do for you?"

"I have need of your services" was the whispery reply.

"Do you now? Well, I'm always ready to do business." Stelft leaned back in his chair, shoved his thick glasses back up onto his forehead, and gestured toward the shelves behind him. "That's my work."

"Fine work it is, too."

"What was it you had in mind, then? Shoes for your mount? Perhaps something of a more delicate nature for your lady friend? Maybe not, considering your attire. Possibly a fine binding for some holy books?"

"Nothing like that," the stranger murmured softly. "Nor any works of art, nor arms or armor."

Stelft frowned. "Well now, I don't see as how there's much else I can do for you, sir. Perhaps if you could tell me what line of work you're in, what profession you claim for your own?"

6

"I am," said the stranger, "a Spinner."

Stelft let out a gentle chuckle. "Indeed, but a spinner of what? Of wool, or of tales?"

"Of many things, some more solid than wool, others more ethereal than tales. Of this and that, bits and pieces."

"Bits and pieces of what? Come now, visitor, let us have an end to this shilly-shallying and be open with each other."

"As you wish. I am a Spinner of space-time, of fragments of ether and shards of reality, of splinters of imagination."

"Do tell," Stelft muttered. "I wouldn't think there'd be much profit in such insubstantialities." He shrugged. "I was bored anyway, so I'll not kick you back out in the street where I think you belong. Amuse me further, if you can."

The Spinner bowed slightly from the waist. "I will endeavor to hold your interest, Shone Stelft."

The smith gestured toward an empty chair. "Sit and drink with me."

"No offense, but I sit only when I am riding and for drink I have no use."

Stelft grunted, then glanced over a shoulder toward the back of the workshop. "Fime! Get out here."

From a far corner came a gangly young man. His hair tumbled across his forehead and he wore an anxious expression on his sooty face. He glanced curiously at the Spinner before turning his attention to his employer.

"What is it, Master Stelft?"

"A flagon of . . . of . . . well, of anything cold you can find lying around the kitchen."

"Yes, Master." Again the quick glance at the silent visitor standing before the table. "One tankard or two?"

"Just one. Get off with you!"

Fime nodded and disappeared through the rear door the

Spinner had noted on his arrival. He reappeared with admirable speed no more than a few moments later, carrying a pewter tankard in one hand and a tall flagon of something golden and bubbly in the other. These he set down in front of his master.

Stelft poured himself a full tankard of the brew, quaffed half in a single prodigious swallow, then put the tankard down on the table and wiped his lips with the back of a forearm.

"Now then, Spinner sir, if you're not interested in my metal work, what exactly is it you want with me?"

"There was a time, was there not, when you did work of another kind?" Stelft stared at the hooded figure silently, one hand resting on the handle of the tankard. "A time when you made your services available to those in need. When you accepted burdens which sent other men fleeing in terror. When you accomplished regularly and with great skill things which most men fear even to consider?"

"That's quite a buildup," Stelft replied slowly. "Yes, I once used weapons instead of just making them. I tried to work only for good, though that's something which seems to vary from individual to individual and from country to country."

"Very true," the Spinner agreed.

"I did such work because it paid very well."

"Then you would not be averse to providing such services again?"

"Oh, I didn't say that. As a matter of fact, I'd be very adverse to so doing. Being a smith doesn't pay as well. Hiring out one's art never pays as well as hiring out one's arm. But I sought out this life intentionally. It wasn't forced upon me. I got tired of dodging spears and spells in search of outrageous fortune. I reached the point where peace and quiet and the possibility of a long retirement began to have more than a cursory appeal to me. I found something I enjoy doing"—and with a sweep of one hand he indicated the well-stocked shop—"married a good woman, and settled down.

"In short, my mysterious friend, I am through with fighting and questing and all that sort of thing. So if that's what you want from me, I'm afraid you've wasted your trip. I'm finished risking my life to solve someone else's petty problems."

"The problem I bring with me is anything but petty," the Spinner informed him. He leaned slightly forward. "Have you ever heard of Shadowkeep?"

Stelft's eyebrows lifted as he gazed hard at his visitor.

"Of course I've heard of Shadowkeep. Any informed person has. They say it's the abode of casual death. No one in their right mind goes there."

A long, breathy sigh issued from the Spinner. "I fear someone must. A vast and ancient evil now threatens this land, threatens all the civilized lands. A time of darkness is coming when all races will be forced to hide from the light. Despair will replace hope, trembling will take the place of laughter, and goodness will be ground into the earth. Unless the evil that threatens to spill out of Shadowkeep can be contained therein and, if possible, destroyed.

"There is also glory for whoever succeeds in this, and treasure beyond belief awaiting the taker."

Stelft shook his head sadly, even as he continued to smile at the Spinner. "I'm afraid the only glory I take anymore is in my sculpture, and my family is treasure enough for any man. It's all very well and good to go gallivanting off on such expeditions when you've only your own life to answer for, but I've a wife and young child who depend on me."

"What becomes of your family if this evil emerges from Shadowkeep to work its will upon the world?"

Stelft sipped at the rest of his tankard. "Maybe it will

work its will in a direction other than this. It's a long way from Sasubree to Shadowkeep. Furthermore I've only your word for any of this, the word of a secretive stranger. Why should I believe a word of what you say? Perhaps you're nothing more than a clever troublemaker, or a traveling sadist. Besides, why would anything that had managed to gain control of Shadowkeep want to spread itself thin? Isn't mastery of Shadowkeep enough to satisfy anyone, or for that matter, anything?''

"You may understand the nature of metals,'' the Spinner replied quietly, "and the nature of daring and of bravery, but you know nothing of the nature of pure evil. It is never satisfied. Left alone it will grow and multiply until it finally destroys not only everything within its power but itself as well. Wishes will not make it go away and indifference will not constrain it.''

"You argue well, visitor, but I'm not your man.''

"I do not seek the services of a man. I need a hero. Sex and race are not important. It is what is inside that matters. You are a hero, Shone Stelft.''

"I was once. Not anymore. Now I'm a simple smith. But you intrigue me. I admire a good storyteller. I've listened to many tales of evil far and near. Every traveling minstrel has different versions. Tell me yours.''

The Spinner sighed again, muttering to himself. "So much explanation for a simple request. Still, better an informed hero than an ignorant one.''

"What, what was that? I didn't catch that last,'' Stelft said uncertainly.

The Spinner ignored the request. "Do you know where Shadowkeep stands?''

"Sure. Doesn't everyone? It's important to know those places to avoid just as it's important to know the good places to visit.''

"What do you know of its origins?''

10

Stelft shrugged, the muscles in his arms rippling. "I always imagined it was raised by some long-gone kingdom as a monument to their memory. The world's full of monuments, though none so impressive, I'm told, as this Shadowkeep."

"A monument it is, but it was not built by the people of a kingdom to perpetuate their memory. It was built by one man."

Stelft grinned. "All of Shadowkeep? That's a bit hard to swallow, stranger."

"He was a sorcerer, perhaps the greatest there ever was in this world. His name was Gorwyther. A good and wise man, though a bit intolerant of his fellows. He designed Shadowkeep and caused it to come into existence. He made it large and complex and imposing to preserve his privacy, to keep out those who would disturb him while he engaged in his studies into the nature of space and time.

"Thus shielded by the castle he had raised, Gorwyther was left to himself to practice his magics and do his research. Much he learned of other worlds, other dimensions. I come from one such, called hither by a last cry from the wizard himself before he came to grief."

"Now, look," said Stelft, "if you do come from another dimension or world, and I don't for a moment countenance that, then why don't you take your otherworldly powers off to Shadowkeep and take care of this looming evil or whatever it is by your solemn lonesome?"

"Would that I could be of direct assistance, but I cannot interfere. My powers in your world are circumscribed by laws you cannot comprehend. I am unable to interact directly. Someone of this world must do what I cannot."

"What happened to this great and wise Gorwyther? Evidently he wasn't all that great and wise or he wouldn't be in the mess you say he's in."

"His intense curiosity about the nature of space-time

11

caused him to ignore what was taking place immediately around him. As I said, there are other dimensions. Some are inhabited by people much like yourself, but others serve as home to those who prefer the Dark. In his work Gorwyther often opened gates between the dimensions. This was not damaging . . . except once. He let through one named Dal'brad.''

"Hey, I've heard that name before," commented the apprentice from his corner.

"Be silent, Fime," Stelft ordered the younger man. The apprentice looked hurt, but subsided. The smith turned back to his visitor. "It's not an uncommon name. He has something to do with the demonic forces, doesn't he?"

"Something, yes. Dal'brad is first prince and then king of all the demons of the demonic dimensions, not only those that haunt this world but the ones who trouble my own, and many others as well. Demons can pass freely between many realms, but usually not directly into such as mine or yours. It was an experiment of Gorwyther's, improperly monitored, that permitted Dal'brad entrance into Shadowkeep without the wizard's knowledge.

"The demon king is clever. One does not become king of anything by acting the fool. So he hid within the bowels of Shadowkeep, planning and biding his time, until he was able to catch Gorwyther off guard. He imprisoned the wizard in a crystal stasis, then took over the castle.

"It is his sanctuary in this world. Safely within he can plot and plan. He cannot be reached, cannot be touched . . . except by one of unsurpassing bravery and skill. Gorwyther's treasures he leaves untouched, and lets word of their availability seep to the world outside. This suits his purposes well, for it so tempts those who might threaten him that they come running to Shadowkeep in search of instant wealth and power. Once they are within, they fall prey to the numerous traps the demon king has set or to the safeguards that Gorwyther constructed. When all have been destroyed, only then will the demon king call forth his legions to ravish the land. Demons are cautious by nature, and Dal'brad is the most cautious of all. Even now he keeps to himself deep within the castle and makes his plans while studying Gorwyther's writings. It is those which must be denied to him, and quickly. The wizard's knowledge combined with his own could eventually render him invulnerable.

"This then is what must be done: someone must go to Shadowkeep, seek out and free Gorwyther. Only with the wizard's assistance can Dal'brad be defeated."

"You make it sound so inviting," Stelft murmured. "A simple excursion."

"Nothing in this world or any other is guaranteed," the Spinner told him, almost apologetically. "There are risks inherent in any difficult undertaking, be it slaying evil or fashioning a fine piece of jewelry. In this the risks are greater than most, but so are the potential rewards.

"I will not try to minimize the danger you would be facing any more than I will the accomplishment. Think of the glory of saving a whole world, not to mention the treasures Gorwyther accumulated which Dal'brad now hoards for himself. All that can be yours if you agree to undertake this quest." The Spinner paused briefly before adding, "I was told that you were a great hero."

Stelft did not reply for a long moment. Then he slapped a big hand down hard on the table, making the flagon bounce, and stood to face his visitor.

" 'Was' is right." He pushed back his chair. "Sorry, not interested. I've plenty to occupy my time right here."

The Spinner sounded surprised. "But I was told . . ."

"I don't know what you were told elsewhere, but listen well to what I tell you here and now. I've a family to look after and a business to pursue. I'm finished with the hero business. I pushed my luck and got away with much and I've no desire to tempt fate yet another time. Most of my friends who soldiered alongside me are well remembered for what they did, but they're remembered in song, not in person, and with flowers set on their graves. Those whose bodies were intact enough for burial, anyways.''

"Someone must do what must be done," the Spinner told him, "or all peoples will suffer."

"That's all peoples problem, not mine," Stelft snapped. "Now if you don't mind, friend, I've had a long hard day at the forge and I'm very tired. I've heard you out politely, and you've no more call on my time.

"As for your tale, I venture that it *might* be true. If so, well, I could do with a spot of treasure. What man couldn't, or woman either? But as far as I'm concerned, the risks of trying to penetrate the depths of Shadowkeep far outweigh any possible rewards. Now, perhaps if you could provide a little of this vast wealth up front . . . ?''

The Spinner spread gray-clad arms. ''Alas, I can offer you only promises.''

"Poor collateral on which to borrow a man's life. No thanks, I'm afraid I can't help you, stranger." Turning, he strode purposefully across the floor toward the back door, stepped through, and closed it firmly behind him. The visit was over.

The Spinner slumped. That was an end to it, then. Shone Stelft had been his great hope. His journey had taken him through many towns. He had spoken to many soldiers-of-fortune and daring adventurers. As each had turned him down they'd said that the man he really needed to engage was the legendary Shone Stelft of Sasubree.

Now he, too, had refused to undertake the task that must be undertaken. There seemed nothing more to be done. He would have to return to his own world and admit defeat, leaving these people to the fate that . . .

A hand tapped him on the shoulder. "Excuse me." The voice was hesitant, deferential.

Turning, the Spinner found himself looking into the hopeful face of Shone Stelft's young apprentice. The apprentice was no less surprised, for in turning the Spinner had allowed the youth an unobstructed view of what lay beneath the gray cowl. Fime took a couple of startled steps backward. He thought he'd prepared himself for sight of anything: grotesque ugliness, facial distortion, blindness . . . but nothing could have prepared him for the sight of nothing. All that lay beneath the visitor's hood was a kind of smoky haziness.

"Do not trifle with me." The Spinner was upset at the harshness in his own voice, worked to modify it. "I have had a difficult day, and a disappointing one. I have no time for casual conversation."

Fime gathered his courage. "I'm not trying to waste your time, sir. My name is Practor Fime, and I'll go."

The Spinner paused uncertainly. "What is this you say?"

"I'll go." Fime smiled at him. It was a thoroughly ingratiating smile. "To Shadowkeep."

"Don't be a fool, young man. Your master was correct in much of what he said. Death waits for any who try to penetrate the mysteries of Shadowkeep."

"Then it'll have a long wait, because I've no intention of dying there. Don't condemn me without giving me a chance, sir. I don't care where you come from, that's not fair. At least I'm willing to try." He nodded toward the doorway leading into the house. "That's more than that old fraud offered to do. He's too attached to his life here. Now, me, I've nothing to hold me to Sasubree, and I'm not afraid of Shadowkeep."

The Spinner spoke softly. "You should be."

Fime slumped slightly. "Well, maybe I am, a little.

15

You'll find me neither overcautious nor reckless, sir. Let me go for you. I'm tired of being an apprentice and I don't think metalworking's the career for me. I'd much rather have a stab at heroing."

"It takes more than good intentions and willingness to endure to make a hero," the Spinner told him, but less brusquely now. Even as he spoke, he was studying the young man standing before him. Fime was taller than Stelft, though not as broadly built. Muscular and in good condition, though. As for the condition of his mind, that lay beyond the Spinner's ability to evaluate. His desire could not be denied, however. It was plain as his face. Might it not be better to employ an enthusiastic if untried hero rather than an experienced but reluctant one?

Did he have any choice?

"I cannot prevent you from going to Shadowkeep. I can only warn you of the danger that lies within."

"Fine. You've already done that. I overheard everything you told Master Stelft."

"What of your own family?"

"I'm long since of age. I make my own decisions and go my own way now." He indicated the smithy, with its still-smoking forges and neat racks of tools. "I chose to be apprenticed to Master Stelft because there was nothing more interesting to do in Sasubree. If I choose to leave, I will do so when I please."

"You lack experience. You've had no training to prepare you for what you talk of accomplishing."

"Could any training prepare someone to enter Shadowkeep?" When the Spinner did not reply, Fime continued, emboldened. "As for experience, I know how to handle myself. See these arms mounted on the walls around us? I've helped to make most of them, and Master Stelft has shown me how each is used.

"Besides, it sounds to me like it's going to take more

16

wits than brawn to defeat this Dal'brad. In that''—he lowered his voice—"I'm at least as well equipped as Master Stelft.''

"It may be that you are, it may be that you are,'' the Spinner admitted. "Very well, then. As you are determined, go then to Shadowkeep. Seek out the imprisoned Gorwyther. Free him and learn how you may restrain or destroy Dal'brad.

"As for myself, I shall continue my search. It may be that I will be able to send help after you, though I have not been very fortunate thus far. I wish you all good luck and success in this venture which you have taken upon yourself, though I cannot keep from feeling that I am sending you to your doom.''

"If what you said earlier about the plans of this demon king are true, then death will be coming for all of us soon enough. So I don't see that I'm any worse off for searching it out now.''

The Spinner was feeling a little better about his trip to Sasubree. "There is no denying that you have courage as well as strength and intelligence. All you lack is experience.''

"One gets experience by experiencing, isn't that the way the world works?''

"Truly. Good fortune to you, Practor Fime. I hope we may meet again someday, if not in this world than in another.'' The hood turned to stare toward the distant doorway. "I hope Shone Stelft will not object to your leaving.''

Practor managed to swagger while standing still. "He has no choice in the matter. I come and go as I please.'' He glanced back over his shoulder. "There's nothing Shone can do to. . . .''

He stopped in mid-assertion. The Spinner had vanished. There'd been no noise of running feet, no final farewell, and it was a fair distance to the street. Frowning, Practor inspected the place where the visitor had been standing only seconds earlier. There was no lingering smell, no footprint in the dirt floor; nothing to show that the stranger had ever been. A most unusual personage.

Unusual, and desperate. He must have been desperate to accede to Practor's request. Not, as he admitted, that he could prevent Practor's traveling to Shadowkeep. No one could.

He looked toward the house. All that remained was for him to pack his few belongings and some provisions and be on his way.

To Shadowkeep. Fabled Shadowkeep, lair of demons and storehouse of unimaginable treasure.

And to think all he'd had to look forward to this day was a visit to the local inn.

Chapter II

What! Have you gone mad?''
    Shone Stelft rose from behind the kitchen table and glared at his apprentice in disbelief. Practor held his ground against his employer's fury while the smith's wife busied herself with kettles and pots and the roaring wood cookstove. Two small children clung to her skirt and stared in wide-eyed fascination at their raging father.

"Go on," Stelft urged the younger man, "explain yourself."

"I am quite sane, Master Stelft. I know exactly what I'm doing."

"Is that a fact? Let me tell you something, Practor. You don't have the damnedest idea what you're about. You heard what that wraith said. Not only is this Shadowkeep secured by every insidious sorcerous device this Gorwyther could devise, it is now home to Dal'brad himself. The prince of demons, or king of demons, or both. Shadowkeep is not a castle: it's the world's largest mausoleum. You go there and inside half a day you'll find a nice cold niche prepared especially for you. Demons like to bury people, and they're not very particular about whether or not you're dead first, either."

"I'm not afraid of traps or demons," Practor told him firmly. "Brains and stealth can carry a careful man past any obstacle."

"Can they now?" Stelft was dangerously quiet. "And just what's that supposed to mean?"

Practor tried to look relaxed and self-assured, but he was trembling ever so slightly inside. "Just what it says."

"I see. You do realize, though, that there are occasions when a little muscle and some small skill at combat is necessary for survival?"

"Certainly, but I'm no novice with weapons. I have your instruction to thank for that." That seemed to mollify Stelft. "I'll manage. I'll have to manage. Not only for my own sake but for everyone's. A lot of people are going to be depending on me to succeed, even if they don't know what's at stake."

Stelft calmed himself, regarded his apprentice evenly. "All right. I'm not going to talk to you as master to apprentice now. I'm going to talk to you as an equal, since that's what you're striving to be."

"That's very decent of you, sir."

"Practor, why do you think I turned down that stranger's request?"

The younger man hesitated. "You gave him a number of reasons, sir. They sounded like good reasons to me."

Stelft was nodding. "They were that, but there is another. I know Shadowkeep's reputation. I don't mean the casual horror stories voluble travelers tell to entertain at the drop of a coin, I mean its *real* reputation.

"When I was your age, I dared many dangers, some of them rash, all of them fraught with peril. That I managed to survive was due as much to luck as to skill and ability. Better fighters than I perished because they weren't lucky. Luck is something you can't pack in your backpack to take with you on an expedition. My point is that you'd need all the luck in the world to succeed in this, and I don't think you have it. I don't think anyone does.

"It's not just you, Practor. I don't think this thing can be done. I don't think anyone can get into Shadowkeep and out again alive, except perhaps another wizard. And you're no wizard. You're just a man."

"You have no proof it can't be done," Practor argued.

"Only this: no one has ever come out of Shadowkeep once they've entered. It's easy to get in, not so to come out with a whole skin. I know my limitations. Always did. Another reason why I'm alive when others are dead. We all have to realize our limitations, Practor."

"The best way to do that is to test them."

"You have some skill, but not the combination necessary."

"Then I'll find help along the way."

Stelft was shaking his head. "What kind of help? Others like yourself? You're a good man, Practor, a fine worker and a decent soul, but you're still a bit headstrong. You're not thinking this through."

"Just because you're too old . . ."

Shone Stelft looked pained. "Common sense is not a province of the old, Practor. Though listening to you, I wonder." He'd chosen to ignore the insult, which was a good thing for Practor. Besides, his wife brooked no fighting in her kitchen. "Listen to me. All you will find in Shadowkeep is an unknown death. You will not emerge covered with treasure and glory. If you enter, you will not emerge at all."

"I thank you for your concerned advice, Master Stelft, but I'm bound and determined to do this thing. To try, anyway."

Stelft let out a tired sigh. "You haven't been listening to me. You haven't comprehended a thing I've said, have you?"

"On the contrary, Mas—Shone . . . I've heard every-

21

thing you've said, but someone still has to get into Shadowkeep to free the wizard so that the world may be spared Dal'brad's intentions."

"So the stranger said. You're a fine one, Practor, for trusting your life to the word of a stranger. There may be nothing to them. The world is infested with troublemakers."

"There may have been nothing to the stranger," Practor replied, remembering his glimpse of that vacant hood, "but there was plenty to his words."

Stelft's wife spoke for the first time. "I know what your problem is, Practor. You've been inhaling too much of the smoke from the forges again. You need a rest." She glanced at her husband. "Don't you agree, Shone? You've been working him too hard."

Practor walked over to the stove. "I am quite clearheaded, Mistress Stelft, and my health's never been better. Nor am I tired. I am well, and confident of my course." He started for the stairway. "Now if you will excuse me, I must pack a few things to take on my journey." He hesitated at the base of the stairs, turned back to them.

"You've both been good to me. I've enjoyed living here and learning the art of the forge. It's been interesting, enlightening . . . and safe. But I always felt the time would come when I'd have to challenge that safety. All my life I've been waiting for one big chance, one special opportunity to prove myself. Now that it's come, no matter how difficult or dangerous, I just can't run away from it. I can't. And there are others whose lives will be affected by whether or not I succeed. Yours too."

"*If* our visitor was something more than just a passing storyteller," Stelft reminded him.

Practor nodded. "I've made my decision. I believe in what he said. I respect your advice as always, Shone Stelft, but this time I have to hold to my own feelings. I wish we could go together, but it seems that's not to be.

So I must go alone.'' That said, he turned and headed up the stairs.

There wasn't much to pack. Practor was not an acquisitive person and over the years had accumulated little he called his own. So while there was little enough to pack, there was also little to leave behind.

At least he would travel well armed, with weapons he had fashioned himself on the forges below. He owned a superbly made sword, a fine knife equally suited to skinning game as well as less domestic pursuits, and a shield of leather and metal. These he placed on his bed alongside his extra clothing and the small pile of savings he'd managed to gather.

That was going to be a problem, he knew. Shadowkeep was too far to go on foot, and he didn't have nearly enough money to pay for a decent mount. Nor did he think Shone Stelft would loan him the balance required for a good horse. Perhaps he could work out some kind of trade, if not in Sasubree then in some smaller town along the way.

He was just folding the last of his clothes into the small backpack when a click sounded from the other side of his bedroom door. He approached it uneasily.

"Master Stelft, is that you?" Perhaps the smith had slipped upstairs to wish him good luck, now that he'd had some time to sort out his own feelings. After all, they'd been together as master and apprentice for many years. It hardly seemed likely that the old hero would just let Practor leave without so much as a word of encouragement.

Stelft was in the hallway outside, all right, but not with the intention of offering encouragement. His purpose became clear enough when Practor tried the door. It wouldn't budge.

"Master Stelft, this isn't right." Practor pulled hard on the handle with both hands, but still the wood refused to move. "Shone Stelft, open this door! I'm a free man, of age, and I can go and come as I please."

"Now, Practor." Stelft's tone was gentle. "I'm doing this for you. You're a fine young man and you'll make a skilled craftsman someday, better than I. You'll be able to set up your own shop or share this one with me and you'll never lack for work. You'll make a fine living . . . if you keep your wits in your head and your blood in your veins."

"I don't have any more time for horseshoes or birthday presents, Stelft. Shadowkeep waits for me!"

"Death waits for you. We'll talk again on this in the morning. Perhaps by then some of this fever will have left you and you'll be able to think clearly again. Visiting wraiths seem farther away in the bright light of day.

"You're a smart young man. I know that. But you're overcome right now with enthusiasm for something you don't understand. I'd be remiss in my responsibilities if I let you go running madly off toward your death."

"Stelft, if someone doesn't get into Shadowkeep and stop Dal'brad we're all going to die. The Spinner's words . . ."

"Spare me another recitation," Stelft told him dryly. "One of your biggest failings, Practor, is that you see truth in everyone else's words. You mistake sincerity for truth. They are not the same.

"Now get yourself a good night's sleep and we'll talk again over breakfast."

Practor could hear footsteps moving away, down the stairs. "Shone Stelft, you let me out of here! Open this door, dammit! *Stelft!*"

He wrenched at the handle, pushed and shoved at the door, but the old wood refused to give, and Stelft had forged the door hinges himself. Gasping, Practor finally abandoned his efforts.

Since there seemed nothing else to do, he did as Stelft had suggested and reviewed the stranger's visit and words in his mind. He went over them repeatedly, and each time he grew that much more determined to make his way to Shadowkeep. No smith was going to stop him, either.

His room was a third-floor garret and it was a long way down to the street outside, but he didn't hesitate. How could he balk at a two-story drop and hope to challenge the gates of Shadowkeep? With sword and knife tied to his belt and his shield slung across his back, he climbed carefully hand-over-hand down the drainpipe which clung to the side of the building. It was a relief to stand finally on the paving stones below his window. There was no sign of alarm from inside the house. He'd made his escape silently.

It was a warm night and there were many strollers out, but only the moon had witnessed his shaky descent from the third floor. He had surmounted his first obstacle on the road into Shadowkeep.

Adjusting the straps of his pack, he stared a moment longer at the building where he had lived for so many years.

Good-bye, Shone Stelft. You were a great hero once. I don't begrudge you your quiet home life, but someone has to do this thing. It might as well be me as any other.

He turned and walked briskly off into the night, toward the busy interior of Sasubree. Down Tarkone Street and then up Greenflight Lane, whistling to himself as he walked. There was something he had to do before he left Sasubree, something even more important than trying to find a horse.

Redface Inn lay at the end of the lane. It was a large, prosperous establishment, one of the most popular in the city. Practor had spent many a pleasant evening there dining and drinking with friends.

A few faces glanced up as he entered and voices were

raised in greeting. He waved casually to his friends, his eyes searching the many tables and booths. The inn was alive with movement and sound. He made his way to a back corner, where the largest wine kegs were stored, and waited there as the waitresses and waiters made their pickups. His interest was more than casual.

The girl he sought was dark haired, not especially pretty but overflowing with a special kind of vivacity and love of life that permeated her whole being. It pleased visitors and customers but had thoroughly captured Practor Fime.

She saw him and glanced behind her, but the owner of the inn was nowhere in sight. Practor gestured urgently, and after a whispered exchange with another server, she hurried over to him.

"Practor, it is you! I thought you couldn't come again for two nights. And then I was supposed to meet you by the Upriver Bridge. Don't you remember? We were going to take a dessert and drink and watch the stars together. We were..."

He put a finger to her lips, quieting her. "There will be no star-watching two nights hence, my love. Something has happened. Something important."

Her eyes widened. "You're not in trouble, Practor?"

"No," he lied. "But I have to go away for a while. Just a little while."

She looked around but no one was watching them. "What do you mean, you have to go away?"

"It's for Shone Stelft," he told her, and that wasn't as big a lie as what he'd already told her. He *was* going for Stelft, and for everyone else as well.

"For the smith?" She smiled then. "I know. You're going to buy some raw plate for him. Or is it ingots this time? That's what you're doing. You're going to buy metals from the dealers in Typur."

"No," he told her softly, "I'm not going to Typur. Not this time. I have to go east, across the Barrens."

She stared at him uncomprehendingly. "No one crosses the Barrens except some crazy traders, and you're neither crazy nor a trader. What's going on, Practor?" For the first time she noticed the pack and shield he'd set down in the corner. "What's happening?"

"It's kind of hard to explain. We had a visitor, at the shop. A most mysterious and wonderful visitor. He told me of a great danger that threatens us all. Someone has to do something to stop it and I—" he shrugged, "I sort of nominated myself."

"I knew you were in trouble."

He smiled fondly down at her. "It's not what you think." Actually, it was much worse than what she thought, but he saw no point in making her worry even more. "I'm just going to deliver a message to someone, that's all."

"What kind of message do you deliver with a sword and shield?"

"That's to protect me along the way," he lied. "Hopefully I won't have to use them. You know me, Rysancy. I've always managed to stay clear of fights by using my wits."

She eyed him uncertainly. "Where do you have to go to deliver this message?"

He couldn't tell her he was going to Shadowkeep, much less what he had to do once he got there. She'd get hysterical right there in the middle of the inn, and that wouldn't do either of them any good.

"It's not important. The important thing is that I'm going to be paid a great deal for this. Enough to set me up in my own business when I get back. Enough so that we can travel and see the world, just like you've always wanted to. Enough," he whispered lovingly, "so that we can finally get married. You're going to have a fine home, and servants; everything you've ever wanted. I'm doing this for more than just myself, Rysancy."

He didn't add that he was doing it for everyone. No harm in letting her think he was doing it for them alone. And as in everything he did, she would be his greatest source of inspiration.

She still seemed uneasy. "Well—if you're *sure* it isn't really dangerous."

"Not at all," he assured her. What could be dangerous, he asked himself silently? All he had to do was penetrate the secrets of the least-visited castle in the world, defeat all its safeguards, free a trapped wizard, and avoid the hand of the king of demons. No danger at all.

"You'll see. I'll be back in a few fortnights and we'll have plenty of time for stargazing." She still looked reluctant, so he took her hands in his and smiled as confidently as he could manage. "You have to believe what I'm telling you, Rysancy. This is more important to me than I can say. I want to go with your blessing, and I don't want you worrying about me while I'm gone."

"What did Master Stelft think of this?"

"He didn't approve," Practor told her honestly. "He advised me not to go. Rather strongly, in fact."

She grinned back at him. "Then you definitely should go."

"Rysancy! I thought you respected Shone Stelft's advice."

"I do—in everything except where you're concerned, Practor. He knows how good you are at what you do. You're valuable to him. It's only natural for him to want to keep you around, where he can keep an eye on you. I've been telling you for a long time that you'll never be able to do anything until you get out from under his wing."

"It's not like that at all, Rysancy."

"Isn't it? No matter. The important thing is that you're doing this thing on your own, for yourself and not for him." She threw her arms around his neck and kissed him long and hard.

He would have been content to stand thus for an hour or two, but she saw something out of the corner of an eye and pulled away from him suddenly. "There's old Strurier." She nodded toward a beefy, bewhiskered individual making his way toward them like a ship breasting a sea full of icebergs. "If he catches me back here with you it'll mean my job, and you haven't been paid for delivering your message yet." She turned her face back up to his. "Good fortune go with you, my love. Come back to me with riches or without, but be sure to come back. That's more important to me than silks and servants."

A last, lingering embrace. Then Rysancy picked up her tray and vanished back into the smoke and noise and movement of the inn before her employer could find her.

Practor watched until he could see her no longer. Then he hefted his pack and shield, slung them carefully across his back once more, and made his way out of the inn. It would have been good to stay and share food and drink with friends, but he didn't think he could stand to see Rysancy again. If he did, he might lose his resolve and never leave Sasubree.

Then too, if Master Stelft thought to check on his ward and found him gone, he was likely to come looking for him. Practor was ready to fight if necessary, but he hoped he wouldn't have to until he was far away from his own home.

Giving the smithy a wide berth, he strode down several side streets as he headed for the outskirts of the city. On its fringes he would find the stables which catered to the needs of the innumerable merchants and travelers who passed through Sasubree. Somehow he had to find himself a good horse.

He wasn't worried about food or lodging. He could live

off the land, or work for his keep. The skills of an accomplished smith were always in demand. The one thing he couldn't do was walk to Shadowkeep. The Spinner's voice had been taut with urgency, and there was no telling how little time remained to the world before Dal'brad felt strong enough to try and extend his sway over the peaceful lands beyond the Keep itself.

Also, the rainy season would soon be upon them. That would not only make travel through the Barrens uncomfortable, it could render it impossible.

He found the stable he was searching for. It was owned by a crafty old codger named Minza. Practor had done plenty of farrying for the old man, both under Stelft's supervision and on his own. Minza was no less avaricious than his fellow stablemasters, but it always seemed to Practor that he'd looked on him with a kindly eye. How kindly he was about to find out. In any case, Minza was his best chance.

The stable was extensive, a testament to Minza's shrewd business sense and dedication to his work. Despite the lateness of the hour, he found the old man near the far end of the stable, brushing down a fine stallion.

It was an unusual hour for customers, however, and the old man drew back uncertainly at the sound of approaching footsteps. One hand reached for the sharp pitchfork he always kept at hand. He leaned forward and squinted into the dim light, his eyes darting from aisle to shadow like those of a mouse.

"Who is it, and what do you want at this time of night?"

"Take it easy, Minza. It's only me, Practor Fime."

The oldster relaxed, set his tri-pronged weapon aside. "Practor? What are you doing here at this hour? I don't recall sending to your master for any work."

"Shone Stelft is my master no longer," Practor told him as he stepped out into the light of Minza's lantern.

"Oh ho! You don't say, you don't say. Does this mean that you'll be setting up your own shop? Perhaps one that will charge more reasonable rates? If so, I think you and I can do a lot of business, Practor. You know that I've always respected your work."

"Not for a while, I'm afraid. Actually, I've come to see you about something else entirely." He leaned against one of the posts that supported the stable roof. Most of the stalls on both sides of the central aisle were occupied. Minza's long hours and careful attention to the health of his boarders had earned him a high reputation among local citizens and visitors alike. No animal at this stable ever lacked for food or fresh water.

Minza was scratching the bald spot atop his head. "Well, my young friend, if this isn't a business call, then what are you doing here in the middle of the night?"

"It is a business call, but this time I'm not here to sell you something. I'm here to buy."

"Oh so, why didn't you say so in the first place?" The old man eyed him shrewdly. "What have you in mind? How about a nice young gigantha? If that's too slow for you, I have a toreledon stabled in the back that I repossessed in payment of a bad debt. He is not too old, and sturdy."

"I need something faster still, Minza."

Minza switched from scratching his pate to rubbing his chin. "You aren't in trouble with the authorities or anything like that, are you, Practor?"

Practor rolled his eyes. "Why is it the first time I decide to take a little trip on my own, everyone thinks I'm in trouble with the law?"

"No offense, youngster."

"I'm not in trouble. Actually, I'm running to it, I can't wait to find it, and I'm in a hurry to get there. So I need a horse. A good one, not some old dray animal." In spite of himself, he kept staring at the proud stallion the old man had been currying.

Minza didn't miss much, and he didn't miss the hunger in his visitor's gaze. "His name's Kaltar. As fine a three-year-old as I've ever seen."

"He's magnificent." Practor moved forward to pat the horse on the nose. "Who owns him?"

"The Riverlord Arnotem. He and his family are away in the south until Springtide. He trusts his horses to my care sooner than to his own grooms. I'm boarding several of them here, but this one's the pride of his breeding farm."

"Beautiful," Practor agreed, stroking the soft muzzle. The stallion nuzzled his hand.

"He likes you, too, it seems," Minza observed. "You have a gentle touch, youngster. He's not for rent, needless to say."

"Needless to say." Practor sighed and turned back to the stablemaster.

"Now then," Minza asked him, "how long would you need this mount for? I'm assuming you don't have money to buy one."

"You assume right. I don't know. Not too many months, I hope. Certainly I'd like to have both my mount and myself home before the worst of winter sets in." He frowned. "Are you saying you'd be willing to rent me a good horse?"

"I might." He walked over to Kaltar, patted the stallion on its neck. "Now, anything I rent to you I would have to have back before winter Second Month, undamaged and in good condition."

"Of course."

"Yes, Second Month should be sufficient. It's just before spring breaks, you know. I'm always busy in the spring. Winter travelers returning from the south and all that.''

Practor discovered that his heart was pounding fit to burst through his shirt. Or was he completely misinterpreting what the old man was saying?

"Just so long as I have him back before spring then?"

"Yes," said Minza thoughtfully, "before spring."

"Which horse," Practor inquired slowly, "should I take?"

Minza waved a hand lazily down the aisle, seemingly indifferent to his visitor's choice. "Whichever suits you. I trust you, youngster. I've known you long enough to do that much."

Practor reached into a pocket and removed his small money pouch. He handed it to the stablemaster, who looked inside.

"I know it's not much," Practor told him worriedly. "My life's savings."

"You're right about it not being much," Minza agreed. "Still, you're not buying. Only renting. Until Second Month. Before spring, when my winter boarders return." He smiled. "You're a fine young man, Practor. I always have liked you. Tell me: what are you about so all of a sudden that you need such a fast mount for?"

Practor didn't meet the old man's eyes. "I'd rather not say. You'd only laugh at me."

"Tut! Haven't we known each other for many years? I tolerate too many fools to laugh at someone I like."

"A stranger passed through Sasubree yesterday. He told a tale full of import and mystery. He was looking for someone to do something and he settled on me. There is much involved. Among the rest is the treasure of Shadowkeep."

"Shadowkeep." True to his word, Minza didn't laugh.

"I've always considered you a clever man, Practor, but that clever? I'm not so sure."

"Don't worry. I won't be riding my mount into Shadowkeep. I'll board it somewhere outside. At worst it will return home by itself."

"That's true, though I'd much rather see it brought back by its renter." He leaned close, his face aglow with honest greed. "What do you know of the treasures of Shadowkeep?"

"Only that they involve wealth and riches beyond imagining. I intend to bring back as much of them as I can carry."

Minza was nodding eagerly. "And would you consider sharing some of this with a poor old man who'd done you a good deed?"

Practor smiled. "I would regard it as a necessity."

Minza looked thoughtful. "I see. That's good to know. Now then, there is the matter of selecting a mount for you." He turned and pointed up the aisle. "You see that seventh stall, the one on the left?"

Practor strained to penetrate the darkness. "I'm afraid not."

"Well, there's a fine mare in there. She ought to do for you."

"Oh." Practor's hopes fell. Apparently he had misinterpreted Minza's words. He sighed. If this was the best he could do, then he would have to manage as best he was able with what the old man was offering him. He'd had no reason to expect anything else.

"Her name," Minza added, "is Gladys."

Practor winced but worked to conceal his disappointment.

"You may have her until the end of Second Month winter and not a day longer."

"I understand." Practor took a step forward.

Minza held him back. "Oh, one other thing. You could do me a small favor, if you would." He gestured at the

34

stallion. "Take Kaltar here and put him into the stall next to Gladys's. It will keep him quiet until morning. Not that he's particularly rambunctious, you understand. Why, for such a spirited, noble steed he hardly makes a sound. I never hear him moving about myself." Minza touched his left ear. "I'm afraid I'm getting a little deaf in my dotage. But that horse, he's so quiet that half the time I worry that he's vanished into thin air."

Practor nodded, still sunk in disappointment as he took up the stallion's reins. "Come on then, Kaltar. It's time you were getting to bed and I was getting on my way."

Minza picked up a bucket and started briskly toward the far end of the stable, carrying his lantern in his other hand. "Good-bye and good luck, Practor. Be sure and remove his bridle before you put him up, and whatever you do, don't let him see the saddle that's back in his usual stall. The one that's slung over the railing in the rear. Every time he sets eyes on that saddle he wants to go for a run, and I have a devil of a time holding him back."

Minza was halfway down the aisle already, his lantern bobbing in the encroaching darkness. Practor called after him.

"I'll be careful, Minza. Don't worry."

He'd led the stallion about ten feet when he slowed. As he slowed, his face broke out into a wide grin.

Hardly ever hear him, never makes a sound, you'd think he'd vanished into thin air—the old man's words tumbled over and over in Practor's mind. Sly old fox. He was covering himself out loud. If the stallion failed to return in time, or came back injured, then all Minza had to do was tell Riverlord Arnotem about the young smith who'd rented the mare next to Kaltar and who in the still and dark of the night had mistakenly taken off with the wrong horse. All unbeknownst, of course, to the stablemaster, who'd only done his duty.

Practor turned back to the end stall. The saddle rested right where Minza had said. He slipped a blanket onto the stallion's back, followed it with the saddle and cinched the latter properly beneath Kaltar's belly. If he returned to Sasubree late, the old man would call him a horse thief to his face and would bear witness against him in any court. Fair enough. But Practor had no intention of returning late. He'd reenter Sasubree in triumph and before Spring—or not at all. Not for Minza's sake, or for his own, but for another's.

Rysancy, he thought. Dear sweet loving Rysancy. You will wear necklaces of diamonds and pearls and skirts of woven gold. Strurier will wait on you for a change, if you so desire it, and you'll never have to fight off the advances of some slobbering merchant ever again. Ever!

Provided, he told himself as he mounted the stallion and sent him galloping off into the night, I can get into Shadowkeep and out again alive.

Chapter III

His enthusiasm waned as he left behind the fertile hills that surrounded Sasubree and entered the Barrens. The chill air of fall, the grasses which were already starting to turn brown and stiff, the drifting of leaves from isolated trees combined to lower his spirits if not his expectations. It's difficult to feel confident and assured when one is cold and alone in a strange country. For the first time, the enormity of what he'd undertaken was beginning to weigh heavily on him.

Out on the Barrens, away from the familiar, warm shop of Shone Stelft, the world seemed much more real, death considerably less abstract. To counter the dreariness of the sky and his mood he had only the words of the Spinner. And why would the Spinner encourage him to try Shadowkeep unless he thought Practor had a chance of succeeding? That thought encouraged him a little, caused him to sit straight in his saddle. He would succeed. He had to succeed.

Yet, what did he know of the Spinner's moral values? He'd been concerned with the evil that infested Shadowkeep, with ridding the world of its influence. What did it matter if a few died to make the world safe? That would be small consolation to the few, Practor mused, especially if the few included him.

But he'd made his decision, as he'd told Shone Stelft so boldly that night. He couldn't go back now. He'd broken with his past. Oh, Stelft would accept him back into his service if he returned now, but in so doing he'd be admitting defeat. He'd be leaving his soul behind, out on the Barrens.

And what of Rysancy? She'd be glad to have him back, but what would she think of his future promises if he failed to make good on this one? Wouldn't there always be the least little bit of hesitancy, of uncertainty in the back of her mind every time he said he was going to do something for her?

No, the fact of the matter was clear. He couldn't go back now if he wanted to. His words had restricted his options as surely as if Mostana Canyon had appeared between Sasubree and the Barrens. There was nowhere for him to ride save eastward. Eastward to Shadowkeep.

Of game he saw little, only the occasional rodent or wild sheep. The rodents were small, elusive, and chewy, while the plump sheep were dangerous to challenge out in the open. The saliva of the Barrens' sheep was toxic and could be spat an impressive distance. They were not like the harmless, domesticated sheep of Sasubree's farms and markets. So Practor took care to avoid the herds he encountered, for all that the aroma of mutton was thick in his mouth.

As the days slid past, the Barrens gave way to the veldt. He'd listened to tales of that verdant land from travelers, but had never expected to set eyes on it, much less to cross it. Yet there it lay before him, an endless expanse of waist-high grass interspersed with clumps of wild, contorted trees that stretched off toward the eastern horizon. Wind whipped the grass into abstract patterns as he started down.

He made camp each night beneath the far-reaching branches of the umbrella trees. Their leaves offered some protection from nightly rains and the vast canopies were reassuring buffers against the large, flying carnivores that were reputed to haunt the expanses of the veldt.

Kaltar proved to be a tireless mount, eager to break a path through the high grass each day and responsive to Practor's every tug on the reins. It accepted his company and directions readily. Practor had planned to ride into Shadowkeep on whatever mount Minza provided him, but as he rode his intentions changed. Kaltar was not his property. He would have to do as he'd said: find someplace outside Shadowkeep to stable the stallion until he came out.

Besides, that way the horse would be well rested for the return journey, and it would need all its great strength to carry both Practor and the treasure he intended to bring out with him. Thoughts of treasure and the look that would come over Rysancy's face when he spread it out before her helped to warm him and to stiffen his resolve.

The veldt grasses bent readily beneath Kaltar's chest and still they encountered nothing larger than the occasional herd of sheep. There were no signs of the large meat-eaters which were known to inhabit the veldt. With luck, Practor thought, most of them were already denned up for the winter.

Several large shauks had been shadowing him for days, but they were primarily carrion eaters. They would drift away as soon as it became clear to them that neither Practor nor his mount was on the verge of dying.

So he was doubly surprised in the morning when the huge scavengers did not appear and Kaltar began to whinny and backpedal uneasily. He had to struggle to retain control of his unexpectedly nervous mount.

"Stay there, Kaltar! Slowly, slowly. What ails you?" He leaned forward to pat the horse reassuringly on the side of his neck. The stallion steadied a little.

Practor tried to see through the high grass. "You smell something? Is that it?" No matter how hard he stared he could find no reason for the stallion's sudden panic. Only the wind ruffled the grasses around them. A thoulun could approach silently, but they never hunted in packs and it was difficult to imagine one's attacking a man on horseback.

Still, something had startled the horse. He put his hand to his sword, looked warily toward the trees. Something high up in the branches, waiting for them to pass? He tugged gently on the right rein and Kaltar started forward. They'd give the umbrella tree just ahead a wide berth. He'd find another place to halt for lunch.

Something struck the middle of his back. Kaltar jerked, rose on hind legs as a strong arm went around Practor's chest. High-pitched screams and hoots filled the air. Again Kaltar reared, and this time both Practor and his assailant were thrown to the ground. Practor fought to free his sword while shouts sounded all around him.

"That's it . . . get him! . . . he's the one . . . !" Each word ended in a whistle and the air was full of strong musk.

Practor finally broke free and rolled through the grass, still fighting to free his sword. His jaw fell as he finally got a look at his attackers.

They were not animals.

The words had told him as much, but it was still shocking to see the three of them standing there before him. They didn't look very threatening, but their actions had belied their appearance. He knew what they were because their kind came often into Sasubree to trade.

Roos. Powerful marsupials standing as tall as a man.

40

Their long ears rose straight and alert from their narrow heads, except for those of the one on the right. His drooped like a lop-eared rabbit's. Oversized feet were counterbalanced by a long, strong tail.

One stepped forward, halted when Practor half drew his sword. The male was clad in a long vest fashioned from strips of leather. They hung down to his knees. Each strip was dyed a different color. The costume was colorful and bright, in a vulgar sort of way.

The roo was rotating his right arm and grimacing. "Did you have to fall on me, man?"

"What am I supposed to do?" Practor snapped back at him. "Apologize for defending myself?" He moved warily to his left to take up Kaltar's reins. The other two held long, thin spears. Could he mount and flee before they spitted him?

The roo whose arm he'd fallen on advanced. His hands were open and empty, all his spears riding in the oversized quiver strapped to his back.

"I guess not." He extended a hand. "I'm Sranul. Nice to meet you."

"Is it? I mean, it is?" A little dazed and wary of deception, Practor reached out with his own hand. The roo took it, shook it enthusiastically. "Practor Fime, late of Sasubree." He glanced at the other two roos, who looked on approvingly. "Listen, what's going on here? I mean, am I your prisoner or what?" Suddenly Kaltar bolted, pulling free of Practor's grasp and dashing off into the grass.

"Hell!" Practor cursed. Now he'd have to run down the stallion on foot.

"Relax," the roo who'd offered his paw advised Practor. "The rest of the boys will catch him. They won't harm him. We won't harm you either, if you'll give us your word you won't try to escape. All we want is your cooperation, if you know what I mean."

"No. No, I don't know what you mean. But okay—I give you my word." He had nothing to lose by doing so. There wasn't a man alive who could outrun a roo in the open. "For a while, anyway. At least until I find out what you want my cooperation for."

"Good enough," said one of the other roos. "We're not capturing you, you know. Only borrowing your services." He put up his spear. His companion did likewise.

Borrowing his services? How did they know what services he could provide? Did he look that much like a smith already? And even if they suspected his profession, what use would a bunch of nomadic roos have for a smith?

"This way," said Sranul, gesturing with his right hand. He fell in step alongside the human while his companions brought up the rear. "How is it someone like yourself is wandering around away out here in the veldt?"

Practor tried to stand a little taller. "I am on an important mission. I'm going to Shadowkeep."

"Shadowkeep!" The roo didn't try to hide his interest. "What business could you have in Shadowkeep?"

"I am bound to try and free the wizard Gorwyther from the grasp of the demon king, Dal'brad—and incidentally, to improve my own fortunes."

"You'd better have more than good intentions on your side, then," declared one of the roos bounding along behind him. "You'd best be on the good side of Mother Fate."

"Especially," chuckled his companion, "if you can't get your sword out of that sheath any faster than that."

Practor felt his face flush. "You startled me, the more fortunate for all of you. I wasn't expecting to be attacked out in the middle of nowhere."

"Never expect not to be attacked," Sranul advised him

solemnly, "and you'll live a lot longer, man. It's the suspicious who survive." He put a comradely arm around Practor's shoulders, confusing him further.

What was going on here? What did these roos have in mind? It seemed they were going to kill him or adopt him, and he was damned if he could figure out which. Would he find himself shaking hands next with a spear?

It didn't make any sense. Roos had a reputation for being unpredictable. All he could do was play along, smile, and see how events developed.

He relaxed a little when they were joined by another half-dozen of Sranul's companions. One led Kaltar easily by the bridle. The stallion looked winded but otherwise unharmed. The roo who led him wore a vest similar to Sranul's, only not quite as garishly colored.

It occurred to Practor that by covering their naturally golden-hued fur with such brightly painted garb, they were forfeiting their natural camouflage. He asked Sranul about it.

The warrior responded with a toothy grin. "Hardly the sporting thing to do, letting oneself blend in completely with the scenery. Besides, who would we need to conceal ourselves from?

"From possible prey."

"Prey?" Sranul let out a short, barking laugh. "Our 'prey' doesn't run from us, Practor." He showed his teeth and for the second time in as many minutes Practor felt embarrassed.

In the rush of the attack he'd forgotten that the roos were wholly vegetarian. In that respect they posed no more threat to him than a herd of cows.

They were leading him down a gentle slope toward a small lake. There were more trees below and the high grass of the veldt receded from the waterline. A pleasant place to camp. He would've ridden straight past without suspecting the lake's existence. But then, he was a stranger to this land, which the roos knew intimately.

The roos were plant-eaters, not hunters. So why had they been hunting him? Did they consider him some kind of threat? That hardly seemed credible. The roos were famed fighters, afraid of no one, least of all a lone rider unaware of their very presence. Or was he a participant in some kind of elaborate game? The roo-folk were famed for that as well.

The roo encampment spread out along the shore of the lake. Young roos bounded and jumped among the high reeds that throve in the shallows, setting up a terrific splashing and yelling. Indulgent adults looked on, ready to step in should the horseplay become too rough or the youngest be trampled underfoot.

Tall, peaked tents were set up haphazardly beside a narrow cove. Each was painted a different color and boasted a specific pattern which identified the clan of the owners. Dray animals grazed peacefully in several temporary corrals. The portles rolled in the dust or threw water on their tough hides with long flexible trunks that could reach all the way to their tails.

At least half of the tents had a cook-fire crackling outside the entrance. The odor of cooking meat was, of course, absent, but Practor could smell rich soups and all manner of spicy vegetable dishes in various stages of preparation. The air was rich with exotic aromas.

Near the middle of the encampment stood several larger tents as well as wooden constructions whose purpose was not immediately clear. It was toward this central location that Practor's captors led him.

As they entered the camp's outskirts they were surrounded by a small mob of unruly roos, all chattering and gesturing simultaneously. They pointed toward Practor and whispered

44

under their breath. What he overheard of their talk was not particularly reassuring.

"Yes, he'll do...He's perfect!...he'll be wonderful... It's about time..."

Wonderful? Perfect? Do for what? The roos were a rough, crude people not noted for their delicate dispositions. Just because they weren't going to eat him didn't mean he was going to leave this place with his skin intact.

He tried to imagine what the younger Shone Stelft would have done if he'd found himself in a similar position, but that wasn't very inspiring because he suspected the younger Shone Stelft would never have let himself be put in such a position.

They passed between the smaller tents, then the larger. By now Practor was so hemmed in by chattering, excited roos that he couldn't have made a run for it even had he wished to. The crowd, with Practor in the middle, emerged into the open area in the center of the camp. Glossy pennants snapped from the crests of long poles. Directly ahead was a raised platform.

A small bench was bolted to the top of the platform. Target practice, Practor thought suddenly. This was some kind of circus, and they were going to use him for target practice. He tried to remember what he'd been told of roo weaponry. They favored long, light spears, which, it was reported, they could throw accurately while simultaneously leaping twelve feet into the air. Sure, that was it. They needed a target on which to test their skill, and he was the lucky bull's-eye.

He was unable to maintain his pose of stoic indifference any longer. "What are they going to do to me, Sranul?"

"Nothing harmful, I promise you, friend Practor. Stand easy and breathe slow."

Sure, Practor thought. Why not? He couldn't do anything else. What a lot of cheery assassins he'd been captured by. They'd probably all laugh when the first spear struck his belly.

They were hustling him up the steps onto the platform. "Have a seat," Sranul told him, gesturing toward the single bench.

Practor hesitated. If he could make it into the water, there was a chance he could outswim them. But by now there were at least fifty adult roos between the platform and the cove. He sat, leaned back against the bench, took a deep breath, and determined not to beg no matter what they threatened to do to him.

Something was placed on his head. It was heavy but not painful. It slid down over his eyes. The cheering around him intensified. When no one moved to stop him, he reached up to shove the object back onto his forehead. Sranul stood nearby grinning down at him.

Using both hands, he examined the thing on his head with careful fingers. It wasn't iron or even wood, and felt too flimsy to serve as an instrument of torture. It seemed to be made of woven reed. Tassels dangled from its sides, strips of brightly dyed cloth and cord attached to small bells.

"What's this?" he asked dubiously, more confused than ever.

"Why, it's your crown," Sranul told him, bending low, "Your Majesty."

Practor gaped at him. "My *what?*"

"It's our custom," the roo explained gleefully. "Every month at carnival time we send out hunting parties to ambush some unwary traveler. We bring them back to our camp to serve as carnival king or queen. If you knew us better, you'd know that we roos will hold a carnival at the drop of a tail. This particular carnival is in celebration of the Fall Harvest. Next month it will be in celebration of the After-Fall Harvest. The month after that we salute First Winter Signs, and so forth.

"There is much competition among the clans to see who will be the first to find a new carnival ruler. The only stipulations are that it may not be a roo and must be an adult. It's quite exciting, travelers through the veldt being scarce this time of the year. We found you and now the other clans must acknowledge our supremacy for another month." He beamed.

"But I don't know how to be a king," Practor protested. "I haven't even had much experience at being a traveler. What am I expected to do?"

Sranul moved close, leaned over and put a paw on Practor's shoulder as he whispered to him. "Just stand up, smile, wave your hand and say, 'I now declare the festivities begun!' "

Practor hesitated briefly, then shrugged and stood. He gestured feebly with his right hand and said hoarsely, "Let the festivities begin."

The crowd went into a frenzy. A couple of fistfights broke out near the back ranks, and there was a concerted break for the fires where food was cooking. Skins of drink appeared as if by magic.

Practor sat down and whispered weakly to his friend. "That's it? That's all I have to do?"

"That's all you have to do, besides lending us your majesterial presence for a while."

"Hmm." So he wasn't going to be used for target practice. Quite the contrary, it seemed. "If I'm king, do you think I could get something to eat?"

"Well, we've no meat for you, but we can't very well let our carnival ruler starve, now can we?"

A female roo who'd overheard stepped forward. "What do you want with meat? We have fruits and vegetables, all the bounty of the earth. Come with me, Your Majesty, and learn the hospitality of the clans.''

By evening Practor was suffering not from a lack of food but from a surfeit of it, since each marsupial matron insisted he try the best of her personal cuisine. He was so stuffed he could hardly walk.

Fires lined the lakeshore, and fighting and drinking gave way to singing and dancing. The roos made music with flutes and drums, and their dancing was, to put it mildly, spectacular. Members of each clan would surround a fire and, in perfect time to the music, twist and spin eight to twelve feet above the ground. Naturally enough, they landed precisely on each downbeat.

There was much good-natured arguing over which dancers were best. None of it was abrasive, all of it high-spirited. The roos were an intensely competitive folk, quick to take exception to an imagined or real insult, quick to fight, and equally as ready to forgive.

In addition to being flashy dancers and fast talkers, they were also master brewers. It was wonderful to taste what they could manufacture from a simple root. He tried to restrict himself as much as possible to those liquids of a nonalcoholic variety.

Much later that night, when he thought no one was watching, he carefully removed his elaborate headdress and set it aside in an empty tent. If he could just find where they'd hitched Kaltar, he could sneak off quietly and be on his way. Not that his duties were anything other than pleasant, but he had a world to save.

Someone was waiting to confront him outside the tent, however.

"What's this?" said Sranul, "abdicating already? Do you find our company so displeasing?"

"Not at all." In spite of all his efforts to prevent it, Practor let out a thunderous belch. "It's just that I'm not

48

sure I can survive any more of your honors. If I have to eat another bite, it'll kill me for sure. I'll explode all over your celebration." His eyes widened as he spotted a portly figure coming toward him. The matron carried a tray piled high with pastries.

"Quick, in here!" He grabbed Sranul's arm and yanked him into the tent.

"What is it, what's wrong?"

"Quiet." Practor peered anxiously around the tent flap, watched until the matron had vanished from sight. He let out a sigh of relief. "That one's been after me all day to try her baking. I couldn't take it, Sranul. I've seen her pastry. It looks delicious beyond belief, but if I have to eat one lousy tart, it'll kill me for sure."

Sranul looked sympathetic. "We can't have that. A dead king's no good at all."

"When," Practor inquired tiredly, "does my reign end?"

"At High Moon tonight. After that you'll be free to leave if you wish."

"Free to leave? Sranul, I can barely walk." He sat down hard on a fat cushion and groaned.

"Come to think of it, you do look a little green. That is not a normal human color, is it?"

"No, it's not."

"What makes you want to leave in the middle of the night anyway? It must be something more than a desperate desire to avoid our cooking. Such haste. And I see anxiety written all over your face, even if it is tinted green." The roo looked thoughtful. "What draws you so powerfully to Shadowkeep? I've heard of the place, and from what I've heard I can't imagine why you or anyone else would want to go there."

Practor told him the story. Sranul listened intently and without interrupting.

"I see," he murmured when the human had concluded

his tale. "So you are going to try and penetrate the castle labyrinth to rescue this wizard Gorwyther while battling the servants of the demon king along the way?"

"I wish everyone would quit trying to sound so encouraging," Practor grumbled. "I don't need any more negative opinions."

"I wasn't trying to venture one." He leaned forward eagerly. "Tell me more about this great treasure you say lies within."

"There is no more wondrous anywhere in the world. Or so I'm told."

"Really." The roo examined his guest appraisingly. "You're going to have a hard time of it, if you don't mind my saying so. You look a bit on the frail side."

"Perhaps I do, by your standards, but I'm pretty strong and agile for a human, and maybe even a bit quicker than you. I'm not afraid. Worried, sure, but not afraid."

Sranul was nodding to himself. "Help. If you're going to have any chance of succeeding in this, you're going to need help. Sounds like a bit of a lark anyway."

"But you just said . . ."

"I know what I said. But where's the fun in anything if there's not a little danger involved?"

Hardly daring to hope, Practor asked, "What are you trying to say?"

"That if you don't mind my company, I'd like to come with you. I'm one of the ten best spear-chuckers in the whole tribe and the best in my clan. I've no family, no immediate plans to start one, and nothing to do tomorrow except drink myself into a stupor. I can do that any carnival time. So what do you say, man? Will you have my company?"

"Gladly!" Practor rose from the cushion and extended a hand. The roo accepted it, enveloped the man's fingers in warm fur.

"That's settled then."

But Practor wanted to be certain. "You're not doing this because you're drunk now, are you, or because you feel sorry for me?"

Sranul looked disgusted. "You talk like a human. I'm going for one reason only: because it's something I want to do. But if I have to spend the whole trip listening to typically silly human guilt fantasies, then I'm going to go without you."

Practor had to force himself not to smile. "I'll try to keep my emotions well hidden."

"Good. You really shouldn't leave until your reign is up, though. Wouldn't be very practical if you snuck away in the dark only to have members of another clan find you and bring you back."

"If you think it best." Practor rubbed his swollen stomach. "But I don't know how much more of my subjects' largess I can handle."

It was much as he'd feared. The following morning the ex-carnival king was forced to endure the largest breakfast he'd ever seen. There were tasary muffins bursting with nuts, half a dozen varieties of fresh bread, more of the roos' extraordinary pastries and several types of drink distilled from rich grains and tubers, plus the usual Brobdingnagian assortment of fresh fruit. Food swamped the tables, overflowed onto the ground where scavenging pets fought and snarled over the scraps. The roo larder was bottomless.

Practor's stomach, however, was not, and he finally had to call a halt regardless of whose feelings he might be hurting.

"Thank you, thank you, my friends, it's been wonderful, but it really is time for me to go." He staggered away from the table and prayed he could mount Kaltar without throwing up.

One of the ubiquitous matrons intercepted him. "Please, good king, just one more bite. You haven't sampled my zuzenza yet." She held out a ball of puff pastry white with sugar coating and bursting with candied fruit. Practor felt himself growing weak.

He waved feebly at her. "No, I really can't eat another thing. Take it away. *Please* take it away."

Sranul stepped between them, gently admonished the disappointed baker. "Enough. We've done well by our king and he by us, but even roo hospitality can be overdone."

"That's true," shouted several onlookers.

"We'll be sorry to see you go," added an elder, whose chest and shoulder fur was turning white. "You've been a right decent carnival king. Maybe we'll be lucky enough to capture you on your way back through the veldt. Then you can serve us again."

Practor put both hands to his mouth and pushed wildly away from his admirers, running frantically toward the lake. The older roo looked puzzled.

"Did I say something wrong?"

"Men are strange," Sranul observed sagely, "and this one, I think, stranger than most. They make good carnival kings, though."

"He doesn't look well," commented another onlooker.

"I'd better see if he needs help." Sranul hopped toward the shore, where his new friend appeared to be suffering from some kind of internal spasms.

It was far from fatal, though, and as soon as a clear path had opened through the food, Practor made a dash for his horse. Sranul bounded alongside effortlessly, content to follow the human's lead. The roo wore a large backpack. Several others had been secured behind Kaltar's saddle. They were bursting with foodstuffs. That, at least, would not be a problem for the travelers. One of Practor's foremost concerns had been alleviated. They would not have to pause along the way to work for their supper.

With the enthusiastic cheers of the clans ringing in their ears, the peculiar pair started off eastward.

"I'd always heard that being a king was a harder job than most," Practor commented as they pressed on through the high grass, "but I had no idea it was so fulfilling. I'm not sure I was worthy of the honor."

"You honored us." Sranul kept pace with Kaltar easily. In addition to his kilt he wore a quiver on his back that held a dozen javelins. Two knives were strapped to his waist, one on either side. The same belt that held them prevented the lower flaps of his leather-strip kilt from flying up into his face every time he took one of his prodigious hops.

"You're sure you can keep up okay?" Practor asked him.

"Keep up with you?" Sranul gave that barking laugh of his and jumped sideways instead of forward. He went right over Practor, clearing the top of the human's head by at least half a foot. The roo landed on the other side of Kaltar and immediately bounded back over Practor again. He performed the feat a dozen times, without apparent strain, while Practor fought to keep the uneasy stallion under control.

"Okay, I believe you. I wish I could jump like that."

"Yes, and I wish I could crawl on my belly through the small places the way a human can. Each of us can do things the other cannot. On a long and dangerous journey, complementary company is the best kind."

"I agree, but I'd have settled for any kind of company at all," Practor confessed. "I had no idea how much the loneliness was going to affect me."

"Tell me, friend Practor, how will we enter Shadowkeep when we arrive at its outskirts, and how will we know how to proceed once we're inside? If it's as big as they say it is, we might not have to worry about fighting this Dal'brad's forces. We might be able to wander through it unnoticed.''

"I don't think we'll be that lucky, but there's no harm in wishing. As for getting inside, that should be simple. It's getting out again that seems to be hard. Once we're in, there must be some kind of guidelines, some kind of markers that enable visitors to find their way about, that we can make use of. Actually, I hadn't thought about it much. My first concern is to get there. One thing at a time.''

"You won't find me arguing that philosophy. We roos live from day to day. Still, it would be nice to have someone with us who can see a little farther into the future, whose perception penetrates deeper than ours in matters demonic and mystical.'' He looked thoughtful, finally stopped alongside a tall dereid bush. Practor reined Kaltar in.

"I've got it!" In imitation of the human gesture, the roo tried to snap his fingers. All he produced was a whispery rushing sound. It's hard to snap one's fingers properly when they're covered with fine rust-colored fur.

"Got what?"

"I know who we should have with us. One of those who possess the foresight denied to us. One not as inclined to impetuosity as a roo nor to fighting as a human. A thaladar.''

Practor looked dubious. "Wishful thinking, Sranul. The thaladar are a proud, snobbish folk who keep to themselves and have as little as possible to do with outsiders. They keep to themselves and do not mix with the other intelligent races unless it's for their benefit.''

"Just my point,'' said Sranul eagerly. "Isn't it obvious? This great evil you speak of, this Shadowkeep danger, threatens them just as it does humans and roos. I'd imagine they'd be more than willing to help.''

''A fanciful hope.'' Still, he was intrigued by the thought of obtaining thaladar aid. ''I suppose we can try. But where?''

Sranul pointed to the southeast. ''A city of theirs, Socalia, lies not far from here. What have we to lose by journeying there and presenting our case? If we explain our intentions, we may come away with advice if not open assistance.''

''We could lose several days' travel time, that's what.''

''Wouldn't it be best to challenge Shadowkeep with as much knowledge as possible? Better to arrive later and better armed than to enter in haste and perish immediately.''

Practor shrugged. ''I've already agreed to try it, though I think it's a fool's detour. I wouldn't know what to say to a thaladar.''

''I'll do the talking if you like. I don't mind talking, not even to a thaladar.''

''No, that's all right. I accepted the challenge from the Spinner, and you're here because of what I had to say. I'll undertake the conversation somehow, though I don't look forward to it.''

''You humans. So optimistic.'' Sranul bounded on ahead.

Their course paralleled a slowly meandering stream lined with the last flowers of the season. Bright red blooms bent to the wind, unwilling as yet to concede the arrival of winter while there was still another day for pollination to occur. As long as the bees persisted, so would the blossoms.

Gradually the veldt gave way to forest. Along with the first stands of trees they sighted thaladar farms, each neater and better kept than the finest human establishment. Strange stares followed them as they continued on toward Socalia. Trading time was past, and it was unusual to see a human riding along the road, much less in the company of a heavily armed roo.

Practor ignored the eyes as best he could and tried to tell himself they were the object of attention because of their presence, not because there was anything wrong with the way they looked or the way he rode. He was, nevertheless, more conscious than usual of his posture and held himself straight as a fencepost on Kaltar's back. The thaladar were perfectionists and as critical of others as they were of themselves. It was a characteristic that did nothing to endear them to their neighbors.

Almond-eyed children watched their passage as quietly as did the adults. Practor noted the resemblances to human children. Like the grown-ups, they were much like humans, though shorter and slimmer. More obvious differences were the solemn, slanted eyes and the narrow, pointed ears.

Thaladar bore close resemblance to the elves of legend, though they were considerably bigger. Some said they were the offspring of humans and elves. Practor didn't know what to think. He was no historian. He saw that only the adults wore the thaladar skullcap over their black hair. Each cap was a different color and bore a different design.

Then there was no more time for observation. They were nearing the city.

Socalia was a handsome community, as large as Sasubree and ringed with a protective wall of pure white limestone. The towers that flanked the main gate were sheathed in black marble. Socalia's flag, a half-eclipsed moon on a blank field, flew from poles stepped into the walls. The gate itself was open and alive with traffic.

It was the quiet that struck Practor, so much in contrast to the constant babble of noise that filled the commercial sections of Sasubree. Everything was so organized and carried out with such precision! Evidently there wasn't any need for casual conversation. There was no cursing or loud hawking of goods. Even the draft animals moved in comparative silence. His impressions were confirmed by Sranul. Socalia might appear silent in contrast to a human town, but compared to a roo encampment it was like a mortuary.

No one tried to stop them as they passed through the gate. Thaladar on foot moved aside to make way for Kaltar.

"Solemn, but polite," Practor observed.

"Yeah. Great party folk," Sranual commented sarcastically. "It's a good thing they're so damned smart or no one would pay them any attention at all."

"I think that would suit them just fine." Practor swerved to intercept a group of richly robed citizens, leaned down toward them. "Pardon me. Could you tell me . . . ?"

Without missing a step, the group turned leftward and walked away, murmuring among themselves. It wasn't as if they'd shunned the visitor. They hadn't even acknowledged his presence.

Practor shrugged it off. Maybe the conversation had been important. He looked around until he located a single soldier standing near the wall, sent Kaltar trotting over.

"Hi! Listen, I wonder if you would . . . ?"

The soldier didn't even look up as he turned his back on Practor. When he tried again, the soldier simply left his post and walked into a nearby shop.

Practor persisted, confronting other citizens both mounted and on foot. They ignored him as though he weren't there. Sranul went so far as to put a hand on one passing elder, grabbing him by the shoulder to keep him from walking past. He was completely bald, Practor noted. Come to think of it, there didn't seem to be a beard or mustache in the whole city. It gave the inhabitants an incongruously youthful appearance, which was belied by the contemptuous look in their eyes as they regarded the outsiders.

The elderly thaladar responded silently to Sranul's overture by disengaging himself from the roo's grasp and continuing on his way as though his progress had never been interrupted. He neither smiled nor frowned.

"I don't think we're going to find much help here," Practor told his companion. "It's pretty hard to get any advice when no one will even let you ask your question."

"They'll listen," said Sranul belligerently. "You get behind one. I'll jump on his chest and hold him down until he talks. Let's see them ignore *that*. I've had just about enough of these skinny snobs, my friend. Yeah, I know coming here was my idea, but that doesn't mean it was a good idea." He stared at the milling crowd, singled out a likely target for his attentions. "There's one. Get around behind him."

"No, Sranul." There were worse things than being ignored, Practor knew. If they actually used force on a citizen, he could envision the thaladar soldiers—silently and politely, of course—skewering them on their gleaming pikes.

As it turned out, he didn't have to worry about restraining his friend. One of the thaladar did it for him, stepping between the roo and his intended target. Sranul reached out as if to push the intruder aside, and hesitated. The reason for his hesitation was clear, for while the thaladar who'd stepped in front of him was no larger or stronger than any other, Practor had to admit that she was exceedingly beautiful.

Chapter IV

"If you'll excuse me, ma'am, there's something I have to do." Sranul moved as if to step around her. She immediately shifted to block his path again.

"What's that?" she asked him. "Make a fool of yourself?"

The roo gaped at her, then nodded knowingly. "What about this, friend Practor? At least one of them can talk. No, ma'am. I'm not going to make a fool of myself. Your friends are doing that already."

"Don't do something you will regret." She indicated those around them. "You may think you are being ignored, but you are not. On the contrary, you are the centers of attention."

"Sure we are," said the roo. "I can tell by the way everyone's come up to give us a friendly hello and a pat on the back."

"You misinterpret our reactions, but it is true that we thaladar are not back-patters. We are more restrained in our relationships with others."

"Any more restrained and you'd all be corpses," Sranul muttered sourly.

She turned to look up at Practor. "Some of us are more curious about outsiders than others. Tell me, how come a man and a roo to be traveling together in this part of the world?''

"Our coming here was Sranul's idea." Practor smiled down at her. She really was lovely, he thought. "We're embarked on a difficult journey and he thought we could use some good thaladar advice. I'm Practor Fime, by the way, and that's Sranul."

"I am called Maryld. So you come to Socalia in search of advice?"

"No," snapped Sranul, "we like to be ignored."

Maryld did just that by talking only to Practor. "What kind of advice do you seek?"

"Any we can get that will help us penetrate and avoid the dangers of Shadowkeep."

The barest hint of a smile creased perfect lips. "At least you don't boast of it. I am not one to pass judgment on the intentions of others, but I may be able to help you. Come with me." She turned and started down a side street without glancing back to see if they were following.

"What do you think?" Sranul watched the woman's progress suspiciously.

"We've nothing to lose by accompanying her and maybe much to gain."

The roo nodded. "Might as well listen to whatever she has in mind, especially since the rest of the population's being so cooperative."

The woman led them down several narrow streets between tall, clean buildings. By now Practor was almost used to the silent stares their appearance provoked.

The street opened onto a wide avenue paved with triangular stones. Impressive two-story homes on manicured grounds lined both sides of the pathway. Maryld stopped before an iron gate, nudged it open, and beckoned for them to follow.

Beyond the gate lay a lush garden full of plants Practor

didn't recognize. They passed a noisy fountain and walking under an archway decorated with mosaic inlay, found themselves standing before a reflecting pool in a central courtyard. A housekeeper appeared and took Kaltar's reins. Practor dismounted, entranced by the beauty of the structure around him.

"My home," Maryld said simply. "Your horse will be well cared for." She moved toward the reflecting pool.

Practor admired the lacy iron grillwork which framed porches and doorways and was a perfect complement to the black tile roof. "What do you do that you can afford to live in such a palace? Are you of a noble family?"

"There are no noble families among the thaladar, at least not in the sense there are among humans, but as you may know, wisdom and learning are well regarded among my people. My grandmother and mother are both highly respected and well-paid sages."

She led them across the courtyard, which was paved with black tiles, past a smaller, inner atrium with another fountain, and into a room whose walls were lined with embroidered draperies and damask streamers.

Seated in a lounge chair in one corner was an old woman of indeterminate age, smoking something through a long pipe. Her hair was white as fireplace ash but her face was hardly wrinkled. It might have been the naturally delicate cast of thaladar features that contributed to the feeling of youthfulness that clung to her, or perhaps it was the winsome smile that played across her lips as she caught sight of her granddaughter.

"You're home early, Maryld." She looked past her. "And you've brought home a couple of strangers, too. What strange strangers they are."

Sranul muttered something under his breath and Practor hastily stepped forward, introduced himself and his companion to "relieve the strangeness." Maryld leaned over

61

her grandmother and whispered in her ear. The old woman listened thoughtfully, making Practor uncomfortable with her stare. Then Maryld stepped back. She did not take a seat but instead stood respectfully at her grandmother's side.

"To Shadowkeep you go, eh? To save the world no less. From what?"

"The demon king has imprisoned the wizard Gorwyther and now claims Shadowkeep for his base of operations."

"Hum. So it is rumored." She smiled at her visitor and said quite matter-of-factly, "You will never leave that place alive."

"That kind of advice we can get anywhere," he shot back. "That's not why we've gone to the trouble of coming here to Socalia."

"It's not advice." She did not react to his anger. "It is a statement of fact. I don't mean to cast aspersions on your intentions, which are nothing if not good, or to impugn your abilities. I'm sure both of you are brave and courageous and good fighters willing to take chances, but you will need more than that if you are to have any hope of succeeding. You will need more of what is here." She passed a palm across her forehead.

Practor tried to control himself. He was beginning to share some of Sranul's frustration. The thaladar were not easy to deal with. "We're not stupid, you know."

"I didn't mean to imply that you were, young man. The kind of knowledge I refer to is not acquired in casual studies of the sort humans favor, or roos either. It is specialized and requires many years of study at the foot of a true master. Only with such knowledge at your disposal can you hope to have a chance of surviving Shadowkeep."

"How many thaladar have done so?"

"We have no reason to go to Shadowkeep," she replied evenly. "We have ignored it just as we have the rest of the world. But if these stories are true, if Dal'brad has overcome the good Gorwyther . . ."

"It happened years ago," Practor told her, interrupting without fear of consequences.

She took no offense. "Yes, so it is said. It is time something was done. You must understand, young man, that most of the thaladar feel invulnerable in their cities. It is hard for us to believe that the outside world can endanger us here."

"You said 'most.' But not you."

"No. I am convinced that we are in as much danger as everyone else. I have argued the point repeatedly with the Council of Elders, to no avail. Even the thaladar are not immune to the perils of overconfidence."

"If you agree that the danger is real, then you'll help us. Tell us how we can avoid the dangers of Shadowkeep, the traps and deceptions that we'll encounter there."

She bestowed on him a copy of that initial winning smile. "Alas, brave human, I cannot."

"Cannot?" Sranul snorted. "I thought the thaladar knew how to do anything."

"We cannot see across the leagues nor penetrate solid walls," she replied calmly. "In order to cope with a danger, one must first be able to study the danger. That must be done in person. A thaladar must accompany you on your journey. Only in that way will you have our learning available to you at all times."

Practor was hesitant. "You mean, one of you would actually consent to come with us to Shadowkeep? We came seeking advice. I never thought that . . ."

"It is the only way," she told him firmly. But that wasn't the only surprise the thaladar women had in store for him.

Maryld moved to stand a little closer to her grandmother, put a hand on her shoulder. "I will go with you."

"Now, hold on," Practor said quickly. "When I said 'one of you,' I thought..."

"A thaladar male?" Maryld was smiling at him. It didn't help that she looked amused.

"It's not that we don't appreciate the offer," he said quickly. "It's just that I thought you meant we'd have the company of someone with more experience."

"You rationalize well, for a man." She smiled and perfect little teeth gleamed in the diffuse light of the sitting room. "I can fight and take care of myself and will be no burden to you on that score. Besides which, it seems to me that between yourself and long ears over there, your expedition is already blessed with a surfeit of muscle. That is not what you need from the thaladar, remember?" She touched her forehead. "You need what I have up here.

"You might indeed manage to find a thaladar warrior willing to accompany you, but he would not be half so skilled in matters mystical as I."

"It's not that," Practor said, acutely uncomfortable, "it's just that I'd worry about you. I won't have time for that in Shadowkeep."

"Your chivalrous concern does you credit, but in my case it is misplaced," she told him. "I am not frail. We thaladar are stronger than we look. If it is my age that concerns you, you should know that we also live longer than human or roo. I am considerably older than a human woman of comparable appearance." She put a hand over her mouth. To conceal a laugh?

He took a deep breath. He was being foolish and he knew it. They'd come hoping for some advice and would come away with something infinitely more valuable: a thaladar volunteer to accompany and advise them. So what if she happened to be extremely beautiful? He would just have to learn how to cope with that.

Still, he would have refused the offer had Maryld's

personality been typically thaladarian. The fact that she was an open, even warm, individual was important. There was no room on the trail for a trio of conflicting personalities.

Maryld's mother joined them later that evening, and the generational line was complete. It was a bit eerie to look from daughter to mother to grandmother, for he saw Maryld in each of them, saw her not only as she was now but as she would be.

As he listened to the three of them discuss Maryld's coming journey, he had an uncomfortable thought. Each of these women was a teacher, Maryld only the latest in the line. Did she look on him as an equal in this venture, or as someone in need of instruction? As a pupil, perhaps? He hoped not, because he'd never be able to think of her as an elder instructor. There was no way of knowing how she felt about him without asking, and he wasn't about to jeopardize this new alliance by doing so. Thaladar vanity was as famous as thaladar wisdom.

Nevertheless, it was hard not to feel a little intimidated by all that knowledge. He confessed his feelings to Sranul.

"Don't worry about it so much, friend Practor. Sure they're smarter than we are. But there are all kinds of smarts. Why do you think the thaladar keep so close to their cities? It's because they're not particularly good in a fight, that's why. They pose and posture like actors, but when they're really threatened, they either talk their way out of a battle or pay off whoever's challenging them. They're not so tough."

"We don't need toughness from the thaladar. As Maryld said, you and I will handle the physical requirements of this expedition. We need her to help us pass Shadowkeep's mazes and traps."

"I know that." Sranul used a long finger to dig at one ear. "Just don't let this one intimidate you."

"She doesn't. It's all three of them together."

65

"Then I'm glad the two older ones aren't coming with us. One thaladar is plenty. I don't think I could take all three of them chattering at once, no matter how valuable their advice."

The proof of the roo's words came later, as the three women held what amounted to a thaladar council of war. Sranul stood it for as long as he could before he excused himself and stole away to the garden, leaving Practor to deal with the three sages by himself.

"You must not assume," the grandmother was telling him, "that you will ever have to confront Dal'brad directly. Shadowkeep is so big that not even the king of demons can keep watch on every room and corridor. With luck, you will be able to reach Gorwyther and free him before the demons realize what you have done."

"That is so," said the mother, whose name was Ferald. "The faster you can find Gorwyther, the better your chances of success. The demon king is known to suffer from overconfidence."

"Yes." The grandmother smiled. "Like us thaladar."

The same thought had been in Practor's mind, but he didn't dare voice it. He was relieved to see the two younger women laughing at the comparison.

"Like the thaladar," agreed Ferald. "It is said Dal'brad relies entirely on the safeguards he has installed in the castle. Since they have worked so well in the past, he will assume there is nothing to worry him in the future. He has no way of knowing that the brave and wise are about to come calling on him."

"Yet caution must ever be your watchword," said the grandmother sternly, wagging a warning finger at Practor. "Take care in everything you do. Attempt nothing without considering all possible ramifications beforehand. You must know when to rush boldly ahead lest pursuit overtake you."

"How do we know when to charge and when to consider?"

"Life, like Shadowkeep, is full of contradictions," said Maryld. "I will be there to advise you." She smiled again. Whenever she did that it was hard for Practor to realize how much older she was than him.

"Look," he said to take his thoughts off that smile, "if the thaladar have known of the danger posed by Shadowkeep for so long, why haven't you moved against it by now?"

Ferald looked from mother to daughter. "There have been proposals made in the past to do something, but as you know, we are not fond of physical combat. Certain things cannot be accomplished through use of logic and reason alone. Many demons are susceptible to logical argument, but the lower orders of imps and devils and poltergeists respond only to the most basic physical or emotional stimuli. You can be as reasonable as possible with them only to find yourself transfixed by an ax instead of an aphorism.

"The result, among the thaladar, has been a lot of talk but no action. I'm not proud of that."

"It has, therefore, been clear to me for a long time," the grandmother went on, "that in order for any penetration of Shadowkeep to take place, it would have to be carried out by a band of mixed individuals. Your coming to us offers us a chance to do just that. The thaladar will benefit if you succeed as much as will humans or roos."

"If you knew this, how come you never organized such an expedition yourselves?"

Again the embarrassed looks. Maryld nodded in the direction of the garden. "The roos distrust the thaladar, as do your own kind. This dislike we have brought on ourselves, by our aloofness and attitudes. Any overtures we might have made, any attempt to form a band of adventurers from all three races, would have been met with suspicion at best, hostility at worst. So we never tried.

"That is why your coming here now is so important. It is a chance we must not let slip away. We three recognize the danger inherent in Shadowkeep even if the rest of the thaladar do not. As teachers, we cannot bury our heads in the sand in the hope that evil will never reach the gates of Socalia."

"I wonder," Practor mused aloud, "if the Spinner knew this would come to pass. That one of you would come with us."

"This Spinner you've spoken of," the grandmother said, "is no Seer, I think. If so, I do not believe his range is great or he would have told you more than he did. He came only to warn of the danger posed by Dal'brad's machinations. If he were capable of more, he surely would have told you of your forthcoming meeting with the roo, at the least."

"That's right."

"It is of no moment. Better in a time of crisis to rely on your own instincts and knowledge than on the word of a wraith with unknown allegiances. What matters is that the three of you get to Shadowkeep and free Gorwyther in time to stop the demon king."

"You realize that once you enter the castle," Ferald told him, "it's unlikely you'll be able to get out again without accomplishing your purpose."

"I expect as much," Practor replied tightly. "I've prepared myself for that possibility."

"Good," said the grandmother. "Prepare for death, anticipate life." She sighed. "It's not good to get old. The machine doesn't work as well as it used to. I'm tired. Too tired to accompany you myself, too tired to talk any longer. Ferald?" Her daughter helped her rise from her chair.

"Rooms have been made ready for you and your friend," Maryld told him. "We'll leave at first light."

Practor nodded. "My thought as well." He climbed to his feet, gazed at each of the women in turn. "Thank you all. You're a remarkable family, and I consider myself fortunate to have met you." He turned to follow the housekeeper toward the stairs, then hesitated and looked back.

"I don't mean to pry into personal matters and I hope I'm not being impertinent, but I see three generations of thaladar women here—and no men." He fixed his attention on Maryld. "Where are your menfolk?"

The grandmother spoke first. "You asked why we had not tried to challenge Dal'brad before and we told you, but we did not tell you all. My husband and my daughter's husband went to Shadowkeep, not to try and free Gorwyther, which they realized they could not do, but to try and learn the castle's weaknesses. They never came back." Her last words had the finality of an ax blow.

Practor swallowed. "I'm sorry."

"So you see," the old woman went on, "our motives for helping you are more than altruistic. Or did you think the thaladar so devoid of emotion that we cannot feel a desire for revenge?"

"No. I never thought that. I just didn't know you had reason for it."

"You know now. You know everything now." She blinked. "I am tired. Ride hard and fast, young human, and bring my granddaughter back to me."

"As long as there is life in me," Practor assured her grimly.

Good as her word, Maryld was ready and waiting for them in the courtyard when Practor and Sranul emerged from their rooms. Her own mount was a mature horse the size of a pony. Saddlebags lay behind the small saddle.

She wore a heavy caftan of iridescent blue worked with silver thread and a matching cape of lighter blue that flowed down to her knees.

Practor spared a curious glance for the horse. No doubt the thaladar had bred them down to size over the centuries. They were good with animals. Knowledge, he thought, was as valuable a commodity as gold.

Kaltar stood patiently nearby, in the grip of a stableman. He greeted Practor with a snuffle. Practor grabbed the pommel and mounted.

Maryld looked questioningly at Sranul. "Your friend does not ride?"

"My legs don't fit comfortably around a horse's spine," the roo informed her. "And besides"—he bounded eight feet straight up—"as Practor can tell you, I can run as fast as any horse, turn quicker, and dodge better. Riding would reduce my mobility, not increase it. I'm built for long-distance hopping and you're not, so don't worry on my account."

Though Maryld had made her farewells the previous night, her mother and grandmother were still there to see her off. Their tender parting gave the lie to everything Practor had heard about thaladar aloofness.

The mother made him bend low so she could whisper in his ear. "See that she comes to no harm, man. I realize none of you may come back, but if you do, you must promise to bring her with you. I could not let you ride away without letting you know how I feel about her."

Practor straightened in the saddle, smiled warmly down at her. "You don't have to tell me how you feel about your daughter, ma'am. It shows in your face."

She stepped back from him, nodding knowingly. "You are wise and understanding beyond your years, young human, though I think you do not realize it yourself. A good omen." She raised a hand as if in blessing. "Go forth in safety and in the knowledge that your cause is just.''

The trio departed, waving until the two older women receded from their sight. They rode out through the iron gate and back onto city streets. They were nearing the city gate when Maryld leaned forward on her mount and frowned.

"This is odd."

"What is?" Practor stared anxiously ahead but could detect nothing amiss.

"The number of soldiers near the gate. Far more than usual."

"Some kind of official function in progress?" he opined.

"I think not."

The reason for the presence of so many thaladar soldiers soon made itself known as they moved to intercept the travelers. Practor found their exit barred. Politely, as always, but firmly. A few curious glances came their way, but for the most part, the citizens of Socalia ignored the confrontation and went about their business.

"What's going on here?" Maryld asked the senior officer. "Is there some danger?"

He stepped forward and grasped the reins of her mount. His skullcap was bright green. "Teacher Maryld. You are traveling in the company of"—and it made it sound vaguely obscene—"a human and a roo. This is not permitted outside the city wall."

She eyed him coldly. "What are you talking about? Who dares to inhibit my free passage?"

"It is done for your own safety. You were observed in deep personal conversation with these two."

Maryld gasped in surprise. "Council spies? In my own home? This is worse than outrageous. This is . . ." she struggled for a term of sufficient magnitude to properly express her anger, "*discourteous.*"

71

"You were not being spied upon," the officer informed her. His eyes flicked in Practor's direction. "The Council was curious to learn what such as these were doing in Socalia."

"They might have asked," she replied frostily.

The officer grinned humorlessly up at her. "Your family is noted both for its wisdom and," he added delicately, "eccentricity. Some on the Council were concerned with motives. It was decided, I was told, to seek enlightenment through less semantically obscure channels. I am sorry if you are offended as a result."

" 'Offended' is too mild a word to use for this invasion of privacy, sir. This is a matter for the courts."

"As you wish. Certainly it is not for me to decide," said the officer. "But I have my orders. In order to ensure your safety and that of Socalia it has been decided that you are not to be allowed to accompany these two beyond this point."

"I'll go when and where I please!" She urged her horse forward. Two more guards stepped up to block her way. The animal bucked slightly, uncertain whose orders to obey.

"Inexcusable!" she growled, fuming as she sought a way around the soldiers. "I will lodge the strongest objection, as will my mother and grandmother!"

"Your family's influence is strong, but not this morning," the officer told her apologetically. "I must ask you to stop trying to ride through my command."

"Don't you know what this is about?" she asked him angrily. "Don't you know where we are going? To Shadowkeep!" This announcement produced a few interested murmurs from the supposedly indifferent soldiery. "I go not on behalf of humans or roos but on behalf of all intelligent beings everywhere."

"I was not given this information," the officer replied

evenly, "but it does nothing to countermand my orders. You will not be allowed to proceed, madam teacher. Think of your reputation and please cooperate."

"Reputation be damned!"

"You will not provoke me into a lapse of courtesy," he responded stiffly. "I am simply following my orders. You cannot pass."

"Now, look—" Practor began, but Maryld put out a hand to forestall any confrontation.

"Never mind. It's all right. There's nothing to be done about it. I don't want you getting into trouble with my people, Practor. Not on my account. There is no excuse for this kind of behavior, and there will be many apologies due, but there is nothing here worth the shedding of blood."

He considered, tried to calm himself, and finally nodded agreement. "As you wish, Maryld. You and your mother and grandmother have already given us much good advice. We will press on to Shadowkeep knowing that you and they are with us in spirit if not in body."

"An unusually sensible attitude," observed the officer, "especially for a human." He turned to his troops. "Let the two strangers pass."

The line of guards separated in the middle, producing a pathway to the city gate. Practor and Sranul urged their mounts forward.

Practor turned to wave farewell to Maryld. "Good-bye and thank you. I know this isn't your fault. As you say, there's nothing to be done."

"I am sorry. I can't tell you how sorry I am."

He gave her what he hoped was a reassuring smile. "Don't worry. We'll manage." He put Kaltar into a trot. Sranul lengthened his bounding strides, easily keeping pace alongside as they exited the city.

"Well," he told the roo later that night as they sat

around a crackling fire beneath the man-sized leaves of a *sombradula* tree, "we *almost* had thaladar help."

"A good idea come to naught through no fault of our own," the roo agreed. He leaned back on his tail and helped himself to another handful of the fruit he'd gathered that evening before the sun had set. He chewed noisily, smacking his lips. They were stained red and blue from berry juice.

"It was no real surprise," he went on. "Just like the thaladar not only to refuse us help but to prevent one of their own from doing so. One of these days I think that race is going to turn so tightly in on themselves that they'll all up and vanish, and you know what the result will be? Not another soul will miss 'em. Good riddance, says I."

"That's not a very charitable attitude to take, Sranul. They can't help acting the way they do."

"Oh, can't they? How can you be charitable toward a bunch of pointy-eared snobs like that? You know why they keep so close to their cities?"

"You told me," Practor murmured, but Sranul continued as though his friend hadn't said anything.

"It's because they're afraid of everything else, that's why. It isn't so much that they dislike strangers as that they're scared. They may be a bunch of brilliant little twerps, but they're still a bunch of little twerps." He slapped an irritating pinecone from beneath his tail. "Didn't you notice the expressions on the faces of those gate guards? They were trying to put on a brave front, but I could tell: they were scared to death. Of the *two* of us."

Practor stoked the fire. "They're not as cowardly as you make them out to be."

"Maybe not, but for all their fine shields and swords it's plain to see they're no fighters. If we'd really wanted to, I'll bet you and I could have sent the lot of them packing and ridden out with that girl."

"She's not a girl," Practor reminded the roo. "She's a good deal older than I am."

"We could have done it, man." He spat out several seeds. "She wasn't such a bad sort, for a thaladar."

"And you're not such a bad sort for a roo," said a voice from the darkness.

Practor dropped the stick he'd been using to stir the fire with while Sranul jumped ten feet straight up. The roo landed on an overhanging branch, which bent dangerously beneath his weight. He tried to penetrate the night and locate the source of the unexpected compliment.

Maryld walked into the firelight, leading her horse behind her. A little embarrassed at having been caught so off-guard, Practor rose to meet her.

"How?" was all he could think of to say.

She patted her mount on the muzzle, let the reins fall, and moved to stand closer to the warming flames. He saw that she was still wearing the same exquisite blue traveling suit.

"Cold out tonight." She put her hands toward the fire, rubbed them together.

A loud thump announced Sranul's descent from the tree. "Yes, what are you doing here? I thought they'd place you under some kind of house arrest or something."

"They tried to." She grinned over at the roo. "Oh, you should have been there! What a fine fight we had! Mother and grandmother let the Council representatives who came to the house know exactly what they thought of them. They argued that I was a free spirit and should be allowed to go wherever I wished, in the company of whomever I chose to travel with. The Elders argued back, but you could see they were embarrassed by their own decision. Their argument was weak, but they had the spears on their side.

"Seeing that they weren't getting anywhere, mother and

grandmother abruptly came around to the Council's way of thinking, acknowledged its supremacy in such matters, and saw to it after the house guards had withdrawn to the gates that I was spirited quietly out through an old and little-used aqueduct access near the back of the city wall.''

"I'm surprised they let you get away," Practor murmured.

"Oh, we're very trusting, we thaladar are." She was laughing at the memory. "As soon as mother and grand-mother conceded the Council's supremacy, they relaxed the watch on our house.''

"What will happen to them if the Council finds out that you got away?''

"Nothing. They will simply say that they locked me in my rooms but that I escaped. The Elders will suspect, but won't be able to prove a thing. They'll retreat to meditate about it. We thaladar meditate a lot.''

"They could send soldiers out to look for you.''

"Away from Socalia? That would be most unthaladarian.''

"Yeah, I'd like to see a bunch of them follow us all the way to Shadowkeep," commented a gleeful Sranul. He bowed in Maryld's direction. "No offense, ma'am.''

"I am never offended by the truth, my good roo.''

"What will the Elders do besides meditate?" Practor wondered.

"They will say that they have done their best according to their consciences and move on to other matters of state. In any case, it doesn't matter what they decide to do now. All that matters, all that's important, is what *we* do. If we can penetrate Shadowkeep's mysteries and stop Dal'brad from carrying out his designs, it matters little what deci-sions the Council of Socalia makes.''

He nodded agreement. "I'm sorry it had to be done this way, but I'm very glad you went to all that trouble to rejoin us. We really value your company, you know.''

"Do you?" There was a coquettish twinkle in her eyes. "For my knowledge or myself?"

"Both," he said without thinking.

Later it occurred to him that he was going to have to listen with utmost care to everything Maryld said. He didn't want their relationship to stumble over any misunderstood double meanings.

Days later they began to leave the last of the thaladar lands behind. Ahead lay the broad, ravine-striped, heavily forested expanse of the Horap Plateau. On its far side was the Valley of the Rift and on the shores of the river that cut through its center, Shadowkeep.

"Tell me something," he asked Maryld. "How came the thaladar to know of Shadowkeep? Since you rarely venture beyond your own cities and farms, how did you learn of the evil that dwells within? Surely your father and grandfather were not the first to learn of it?"

"Some few of us do travel widely. My family is not the only group of 'eccentrics.' Thaladar traders move between thaladar towns, and in addition to goods and produce, they carry information with them. If not for them, each thaladar city would remain truly isolated from its neighbors. Socalia, for example, carries on a steady if not spectacular commerce with the towns of Sorsen and Sulahu."

"If the people there were more like you and your parents," said Sranul, "I think the thaladar would be a lot better off."

She shrugged. "We are what we are, roo. We like our privacy. Myself, I agree with you, but most do not. Perhaps someday that will change. Grandmother says that it must or one day the other races will join together out of envy and hatred to attack and destroy us. As you have seen, we are reluctant to fight, even to defend ourselves. We should have used our knowledge against Shadowkeep long ago, yet only my father and grandfather had the courage to do so. If you two had not come along, then Dal'brad would like as not never have been challenged." She gave Practor a look that was enough to make him shake in his saddle.

"It was an accident," he blurted. "We didn't plan it."

"Now don't be modest, my friend." Sranul was grinning. "You instigated this expedition. Don't deny it."

"Nonsense. I'm only an instrument. The Spinner was the instigator."

"Sranul is right," Maryld insisted. "You are an extremely brave man and I won't have you denying it. You do yourself an injustice."

Practor hoped he wasn't blushing. "You can tell me how brave I am once we get into Shadowkeep. It doesn't take a brave man to play tourist, and so far that's all I've done."

They would have continued the argument had not Sranul suddenly bounded on ahead. Practor looked after his friend curiously.

"I wonder what got into him?" They followed without increasing their pace, and the roo rejoined them moments later. He put up both hands, forcing them to stop.

"What's wrong?"

The roo glanced back over his shoulder. "I thought I heard noises up there, so I went to check. I was right. There's fighting going on ahead of us. I'm sure of it."

Practor strained his ears, looked doubtful. "I don't hear anything."

"Neither do I," said Maryld, "but I wouldn't doubt a roo's hearing."

"I could be wrong, I suppose," Sranul muttered, "but I think not. Both my ears and my nose say we should proceed cautiously from here."

"Can't we get around whatever it is?" Practor asked

him. The last thing they needed was to be involved in someone else's fight.

"I don't know. The forest becomes very dense off that way," he pointed to his right, "and somewhere to our left is the first of many steep canyons. We must continue on this course, but once we see what we're up against, we may see a way around it."

They followed the roo onward. After a short ride he had them dismount. In this manner they continued through the woods on foot. Before long even Practor was able to overhear the unmistakable sounds of fighting not far ahead.

"This way," Sranul whispered, leading them off to the left.

They left their mounts tethered at the base of a pile of smooth granite boulders and started to climb. Sranul had to wait for his companions, who could not bound easily past the difficult places. Soon all three of them were lying on their bellies atop the rocks, overlooking the trail below.

It dipped into a narrow ravine which widened out again only at its far end. It was an easy way to descend to the next level of the plateau, but this morning it had been turned into a trap.

A group of travelers were under attack in the defile. Practor saw that the far end of the narrow ravine had been sealed off with bundles of straw and thorn branches, blocking the only avenue of escape. Then he let his eyes rove over the cliff tops, and shuddered as he got his first look at the attackers.

Goblins.

Chapter V

The squat, ugly parodies of humankind were jumping up and down, grunting and babbling disgustingly as they threw rocks down on their trapped prey. A few of them used short, thick bows to shoot at those below. Here was a collection of bandits who did not have larceny on their minds.

They were after food.

Some thirty individuals had been trapped in the ravine. They'd pulled their wagons into a defensive square, but by now nearly all the dray animals had been slain and there seemed no hope of escape for the survivors. From time to time several of the besieged would break from the cover of their wagons and try to force a path through the far end of the canyon. Each time they were driven back by a hail of goblin arrows and throwing stones.

These poor unfortunates were man-sized but even less human-looking than their attackers. Their tails were shorter and bulkier than Sranul's. Instead of fur or bare skin they were covered with interlocking gray scales. Their bodies were broad and muscular.

"Zhis'ta," said Maryld softly, "making their way down to warmer country before the onset of winter."

"Why can't they break out of this trap?" Practor wondered aloud. "The Zhis'ta are supposed to be the best warriors alive."

Sranul put a paw on his shoulder. "Strength is a poor substitute for tactics, my friend. They are badly outnumbered and the goblins have them well and truly trapped. And that's not all." The roo pointed toward the lead wagon. Gray shapes could be seen huddling beneath the woven roof.

"Females and young ones. That's no war party down there. It's a Zhis'ta extended family. They're all related. The males could possibly break out, but then the goblins would swarm down to slaughter the children. So they'll all perish together."

"No they won't." Maryld's expression was grim. "Because we're going to help them."

"We are?" Practor looked dumbfounded.

So did Sranul. "I'll be damned for a newt: a fighting thaladar. I didn't think such a thing existed."

Maryld's eyes were blazing as she glared down into the ravine. "I will not stand by while the children of any intelligent race are murdered."

"Wait a minute." Practor hurried to follow her back down the rocks. "Aren't you forgetting something, Maryld? We have to deal with the evil that lies within Shadowkeep. That threatens all children, everywhere." He was hard pressed to keep up with her. Sranul simply bounced from boulder to ledge, heedless of missing a step.

"We've got to talk this over. Maryld, listen to me! What happened to thaladar logic? Hey, wait for me!" She was already mounting her horse. For the first time he saw that she carried a small rapier. It had been kept hidden beneath her cape. It was a delicate, feminine, altogether deadly-looking device.

"If we're going to do this, we ought to do it right," Sranul muttered. "The first thing we need to do is clear away the barrier that's blocking the far end of the canyon so they can get their wagons out. We ought to be able to circle all the way around the battleground without being spotted. The goblins are so intent on massacre they won't be bothering to watch their rear.''

"A sound plan." Maryld eyed Practor. "Don't you agree?"

"I don't—oh hell, I guess so. Do I have a choice?"

"Not morally." She turned her steed and galloped off with Sranul.

"Thaladar." Practor drew his own sword and spurred Kaltar forward. What he couldn't admit to himself and what really troubled him about the discussion was that until Maryld's arrival, he'd been the clever one with words.

Sranul's estimation of the goblins' state of mind turned out to be correct. Not one of the attackers noticed the trio as they made their way stealthily through the woods and circled back behind the blocked end of the ravine. Not that they had to be especially quiet. The howls and screeches of the goblins, inflamed as they were by the smell of blood, were overpowering. You couldn't hear the Zhis'ta at all.

Practor asked Sranul about the silence of the besieged.

"They utter no battle cries, not even to exhort each other," the roo explained. "I always thought it a strange way to fight. They do battle silently, in a most businesslike manner. Not that I've ever seen them in combat myself, but such are the stories I've heard. They are the best."

"Better fighters even than roos?"

Sranul was not offended. "So it is said. It's difficult to make comparisons because they aren't involved in many wars. Sensible folk leave them alone. One would not expect goblins to act in a sensible manner, of course." He glanced at the anxious Maryld, who was staring toward the ravine, and lowered his voice.

"They're not standoffish, like the thaladar. Friendly enough, I'm told, but not exactly the life of the party, either. Taciturn's the word my clan elder once used to describe them. Then too, there aren't a lot of them living in this part of the world. They prefer the hot southern lands. The way I understand it, their blood is not warm like ours, but cold. They have to lie in the sun or next to a fire to warm themselves, so our winters can be deadly to them.

"That's why this family group is moving south, to beat the winter weather. Perhaps this bunch lingered too long and became separated from a larger group. This I do know: unless they were awfully sure of their strategy, the goblins would never take them on, not even a single family. But the rotten little things know that the warriors won't abandon the children, so they feel safe in attacking."

"I'm still not sure this is any of our business," Practor muttered. They were starting to pick their way back up the canyon, toward the blocked end of the ravine. "The goblins are warm-blooded and look more like you and me than any Zhis'ta."

"In some ways you are wise beyond your years, Practor," Maryld told him, "but you still have much to learn about the world and those who inhabit it. Shape and appearance and internal makeup are not what makes a person. For all their strange, solitary ways and cold blood the Zhis'ta are people. The goblins are not. Laws and attitudes, art and compassion make people. Not looks."

Practor accepted the mild reprimand because he knew Maryld was right about at least one thing: he did have a lot to learn of the world. Another might have gotten mad, but this was one of his greatest attributes: that he recognized his own limitations. He knew that wisdom grows from ignorance, that learning was more important than defending one's ego. Although he did not realize it, this attitude in itself made him wise.

But he still wasn't completely convinced that they had any business risking everything to save a bunch of strangers.

They were quite close to the bottom of the ravine now and could make out the bundles of brush and thorn that had been used to block the exit. Sounds of battle came from above.

"Ready then?" Sranul asked him as he pulled a couple of javelins from his quiver and hefted one in each hand. "I'll try and clear out as many of them as I can from the rocks on either side of the gap. You two make a break through the barrier."

"You sure you can keep up with us?" Practor asked him. "I don't mean now, but when we're retreating. I don't want you falling behind for the goblins to overtake."

The roo grinned up at him. "It'll be a cold day in Coscatua when there's a goblin alive who can run me down. Don't worry about me. Worry about staying on your horse."

"Wait until we are right on them." Maryld's eyes glittered and she held her dainty blade tightly in her right hand.

"Right. Let's get to it." Sranul turned and took a twenty-foot leap up the canyon. Maryld and Practor followed.

He found himself trembling slightly. He'd never been in a real fight before, not one where blood was to be spilled. Angrily he shook off the tremors. If he couldn't control his nerves now, what would happen when they reached Shadowkeep? Compared to that, this was nothing more than a mild diversion.

The blood was real enough, though, and so was the prospect of dying. Practor and Maryld fell on the barrier that the goblins had erected at the back end of the ravine, taking those few at its base by complete surprise while Sranul overwhelmed those atop the brush. In the surprise and confusion, they gave the impression of being many more than three. Goblins fled in all directions as Maryld threw a rope around the first stack of thorn branches. With the other end looped around the pommel of her saddle, she urged her mount downhill, pulling the pile clear. Several other bundles of brush toppled down around it, opening the first hole in the wall. While Practor guarded her, she unhooked the rope and returned to repeat the maneuver.

He was surprised the first time he ran a startled goblin through with his sword. The squat creature had charged straight toward him, waving a spiked club over its head, and there'd been no time to think, only to react. What surprised him was how easily the metal point penetrated the gray flesh. The goblin choked and fell backward, pulling free of the shaft. How simple it was to kill! He discovered he didn't like it one bit, not the actuality of it nor the ease with which it could be accomplished.

He often helped with the slaughter of animals for food, but this was something quite different. Could there be varying degrees of death? He struck at another goblin who came at him from behind, slicing its throat. It reeled away, blood pouring out of it.

How strange to see his sword as something more than a mere decoration, to be worn proudly at the waist at a parade. It was an instrument of killing, not of beauty. All his life he'd helped to fashion such devices—swords and knives, battle-axes and quashoggis, never thinking of their ultimate use. He took pride in putting a fine edge on a blade without ever imagining it passing through living flesh.

Another goblin rushed at him and he ran it through. No, he didn't like killing, skilled as he was in the use of death's instruments. But there were children depending on him, even if they were cold of blood and skin. Would a Zhis'ta have defended him as a child from a similar attack, or would they have gone on their way without getting involved? If he asked one, would it answer truthfully?

No matter. He knew that what they were doing was right, and necessary, and not just because Maryld said it was so. He knew what was right.

Maybe that was one reason why the Spinner had settled on him.

The rest of the goblins guarding the barrier turned and fled as Maryld pulled another mass of brush from the exit. Sranul jumped down from the rocks above and joined her, leaning back and balancing himself on his tail while he used his huge feet to kick with, sending bale after bale flying. Then the roo dashed through the opening and shouted at the trapped Zhis'ta, dodging rocks and the occasional arrow that flew his way. Most of the goblins lining the lip of the ravine continued to concentrate single-mindedly on their prey, unaware that anything was amiss.

Practor and Maryld waited anxiously, ready to keep the gap clear. But there was no counterattack. Sranul finally managed to get the attention of several of the Zhis'ta females and show them that the way was now open. They jumped from their wagon and ran to the others, passing the message along. While the strongest males continued to defy their attackers, the others bent to the harnesses. The wagons abandoned their defensive square and began to move toward the exit.

The children hid beneath the cloth covers while the adults struggled to run the gauntlet of goblin arrows and stones. They burst through the gap in the barrier without pausing to thank their rescuers.

By now the goblins had figured out what was happening, and they began to drop down into the ravine themselves, to pursue their fleeing quarry. Howls of triumph turned to cries of outrage as they saw their once hopelessly trapped prey escaping. Several of them jumped onto the back of the rearmost wagon.

Seeing this, Practor let out a yell and sent Kaltar circling round behind them. His sword cleared the back of the wagon rapidly and kept it clear. The goblins didn't have the stomach to confront a man on horseback.

Several pairs of small yellow eyes peeped out at him. He smiled toward the wagon, feeling suddenly that no matter what happened now it had all been worthwhile, and galloped around to rejoin his friends.

As he did so he passed a number of Zhis'ta bodies. Several of them were small and hardly formed. All had been mutilated. He started looking for goblins to kill.

But the majority of the killing was over. The last wagon cleared the gap in the brush barrier and plunged noisily down the trail. Only a rare, fitfully aimed arrow threatened the escapees, save for one or two goblins who were so mad with rage that they were foolish enough to challenge their intended prey on foot.

This provided Practor with the chance to see just how accurate Sranul's assessment of Zhis'ta fighting ability was. If anything, he decided, the roo had underestimated them. They were unbelievably fast, with reflexes that would put the quickest human fighter to shame. The few goblins who pursued never had an opportunity to use their weapons. The Zhis'ta cut them down as soon as they came within arm's-length, and they did so silently. Out in the open, the goblins didn't have a chance. Most of them knew it and didn't try to pursue.

Practor also saw how the Zhis'ta had managed to survive the trap until they'd been rescued. They had no archers of their own, but so fast were they with their swords and axes that they were able to deflect the majority of arrows and rocks that had been directed at them.

With Maryld and Practor riding cover on the flanks and Sranul bringing up the rear to discourage any lingering belligerents, the re-formed line of wagons made its way out of the canyon onto the next level of the plateau. Not a thousand armed goblins would challenge the family on an open plain.

The wagons slowed and again formed a square. Quietly, patiently, the wounded waited their turn to be treated for their wounds. An elderly male went from wagon to wagon, counting the missing.

Practor brought the foaming, exciting Kaltar to a halt. Blood was congealing on his sword. Maryld rode up alongside him, panting as hard as her mount.

"It's finished," he gasped. "We did it. Now we can continue on to Shadowkeep."

"No, not yet," she told him. She dismounted. "First we must see if there is any additional help we can render. They are tired and many are injured. You saw back in the canyon? The young ones who did not get out?"

"Yes," he replied quietly, "I saw." He looked back the way they'd come. Only the distant hooting of goblin obscenities came from the vicinity of the ravine. There would be no more fighting this day. "It made it a lot easier for me."

"I watched you fight. Were you trained as a warrior? You handle a sword exceedingly well."

"No. But I've helped to make more swords than most men ever see, and my master was a great fighter. He said that as long as I was going to make them, I might as well learn how to use them."

She nodded. "He taught you well. I did not expect you to fight with such skill."

"Nor I you. What of the peaceful, pacifistic thaladar? What of Maryld of the family of sages?"

"Merely because we chose not to fight does not mean we

do not know how to. This, too, is knowledge, even if little used." She turned and started walking toward the wagons. "Come. Let us see what we can do to help the injured."

Of those Zhis'ta who had been wounded, however, most seemed to require only perfunctory attention. Their thick, scaly skins protected them from all but the most powerful goblin bows and they had actually suffered far more from the rocks which had been flung down on them. It seemed that if a Zhis'ta was not slain on the spot, it would eventually recover completely not matter how severe its wounds.

"We do not die from injuriess," the mature female explained to him. "That iss why we never leave behind any of our wounded. We do not have the equivalent in our Old Tongue for 'fatally wounded.'" She gestured behind her, toward the wagons. "All of my family who are here will live."

"You're all related, then?"

"Yess." Her voice was unexpectedly soft, not at all the harsh reptilian rasp he expected. As she spoke she continued to work at binding up the gash in the shoulder of the young male seated in front of her. "We are all family, man. Unlike thosse of the other races, we Zhiss'ta do not believe in resstricting the upbringing of a young one to only itss natural parentss. Any male or female may help to raisse up any child, and our children resspond well to all thiss attention." She looked back toward the canyon. Practor tried to read her feelings from the tone of her voice but could not. He did not know the Zhis'ta.

"Perhapss we devote sso much care to the raissing of our children becausse we have sso few. We do not give birth ass often ass humans or rooss. That iss why we fought so hard. The goblin folk may have believed we would run and leave our wounded behind, or would ssurrender to them. They do not realize that a family of the

Zhiss'ta with children will fight ten times ass hard and long ass any war party.''

Practor nodded understanding, turned his gaze back to the wounded male. The cut was wide and deep, and he was still bleeding quite a bit despite the older female's efforts to staunch the flow of blood. From the moment she'd begun, even when she'd poured disinfectant into the wound, the warrior hadn't uttered a sound. He acted more like a silent participant in the conversation than someone in need of vital medical attention.

Certainly he was aware of Practor's stare. Now he spoke for the first time, without a hint in his voice of the pain he must be feeling.

"Tell me, human. Why did you help uss? Humans have no particular love for the Zhiss'ta."

Practor tried to shrug it off. "My friends and I decided we couldn't just ride past and let you all be slaughtered." He searched the wagons until he located Maryld, pointed. "The thaladar said that you are people and the goblin-folk are not, and that all people should stick together. I confess I hesitated at first, but what she said makes much sense."

The warrior nodded, a faint, slightly sideways movement of the head. "Sometimes what the thaladar say does."

The old female continued to bind up the wound. "I am as surprised to see a thaladar stand up for the Zhiss'ta ass I am a human. Their wisdom cannot be denied, but they are not famed for rissking their livess for otherss of another race. Now, the roo, I can undersstand. They love a good fight and are all a little crazy bessides. But the actionss of the thaladar I do not undersstand."

"This isn't your usual thaladar," Practor told her. "This one is different."

"Different sso," she murmured. Cold, thoughtful eyes turned to regard him. "Different ass are you, man." She hesitated, then returned her attention to the male she was nursing.

"How doess that arm feel now, Torun?"

The warrior stood, experimentally flexed the injured shoulder. "It hurtss a great deal, ssenior mother." This was spoken in an unstressed, perfectly normal tone of voice. "But the movement iss much improved."

She gave him that brief, sideways nod. "Usse it ass little ass possible for five dayss. Give the flessh and musscle a chance to heal. Then you can usse it again if you musst."

"Thankss to your sskill, senior mother." He bowed back to her, turned and trotted off toward several other warriors who were talking in low tones nearby. To see him move, Practor thought admiringly, anyone would have thought he'd suffered nothing more serious than a scrape.

"Tell me, man," said the senior mother, speaking to Practor as though to an old friend, "how come a human, a thaladar, and a roo to be traveling together on the plateau? And ssuch an unussual trio."

"I met both of them along the way."

"Along the way to where?"

"To Shadowkeep."

She mulled this over in her mind a moment before asking the inevitable second question. "And what doess ssuch a sseemingly ssenssible young human like yoursself sseek in SShadowkeep? That iss a place to be sshunned, not ssought out."

"So everyone says. It's not very encouraging."

"The truth is not always encouraging, my warm young friend."

He sighed. "I go to try and free the wizard Gorwyther so that we may prevent a great evil from spreading out across the world. As to my friends, the roo comes with me for adventure and the thaladar to help with advice. I don't

91

suppose you have any, other than advising me not to go there?''

"We know little of SShadowkeep ssave itss reputation. We musst travel ssouth and quickly, lesst the cold of winter trap and kill uss here ass ssurely as the goblinss would have. We can ssurvive the cold of the plainss and the plateau, but the children could not." She smiled at him, showing a multitude of small, sharp teeth. "You undersstand, we cannot linger."

Practor nodded solemnly. "My friends and I are not afraid of Shadowkeep as much as we are what may be festering deep within its walls. The demon king has taken it over and uses it as a sanctuary from which to plot against the rest of the world. Whatever he intends, if it is not stopped now, will spread out to infect the entire world. Including," he added significantly, "the warm countries of the south."

Her reply was chilling in its import. "Not even demons dare to trifle with the Zhiss'ta. SStill, we are firm believers in preventive medicine." She turned and Practor admired the play of muscles in her upper body, wishing he were half so powerful himself. But no human was. Shone Stelft, as strong a man as Practor had ever seen, would not be capable of lifting as much as this elderly Zhis'ta female.

"I had not thought to ssee the family ssurvive. We would all have perisshed in that canyon if not for the intervention of you and your friendss.''

He frowned uncertainly. "What are you trying to say, senior mother?''

She glanced back at him, and the tendons in the thick neck twisted like cables. "That we have a debt to pay.''

"Oh no," he said quickly, raising his hands. "We didn't help you because we expected some kind of reward or payment. We did it because it was the right thing to do.''

"SSpoken like a true thaladar—or an exceptional human. All three of you are unussual—nay, unique. Therefore the fourth member of your party should be equally exceptional." She started off toward the gathering place where the wagons formed a central square with Practor protesting in her wake.

"You shouldn't feel obligated. I don't *want* you to feel obligated to us. We would've done what we did for anyone trapped like you were."

"But you did not rissk your livess to ssave 'anyone.' You did it for uss. SSo the obligation iss incurred whether you wissh it or not. You no longer have a choice in thiss. I no longer have a choice in thiss. It hass been decided." She eyed him firmly. "We have our lawss too, you know, and we musst adhere to them."

"I'm not sure what you're proposing," he muttered, "but wouldn't it be simpler all around if we just went on our way? Wouldn't that free you of this 'obligation' or whatever it is?"

"That would only make matterss ten timess worsse, man, becausse we would have to follow you until you agreed to accept payment for the debt or until we perisshed from the trek."

"Oh." Practor was subdued. "I guess I'm stuck with it, then."

"I am sorry, but it iss our law."

"Oh, okay." He considered. "I guess we could use a couple of extra swords, something along that line if you have them to spare. Or fresh food to replace what we've polished off the last few days. We're pretty well stocked and we haven't had any trouble finding food along the way, but if that will help clear up this problem, we'll take whatever you want to give."

"It iss not sso ssimple, man. You rissked your livess for uss. We musst repay the debt in kind."

"Huh? I don't follow you." But, of course, he did, right into the center of the square where the surviving Zhis'ta had gathered.

Everyone looked up when she entered, and a respectful silence fell over the extended family. They waited patiently and with interest for whatever the senior mother had to say.

She gestured at the man standing next to her. "This iss the human called Practor, foremosst among thosse who ssaved us from the handss of the goblin-folk."

Immediately and without further instruction, the entire family, from the eldest to the youngest, performed that strange sideways bow of the Zhis'ta. They repeated the genuflection while Practor looked on uncomfortably. When they had finished doing him homage, at least half concentrated their attention on him instead of the senior mother.

"He offered up hiss life for ourss. With what sshall we repay him?"

"With life," declared a chorus of solemn, softly modulated reptilian voices.

She turned to face Practor. "There, you ssee how it iss with uss? I did not prepare them."

"You're not planning some kind of crazy sacrifice or anything, are you? Because I won't stay around for something like that, and I don't give a damn if it is your law."

She let out an amused hiss. "Do you think because we choosse not to live in cities that we are not civilized? We do not make ssacrificess. We give life for life, not death." She turned back to face the members of the family, scanned their attentive faces. "Who volunteerss to ssatissfy the debt?"

The strongest of the Zhis'ta rose from his squat. "I, Hargrod, will go. The children will not miss me ass they would some others, and I can stand the cold better than mosst memberss of the family."

"All of what you ssay iss sso," agreed the senior mother, "but who will lead uss in battle if the family iss attacked again?"

Another elder rose to speak. "I do not think the goblinss will trouble uss further. Not after the lossess they have suffered. From here to the river valley the way iss wide and clear. There are not more narrow placess in which we could be trapped. I think we are ssafe now." He eyed the younger warrior. "Hargrod sshould go." Other adults murmured their assent. "It iss owed."

"SSenior father iss right," said Hargrod. "The family will be ssafe now. Out in the open none will challenge uss, and I will rejoin you all ass ssoon ass the debt hass been paid. Do any object?"

"I object." All eyes turned to where a young female had risen near the back of the group. "I object from memory, so that my objection may be remembered, though I, too, agree that the debt musst be disscharged." Practor saw the way in which Hargrod and the female stared at each other and felt guilty, but he'd done everything possible to dissuade the Zhis'ta from their course of action, with no success. Raising further objections would only make things worse. Apparently this Hargrod was bound and determined to accompany them to Shadowkeep, whether Practor wanted him along or not.

After a moment the female sat back down and Hargrod turned away from her. There was no touching, no exchange of embraces, but the pair had already made their farewells.

The warrior picked his way through the rest of the family until he was standing before Practor, who looked the new addition to their little company over carefully. Hargrod was shorter than any of them except Maryld but was much heavier than Practor. A double-bladed ax was slung across his back. Each blade was nearly as long as the thick, leather-wrapped wooden handle. A short handle and a short reach, he thought, but anything that moved within range of those swinging blades would die.

The Zhis'ta's arms were as thick as his legs. Diffuse sunlight shone on gray scales. Hargrod reached out and ceremoniously placed a hand on each of Practor's shoulders. Though he squeezed gently, Practor could feel the power in those steellike fingers. He didn't doubt that if the Zhis'ta chose to contract them with all his strength, he could snap Practor's collarbone like a pencil.

Perhaps he shouldn't seem so reluctant to accept this offer of assistance. Hargrod would be a valuable ally. And as the senior mother said, he had no choice in the matter anyway.

So he put his own hands on the Zhis'ta's shoulders. "I hope we will become good friends and that we will find glory together."

"Only enough so that I may disscharge the obligation," Hargrod replied evenly. "Then I will leave you. I have other ressponssibilitiess."

"I know, and I accept that. You are free to leave whenever you feel you've done enough." He dropped his hands at the same time as the Zhis'ta did. "If it was up to me, I'd just as soon that you stayed with your family, but senior mother says that wouldn't be right."

Hargrod nodded tersely. "I would have ssaid the ssame things as sshe hass ssaid. A debt is a debt and musst be repaid. Do not think thiss painss me, man. We owe you far more than my mere pressence. Let us sspeak no more of it." The Zhis'ta made an effort to change the subject.

"You ssay we go to find glory. Where?"

"To Shadowkeep." Practor was very interested in the reptile's reaction. It was much as he expected. Hargrod simply nodded.

"I go to gather my belongingss." He turned and headed toward the far wagon.

The senior mother moved a little closer to Practor. "He will prove a great help to you, man, even more so within the confines of Shadowkeep than out here in the open. Few beings can sstand for long against a Zhis'ta in close-quarter conflict, and Hargrod is the besst fighter in the family."

Practor rubbed his left shoulder, which still tingled from Hargrod's gentle grasp. "I believe that." A sudden thought made him frown. "Maryld and I have horses and Sranul there needs none."

"Neither does Hargrod. Hiss sstride may not be ass long ass thosse of your mounts and he may not bound ass high ass the roo, but he can run for dayss without tiring. Hargrod is a warrior'ss warrior." This last was said with unconcealed pride.

"What if winter comes early, before we've finished our work at Shadowkeep?"

"Do not worry yoursself on that concern, man. Hargrod will manage." Again the show of sharp teeth. "Not only can he take care of himsself, he will alsso take care of you."

Practor was a little miffed. "We've done all right so far. Not that I'm not glad of all the help we can get."

"Wissely sspoken. Then I am right in ssaying that you accept Hargrod'ss sservice as full ssettlement of the debt we of the family Zorphendia owe you?"

"Yes. Would you like it in writing?"

She made a peculiar expression. "Why would we need it in writing?"

He tried to make light of it, not wanting to offend her. "It's a human custom. When such agreements are commit-ted to paper, then there's always a record of them to refer to. Nobody has to worry about being cheated."

"The Zhiss'ta," she informed him gravely, "are never cheated. More than once." She smiled again and put her hands on his shoulders just as Hargrod had. Her grip wasn't much weaker, he noted. "Thank you for your kindnessess, man. We can continue southward relaxed in mind, knowing that we leave no unpaid billss behind uss."

"You can go with more than that in mind," he told her. "There's treasure as well as danger to be found in Shadowkeep. If we're successful, Hargrod will return to the family with his share."

"That would be nice," she said slowly, "but I would conssider mysself well rewarded to have Hargrod back alive." She removed her hands from his shoulders. "Go now, and be a credit to your family."

Maryld was pleased to learn that one of the Zhis'ta would be joining them, but Sranul's reaction was something less than enthusiastic.

"What? One of those cold-bellied, unblinking snakes is coming with us?" He spat to one side. "That's great. That'll lighten things up even more. They aren't exactly the life of the party, you know."

"This isn't a party, Sranul," Practor admonished the roo, "no matter what you think. This is a serious business."

"Pagh. No business is so serious that you can't have a little fun with it, but with a Zhis'ta around to put a damper on things . . ." He hesitated, acquiesced with a sigh. "Oh well. Maybe I can loosen the leather-head up a little as we go. Though those scaly facades are pretty hard to crack."

"Just don't try any practical jokes," Practor warned him, "and be grateful that he's joining us. He's as strong as the three of us put together."

"Yeah, and I'll bet the muscle goes all the way through his head. Although I guess I shouldn't complain too much. You're the nominal leader of this little expedition. It's your responsibility to hold up the conversation. So you talk to him.'' The roo bounded off toward a nearby stream.

"I wonder if that roo's going to give us trouble?'' Maryld murmured.

"I hope not. If he provokes Hargrod, we'll be short one talkative companion. Though the Zhis'ta would have to catch him first.''

Chapter VI

They lingered long enough for Hargrod to bid good-bye to each member of the family. They might be solemn in manner and terse in speech, Practor mused as he watched the Zhis'ta make his farewells, but there was no lack of affection among them.

When it was over Hargrod walked over to where they waited and looked up at Practor. "I am ready."

"You're sure you'll be able to keep up with us? We can go slowly for a while, if you wish. This is no time for a demonstration of false pride. A man named Shone Stelft taught me all about that. You won't be any help to us at Shadowkeep if you run yourself into the ground getting there."

"Go at whatever speed you wissh. I will sstay closse at hand. The faster we travel, the ssooner I may rejoin my family."

"Right, enough talking," snapped Sranul. "Let's get moving." He took off down the trail that led downhill through the trees.

The Zhis'ta family would follow more slowly, eventually turning onto another branch of the road which led due south. Practor spurred Kaltar forward and Maryld followed. So did Hargrod.

True to his word, he did not slow them down, matching the horses' pace with ease despite his short, thick legs. He was not built like a runner, but he ran tirelessly and seemingly without effort as the hours and the plateau slid past. Practor forgot his initial concerns. Hargrod was not only as fast as Kaltar, he was probably stronger.

The trail led down into the great valley of the Charycun River. As they descended, the temperature rose and Practor was able to dispense with his heavy outer cloak, stuffing it in a half-empty saddlebag. The trees grew slimmer and thrust out fewer branches, while flowers burst forth from crannies in the rocks. It was easy to imagine he was traveling through harmless country, on a casual sightseeing jaunt with friends, and was not engaged in a life-or-death mission on behalf of the civilized world. Much simpler to smell the flowers and think of more pleasant diversions.

They reached the river valley and turned upstream. The water flowed slowly, lazily alongside the road.

Sranul knelt to study their path. "A good road, this, made to handle regular commercial traffic. Nothing's passed this way for some time, though." He hopped to his left. "No, wait, here's evidence of passage. Many animals, humans, roos as well." He looked up the trail. "All traveling in the same direction: south."

"Away from Shadowkeep," said Practor. "Then we have even less time than the Spinner suggested." He chucked the reins and Kaltar broke into a trot.

"You know, Maryld," he said, "now that we're actually almost to Shadowkeep, I'm beginning to wonder if perhaps you shouldn't remain outside. We can come out and consult with you whenever we have a problem."

She laughed. "Sure you can. What was that you said many days ago about Shadowkeep being easy to enter but hard to escape from? I'm sorry, Practor Fime, but you're not going to get rid of me that easily. Though I appreciate

101

your gallantry. But my knowledge and advice will be no use at all unless I am with you when it is needed. You will not have time to come searching for me. Besides," she added with a sly glance, "you're big and strong. You'll protect me, won't you?"

"Don't tease me. It's not fair."

"But Practor, I thought you liked me."

"I think I've already made that clear, but I'm promised to another. Your teasing me only complicates matters."

"Poor Practor." She laughed then, a much richer and more full-bodied sound than should have come out of so slight a form. "You are quite right. I am not being fair. I will strike a bargain with you. I will stop playing the fragile flower if you'll stop treating me like one. You must stop thinking of me as something delicate and easily broken. Size is no measure of toughness. You must treat me the same as you treat Sranul or Hargrod."

He spared her a quick, sideways glance, admiring the way she held herself in the diminutive saddle. "That's not going to be easy. You don't look much like Sranul or Hargrod."

She pursed her lips. "Really, Practor, you must. I'm being serious now. If you should hesitate at some critical moment out of fear for my safety, it could mean your end as well as mine or any of the others. We must each of us be as one side of a square: if one side is weaker than the others, all will collapse under the pressure.

"I imagine there will be times when you will have to protect me, but there will also be occasions when my knowledge and skill will be called upon to shield you. Each must defend the other, but we must have a defense based upon equality."

"It's not going to be easy."

"Nothing about this expedition is going to be easy. Unless we work together, each of us learning to rely upon the skills of each other, we'll never leave Shadowkeep alive. Individually we are no threat to Dal'brad. But if we can function in concert, combining our disparate skills, we may yet surprise the demon king. We already have one advantage.''

"What might that be?"

"Surprise." She smiled thinly. "I dare say that those who have entered Shadowkeep in the past have traveled no farther than the first room or chamber. Either one of the demon's traps overcomes them, or else they are blinded by their lust to find the castle's treasure. We four will not be so easily diverted or surprised."

"No, we won't." He nodded grimly. "The last thing Dal'brad will expect to encounter in his sanctuary are intruders who are looking to find him, not avoid him."

Sranul took a backwards bound and landed between the two horses. He nodded ahead. "People coming."

"What kind of people?" Practor asked him. "Roos?"

"Sadly no. Your own kind." Practor's hand went instinctively to his sword hilt, and the roo hastened to reassure him. "They're not going to cause trouble. The band is full of women and children, as was Hargrod's."

There were three times as many in the wagons that came rumbling down the trail as there had been in Hargrod's extended family, however. Their dray animals, mules and yozen, were fat and strong. They pulled wagons piled high with goods and furniture as well as with people. But the people themselves, though obviously healthy and well-fed, looked uneasy, and their leaders were tired from lack of sleep.

Practor turned Kaltar around to walk alongside an old man who rode the back of a striped yozen. "Where do you come from, stranger, and where are you bound?"

The man was on the portly side. He wore earrings of silver, and silver wire was twisted in his beard. "We come from the Kept Basin and we go anywhere else. You ride upriver?'' Practor nodded. "Have you not heard?''

Practor exchanged a glance with Maryld, who had turned back to parallel the two men, then asked, "Heard what?''

"Of what is happening in the Kept Basin, at Shadowkeep.''

"No. We've just come down off the plateau. Why? What is happening at Shadowkeep?''

The man halted his mount, spoke as wagons and animals trundled past. "We who lived in the Kept Basin ignored the castle. For years and years it was nothing more to us than another pile of stone, a man-made mountain. We warned those adventurers who entered it seeking gold and prayed for their souls when they failed to come out again, but we never tried to penetrate its mysteries ourselves. Our gold lay in our lands and shops.

"Several fortnights ago strange lights were seen moving about inside the few windows of the castle. The bravest among us crept close to the gateway. They heard noises coming from within, noises fit to freeze the blood of a saint. At all hours of the day, though in the Kept Basin even day seems to have fled in fright from Shadowkeep. The sun shuns our land and mornings and afternoons are as gloomy and gray as the night.

"Smoke wraiths began to visit us even in protected homes, and—other things." He looked upriver and the fear was plain on his face as well as in his voice. "Of themselves these visitations would not have driven us away, for we are not cowards, but one thing about them made us leave.''

"What might that have been?'' Maryld inquired understandingly.

The man looked over at her. "All these manifestations that afflicted us came from *within* Shadowkeep. We of the

Basin decided not to wait to see what might emerge next from that cursed place."

Maryld looked grim. "It has begun. Dal'brad has sent his first scouts out into the world to study and to seek. When they return and he learns that there is no one to oppose him, then he will gather his dark forces and move against the civilized people of the earth. We have little enough time left to us. We *must* stop him before he learns that there are none to equal the imprisoned Gorwyther. Shadowkeep must become the demon king's coffin, not his palace."

The traveler's eyes narrowed as he listened to the thaladar. "What madness is this?" He let his gaze shift to Practor, sitting quietly nearby, then back to where Sranul and Hargrod waited, watching the long line of refugees. "Who are you people? Where do you come from?"

"We come from everywhere," Practor informed him, "and we go to Shadowkeep."

"Then you go to your deaths," the man told them.

"Perhaps." Maryld shrugged. "Death comes for everyone eventually."

"Yes, eventually," the traveler agreed, "and better later than sooner, and without encouragement. And in between making its regular rounds, Death rests in Shadowkeep. If you go there you will disturb it and it will go badly with you."

"Nevertheless, that is our intention," Practor told him. "We're not afraid of death or of Dal'brad."

The traveler stroked his beard, playing with the silver wires. "You are a peculiar lot, that much is certain. You might be heroes. I've lived a long time and I've never met any real heroes. Or you might be mad. Or perhaps you are half of each, yes, four mad heroes. You will need more than madness to get you through Shadowkeep alive."

"What help can we expect to find in the Kept Basin?" Practor asked.

The traveler rocked with laughter, though the sound was bitter. The last wagon had passed and he was alone on the trail with the four mad strangers.

"We of the Basin are sturdy folk, but mad we are not. Why else do you think you find us here like this, on the road traveling south with everything we own? Help? You will find no help in the Basin because everyone has fled the place. Everyone! Only fools remain where evil thrives. We left as quickly as we could, abandoning everything we could not carry with us: homes, businesses, farms, goods. Wealth is useless to a dead man." He smiled humorlessly at Practor.

"It is said that one benefits from doing a kindness to a madman, so you may make use of whatever you can find in the Basin. I will ride more easily knowing that through charity I may have helped make your last hours more comfortable."

"If Dal'brad is allowed to break loose of Shadowkeep's constraints, he will come for you and your neighbors soon enough," Maryld told him.

The man shrugged. "What else can we do? Join with you? I am no hero, mad or otherwise, and neither are my neighbors. Myself, I am a shopkeeper, not a Shadowkeeper. I am no fighter and I prefer to run. So you four go to Shadowkeep and confront Dal'brad in his lair. All our blessings will accompany you, for all that I think you go on a fool's errand to find only a fool's death for a reward. We will hope for your success while we honor your memory—from a safe distance. Help?" He nodded down the trail. "These people, good folk all, my neighbors, can give you no help. Although..."

"Although what?" Practor pressed him.

"I was just thinking, who better than a crazy man to aid

a fool? There is an inn, the Inn of the Keep. It lies next to the river.''

"But you said all the people of the Basin have fled,'' Maryld reminded him. Sranul and Hargrod had walked over to join them. They listened quietly.

"Perhaps—not all.'' The shopkeeper looked yearningly down the trail. The last wagon was disappearing down the slope. He was anxious to rejoin his neighbors and friends, Practor thought, yet he remained behind to offer what advice he could. Despite his disclaimer, that in itself was a kind of courage. Practor hid his amusement. The man preferred to be thought of as a coward, so there was no point in shattering his illusions by complimenting him.

"The proprietor of the inn is a strange one himself, name of Norell. Strange, but honest and straightforward. As honest and straightforward as any crazy man can be. I myself have sold him wine when there was enough to spare from my personal stock. He paid me a fair price every time, on time. There are plenty of sane folk I cannot say that about. But most of his dealings were with the transients traveling through the Basin, so I did not see him often.

"My point is that Norell is just crazy enough to remain even after all the rest of us have left. The thought of a traveler having nowhere to sleep would upset him, you see, and he is not the sort to be forced out of business by anyone. Or in this case, anything. I think he'd offer the demon king himself food and lodging, but he'd fight to the death to keep from having to close down his business. There are those who say that Norell has gambled with the dark forces before and has won every time.''

"He sounds like a potential ally,'' Practor commented.

The shopkeeper shook his head. "Nay, Norell's no ally of anyone. He'll sell you a soft bed and a hot meal, but he's interested only in building up his business, not in something as immaterial as the survival of the world. You see, if everyone else perishes, he's convinced he'll still have a business catering to the needs of travelers from the underworld.

"That is the only help I can offer you, stranger. Seek out the Inn of the Keep. If the owner remains, I'm sure he'll be happy to put you up. At least you won't go to your deaths on empty stomachs. Not if Norell has anything to say about it." He turned his mule about, hesitated.

"There is one thing more you should know about the Basin's resident crazy man. I can't vouch for the stories myself, since I only sold him wine, but it is rumored that when he is so inclined, Norell can supply travelers with more than just food and lodging."

"Like what?" Practor asked.

"How should I know? I'm only a simple shopkeeper and my wants are uncomplicated. I've no wish to know what Norell keeps hidden in the secret places of his establishment, nor how he can operate it so efficiently all by himself. Maybe you'll be lucky enough to find out.

"And now I really must go. I am one of those in charge of our little band of refugees, and sometimes even a coward may help to direct a retreat."

"You're no coward," Practor told him, unable at the last to let the man leave without some kind of thank-you. "A realist at worst, but a coward, no."

"Your words are kind. I wish you luck, travelers. If by some miracle you should succeed, then maybe someday I'll be able to reopen my shop. Unlike Norell, I don't think I'd be very comfortable selling to demons." He spurred his mount onward and soon vanished down the trail.

"What do you make of all that?" Practor asked Sranul.

"Nothing good," the roo replied tersely. "It's one thing to see people running and screaming from something they don't understand and can't cope with, but this hurried, anxious flight is something else again.'' He nodded down the trail. ''That's a sturdy, upright human, despite his words. I think he'd stand and fight for what he's worked to build up over the years, if he thought he and his neighbors had the slightest chance of holding on. If mere sights and sounds are enough to frighten him off, then I don't like to think of what might lie behind them.''

''Talking will not slay Dal'brad, nor get me back to my family.'' Hargrod pivoted and started up the trail, retracing the wagon train's wheel tracks.

''Now what's that supposed to mean, snake-legs?'' Sranul bounded to catch up to the Zhis'ta. Maryld and Practor followed at a less disturbed pace.

''What do you think, Maryld?''

''The human may have been exaggerating. It is a quality many humans have. But Dal'brad's scouts will roam far and wide. We should still be able to slip unnoticed into the castle.

''The sending out of scouts is a sign that Dal'brad is feeling confident, though not confident enough to move against the civilized peoples in full strength. Not yet. If we are very lucky we may catch him in an overconfident mood, unawares and lightly defended. The fact that he has frightened everyone out of the Basin is to our advantage. He can turn his attention to planning, certain in the knowledge that he has secured his immediate surroundings.''

''Except for one crazy innkeeper.''

''Possibly. We still don't know if this Norell has stayed behind. He may have fled after these others, in a different direction. But we must certainly find out for ourselves. If naught else, an abandoned inn would be the best place in the Basin for us to scrounge a bit of food and catch some sleep. But I would far rather find this Norell, crazy or not, running his establishment. Because if he has remained behind he may have more to offer us than just food and drink."

"You mean, the mysterious unknowns the shopkeeper mentioned?"

"No. I mean information." She urged her mount to a gallop lest they fall too far behind and lose contact with Sranul and Hargrod.

Destiny lay another four days' easy ride upriver, in the Kept Basin. There the land was flat and level and the river spread out to fill much of the shallow valley thus created. Hills surrounded the Basin on two sides, while farther to the north the Tetuock Mountains climbed toward the sky.

In the center of the Basin the shallow lake became a marsh, full of high reeds and drifting moss. Flowers gave way to foulness and healthy trees were reduced to scabrous gray skeletons devoid of needles or leaves. A sickly mist rose from the surface of the marsh, forming damp clouds that drifted aimlessly back and forth across the Basin as if seeking a way to escape. Of the fertile farmland that had once filled this valley, only a few signs remained.

Staring at it thus transformed by the evil which was leaking out of Shadowkeep, Practor could easily understand why the inhabitants had taken flight. They had been driven out not by threats or weapons, but by the malaise which had infected the very soil beneath their feet. You cannot grow crops in corruption, and something had certainly corrupted this once beautiful river valley.

Barely visible through the cloying mist was an island in the middle of the marsh, an island built of solid rock. Shadowkeep. It was plainer than he expected it to be, devoid of external decoration or charm. It towered over the surrounding marsh, resting heavily on its inundated foundation. Despite the fog Practor could see that the lower portion of the castle was constructed of individual blocks of cut stone weighing hundreds of tons apiece.

110

Something stronger than human hands had hewn and moved those immense blocks and set them into place without mortar in the center of the lake. Something directed and controlled by the greatest wizard the world had yet known.

But not so great, he reminded himself, that he could keep himself from being trapped in a careless moment by one who sought to supplant him. One whose designs and plans for Shadowkeep were founded on evil rather than a simple desire for privacy.

As the shopkeeper had said, there were few windows. Peering through the shifting mist, it was difficult to tell if they were actually openings cut in the rock or just dark cracks between the building stones. No banners flew from the silent turrets. No guards (no *visible* guards, he reminded himself) stood watch atop the battlements. No gatekeeper waited to greet visitors. A great wizard Gorwyther might have been, but Practor decided as he studied the vast castle that its builder was no artist. It was a grim, stolid, dull edifice: a fit home to danger.

He discussed his feelings with his companions. All agreed with his appraisal except Sranul, who felt it didn't go far enough. To the roo the building was more than just dull; it was downright ugly.

"See the causeway?" he said, pointing. "It's narrow, but dry. I can't tell if the main gate is open but it certainly looks to be unguarded."

"'Looks to be'?" Maryld tried to see beyond the entrance, but her eyesight was no better than the roo's. "We must proceed from now on as though we can expect to be attacked by anything at any time. It may be that Dal'brad is sure enough of the safeguards within to leave the entrance unwatched, or it may be that his seeming indifference conceals unpleasant surprises which will only manifest themselves when we try to step inside. Nothing is

111

more deceptive or more dangerous than apparent peacefulness. Keep that in mind when we go in.''

Sranul took a short hop forward. ''Do we try the entrance now?''

''No,'' Practor told him. ''First we try to find this inn we were told about.''

''It's probably deserted.''

''Probably, but we must find it nonetheless. I was always told the roo are an impatient folk.''

''Not at all, friend Practor. We just hate to waste time.''

''Don't worry,'' Maryld told him. ''You'll have your chance at Shadowkeep soon enough.''

Hargrod was turning a slow circle, trying to peer through the mist. Finally he pointed. ''Over there. A structure.''

''Farmhouse probably,'' Sranul grunted, but he recognized the wisdom of Practor's words. And he *was* hungry. Health before wealth. They would eat and rest before challenging the fortress.

As they approached he saw it was much too large to be a farmhouse. The walls were built of river rock halfway up the first story and had been completed with peeled logs. A second building stood nearby, closer to the river.

''Most likely a stable,'' murmured Practor. ''There should be a place to leave our horses.'' He glanced to his left. The outline of Shadowkeep was still visible through the mist. ''Surely this Norell has fled along with the rest. It's so close to the castle.''

''That may not mean anything to a crazy man, my young friend,'' said Maryld.

Practor pulled hard on Kaltar's reins, coming to an abrupt halt. She turned in her saddle and eyed him curiously.

''Something wrong?''

''Just one thing, Maryld. I don't mind you calling me your friend, but I would rather not be called your 'young'

112

friend. Not unless you want me to start calling you grandmother, or elder.''

She laughed that full, mature laugh again. ''All right, Practor. I declare a truce on the matter of age. And if that is settled to your satisfaction, then mayhap we can see what this inn has to offer.''

''My feelings exactly.''

As they dismounted and secured their horses outside the inn, he was certain he could feel the pressure of other eyes on the back of his neck, eyes that belonged neither to human or thaladar, roo or Zhis'ta. Eyes that saw the world differently because they came from elsewhere. He turned twice but saw nothing behind him. There was only the mist and the dead and dying trees.

He shrugged. Like as not it was only his imagination, stimulated by their proximity to the castle and magnified by the suffocating mist, a moist lens which served to intensify his inner fears.

Together the four travelers stood and examined the sturdy, silent building before them. Katlar nuzzled Maryld's horse. Somewhere off in the marshes a wading bird cried uneasily.

''Looks deserted to me,'' said Hargrod. ''So is the stable.''

''How do you know that?'' asked Sranul challengingly. ''We haven't looked through it yet.''

Hargrod smiled thinly at the roo. ''I would smell any mounts.'' He nodded in the direction of the stable area. ''There are only old odors.''

Sranul sniffed several times. ''I can't tell for sure, but I guess I'll take your word for it. I didn't know the Zhis'ta had such sensitive noses.''

''We do not brag of our abilitiess,'' he replied. He nodded toward the door. ''However, I do ssmell life

113

insside. It iss faint. The wood iss thick. But there iss something alive in there.''

"You can't tell what it is?" Practor asked him hopefully.

"No. Not a mount, though."

"There's only one way to find out for sure." He moved forward, put one hand on the hilt of his sword and the other on the door, and shoved.

It opened without resistance. Beyond was a hall that twisted to the left. They entered the weather alcove and opened a second door. This admitted them to a spacious, warm room with a sunken floor of hard-packed earth.

Simple tables of heavy oak filled the open area. The matching chairs were of different sizes and shapes, designed to accommodate customers of varying dimensions and backsides. Casks were lined up behind the short wooden counter. At the near end the counter doubled as a desk. Oil lamps lit the room, and their flames danced in the breeze that entered with the quartet of adventurers. Hargrod closed the door behind them.

"Well, don't just stand there gawking."

The voice came from the huge human who stood behind the counter staring back at them. He rested massive hands on his hips, just above the edge of the greasy apron he wore. Once it might have been white, but clearly it hadn't been washed in a hundred years. The residue of a thousand meals decorated the weave.

Thick black curly hair covered the man's head and face, viscous locks that looked as greasy as the ancient apron. Grease aside, Practor guessed their greeter's weight to be close to four hundred.

His expression as he walked out from behind the counter was carefully neutral. He neither smiled or frowned as he approached them.

"Are you Norell, the crazy innkeeper?" Sranul asked,

displaying an extraordinary lack of tact. The roos were not noted diplomats.

"No, fatfeet, I'm a jockey come down from the highlands for the Falltime races."

"I asked if you were crazy, not sarcastic," commented the roo, not in the least embarrassed.

"Sanity is a matter of perception, my long-snouted friend. You may make your own judgment. It won't matter to me one way or the other, so long as your money's good. Pay full rates and you can call me anything you wish, except poor."

"Then you didn't run off like your friends and neighbors?" Practor said. "We encountered them four days south of here."

Now that neutral expression gave way to a suggestion of a smile. "And still moving south as fast as their feet will carry them, I'd wager. No, I chose to remain here. This is my home and my profession, and I'm not afraid of a few moans in the night or a little witch-light. This is the Inn of the Keep, so why should I be frightened of the Keep?"

"Considering what's going on within it, I'd think a little fear would be a healthy thing for someone living so near."

"That's respect you're talking about, traveler. Not the same thing as fear." Again the slight smile. "Of course, if I'm crazy, that explains everything, doesn't it? Well, it's apparent you four aren't afraid or you wouldn't be here now." Small black eyes regarded each of them in turn. "You'll be wanting lodging then, and something to eat?"

"Indeed we will." Sranul hopped forward and stuck out a paw. "No offense, fat man. My name's Sranul."

"No offense taken, big ears." Man and roo shook hands.

"You already know my name." He glanced at Practor, who introduced the rest of their party as well as himself.

"You are welcome." Norell turned and shuffled back to

the counter. There was a massive black-bound book on the part he utilized as a desk. He flipped it open, searched the pages until he found one that satisfied him, then dipped a quill into a nearby inkwell and held it out to them.

As he signed his name, Practor noted uneasily that the ink was a rich, thick shade of crimson. It also had a peculiar odor, but he forbore from inquiring as to the reason for this.

"We may not stay long."

"No matter. All my guests must register." A wider smile this time. "Sometimes all I have to remember my visitors by is their names," he added enigmatically. "Sometimes they only stop at the inn once and then I never see them again."

"One's true name cannot be used against one unless another knows all the proper words," Maryld told him as she signed.

Norell's eyes went wide. "Is that what you think of me? Have no fear of that, little lady." He put both huge hands on his chest. "I am an innkeeper pure and simple. The only use I have for names, true or otherwise, is for purposes of record-keeping."

"Not shadow-keeping?" Practor asked.

Thick black brows drew together as Norell shifted his attention from Maryld. "I have no love for whatever has taken possession of Shadowkeep, traveler. I make no moral judgments one way or another. If that marks me as crazy, than so be it. But I do not care for whatever now dwells within. I sense it sometimes, here alone in my inn. I can feel its presence around me. Perhaps it takes no notice of my presence here. Perhaps I am beneath such notice. But I do not like it. Unrepentant, rampant evil is bad for business. I would like to see it go away, but there is nothing that can be done."

"You may be an innkeeper pure, but you are not simple

as you choose to appear," said Maryld shrewdly. "You know that we're not passing traders. So I will tell you that we have come here to try and do what you and everyone else says cannot be done: cleanse Shadowkeep."

"Since it troubles you so," said Hargrod, "will you help us do this thing?"

"I've said that I've no love for whatever now dwells within Shadowkeep and I meant that, but I will not chance my survival by opposing it. It may be naive of me, or crazy, but I fancy that my neutrality is what protects me here. I am left alone in something approaching peace."

"There can be no middle ground where Dal'brad is active," Maryld told him.

"So that's who's mucking about within the castle, is it? The old demon king himself." Norell chuckled softly. "Of course, I've only your word for that. I'm not as gullible or easily frightened as those poor fools who packed up and left at the first howl." He carefully put his quill aside and closed the registry. To Practor it sounded like the closing of a heavy door. There was a finality to it.

His imagination again, working overtime.

"If you don't mind my saying so, you're a strange lot to be traveling together."

"We don't mind you saying so," Sranul replied. "Everyone we've met has said the same thing."

"Yes, an odd lot." Norell seemed to bring himself back from some distant contemplation of matters beyond their ken. "Have a table! We're not crowded tonight, sit anywhere you like. Give me but a little while and you will see food aplenty: all vegetarian for you, roo, plenty of fresh meat for our soft-spoken Zhis'ta, and a suitable mixture of both for human and thaladar. I pride myself on my humble cuisine and have had little enough occasion lately to practice it." He spat into a corner, striking the exact center of a pewter spittoon, then glanced sideways at Maryld.

"So old Dal'brad himself has taken up residence in Shadowkeep, eh? And what of the rightful owner?"

"We do not know what has happened to Gorwyther, but we hope to find out," she told him.

"Do you, now?" Norell's eyebrows rose and he stroked his beard absently. "I know that the thaladar are well versed in the mystic arts, but are you that accomplished, little lady? Your pardon, but I sense no necromancer among you. Not even a studious monk or mage. Strength at arms I can see you have, but that will not get you far into Shadowkeep." He nodded toward the thick black registry. "Others have tried."

"We know what we're about and we're quite capable of taking care of ourselves," Maryld informed him dryly, "no matter what form the opposition may take."

The innkeeper responded with a grunt. "If all are as bold and confident as you, little thaladar, such may be the case."

"Do not think to question our courage or determination," Hargrod said warningly.

"What, I question the courage of a Zhis'ta, or a roo?" Norell raised both hands and made a show of being surprised. "Not I. I tell them all the same things, and they respond with the same replies—before they go into Shadowkeep.

"But I am not going to weary you with my concerns or uncertainties. I am neglecting my duties. However long you remain with me, I hope you will enjoy it. I would not want you to leave with any unpleasant memories. I wouldn't want that on my conscience." He bent below the counter, and they could hear him rummaging through metal drinking utensils.

"You said that you tell 'them' all the same things." Practor looked toward the counter. "Have many preceded us?"

Norell stood, lined up four tankards on the counter. "More than you might think, less than you would suppose. They came seeking the treasures of Shadowkeep. I do not know what they found, but I never saw any of them ever again. Many have gone through that front entrance. Not a one has ever come out again."

"Maybe that's why," Practor observed thoughtfully. "They entered with only one thing on their minds: treasure. Their motives were base."

"Then you're not interested in the treasure?" Norell asked him, obviously amused.

"It's our hope that all peoples will profit by our visit."

Maryld leaned over and put a small hand on his arm. "Well spoken, Practor Fime." He felt unaccountably pleased.

"Even so," Sranul murmured, "we wouldn't be adverse to bringing out a bit of gold, or just a small gem or two. For decorative purposes, of course."

Norell nodded somberly. "Of course. For decorative purposes." He glanced significantly toward the horses tethered outside, making a show of peering through the single window. "You appear to be well equipped. Are you sure you have everything you need?"

"I think we've prepared well," Maryld told him.

"Still, there's always the last item forgotten and left behind, the special something you think of only at the last moment." He winked at Practor. "Now, I might be able to round up a few tools, the sort of thing you'd find very useful in this enterprise you propose. For a small fee, of course."

Practor recalled the shopkeeper's words. "We have everything we need, thanks."

"Well then, four seems like a small number to me to be challenging all the dangers of Shadowkeep. I might be able to find you some soldiers willing to accompany you a ways."

"I thought you said everyone but yourself had fled from the Basin?"

The innkeeper's eyes twinkled again. "Did I? Perhaps I did. But there are ways of finding such fighters—if you know where to look."

"Our number is complete," Maryld told him.

"Have it your way, little lady."

"Your offerss do not sstrike me ass thosse of a neutral man," Hargrod ventured aloud.

"I will sell to any who have the wherewithal to pay," Norell informed him evenly. "Man or Zhis'ta, demon or devil. My inn is open to all. One who sells does not take sides if he wishes to profit."

"There are many kinds of profit and some are more bankrupt than others," Sranul told him.

Norell's eyes narrowed as he stared over at the roo. He filled the tankards smoothly, without spilling a drop.

"So your primary interest is in making a profit," Maryld said casually.

"I am a businessman. Yes, that is my primary interest, thaladar."

"Even at our expense?"

"How else does one make a profit except at other's expense? One man's expense is another man's profit. That's the way of the world."

"Dal'brad wouldn't like you helping those who plan to try and destroy him."

"Well, I tell you what, little thaladar. When you confront him you tell him that, and I will worry myself as to the consequences." He walked over and set the four full tankards down on their table. "Drink and make merry, while you have the time. You'll find no one to serve you inside Shadowkeep." He paused a moment, then said to Maryld, "I would think a thaladar would chose a different class of comrades for such an expedition."

Hargrod started to rise, but Maryld put a small hand on his shoulder, and he resumed his seat without saying a word. She smiled pleasantly up at the innkeeper.

"I do not think I could find three better companions, thank you. As for myself, I was chosen." She nodded at Practor. "He is the instigator, not I."

Norell's attention shifted to Practor. "You don't say? It's a truth, then: the world is still full of wonders."

"Just act as neutral as you claim to be and spare us any more of your encouragement," Practor told him.

"I hope you're as quick with your sword as you are with your wits, friend. I will prepare your supper, which I assure you will be encouraging, and not at all sarcastic." He turned and vanished into a back room.

Sranul leaned forward. "Well, friends, what of our happy host? Do we eat his cooking and sleep in his beds, or would we be better advised to camp out beneath a tree with a solid wall at our backs and our swords at the ready?"

"I don't like him much," Practor muttered, "but I believe him when he says he's trying to stay neutral. I don't think he'd try to poison us. There's no profit in it."

"Unless he hass made a bargain with the demon king," Hargrod pointed out.

Maryld looked doubtful. "I agree with Practor. I think we are safe from everything except this man's tongue, which he likes to wag to see what reactions he can provoke with it. Dal'brad does not need to strike bargains with talkative innkeepers. And what Norell says about this miasma of evil having driven away his clientele also makes sense. I think we can eat and sleep here in safety. We all need a good night's sleep."

"I confess it will be a pleasure to sleep on something besides the ground," Sranul admitted. "Besides, how can we hope to penetrate Shadowkeep if we can't handle one simple innkeeper? I agree with you and Practor. We stay here tonight.''

Hargrod nodded acquiescence. ''I will not argue with the resst of you. It iss jusst that we Zhiss'ta are naturally ssupiciouss.''

''That caution will serve us well inside Shadowkeep,'' Maryld told him, ''but I think we can safely dispense with it here.''

''Ass you wissh. It iss not for me to ssay in any casse, ass I am bound to sserve you.''

''Forget that,'' Practor said sharply. ''You're one of the group, and just like Maryld said to me earlier, each of us is an equal side of a square. No one's 'bound' to anyone in this.''

The Zhis'ta was silent for a long moment, then he said, ''You are good people. That I knew becausse you helped uss againsst the goblinss. But I did not know how good.''

An embarrassed Practor hastened to change the subject....

Chapter VII

True to his word, the most wonderful smells began to reach them from the vicinity of Norell's kitchen. They were salivating by the time he finally emerged, pushing a heavily laden cart in front of him.

Practor viewed the forthcoming meal with suspicion. To his great surprise, the innkeeper's cooking demonstrated a light touch. There were puff pastries stuffed with some kind of sauteed, shredded meat, several kinds of vegetables, and lightly spiced potatoes and other tubers. Long strips of fried fowl were encrusted with pepper and coriander, and there were enormous loaves of some yellow bread that had been sweetened with honey.

The famished travelers dug into the unexpected feast with gusto. Even the usually taciturn Hargrod was moved to compliment grudgingly, "I am impressed, innkeeper."

"Me too," Sranul's words were blurred because his mouth was full of steaming vegetables. "Never expected anything like this. Sure is a change after weeks of scrounging for fronds and berries."

Norell looked embarrassed. "To tell you the truth, my friends, I don't usually lay on this kind of banquet for my customers. My regular dinner fare is not nearly so elaborate. In fact, I don't usually have time to cook at all. But you all looked hungry, and you're going to need your strength, and besides, all my help has run away.''

"This is most considerate of you.'' Maryld had distanced herself somewhat from her three male companions. She ate slowly and precisely, watching distastefully as they assaulted their plates. To see them you would've thought that the food on their dishes was still alive.

Norell stood nearby, attending them with a jug that rested on his right shoulder. It had a long, flexible spout attached to one end. By keeping a firm grip on it with one hand he was able to regulate the flow precisely.

"My best golden ale,'' he told Practor as he refilled his tankard.

"I'm not sure we can afford—'' he began, but Maryld shushed him.

"I have resources of my own to draw upon, and who knows when we may again have the opportunity to enjoy so fine and nourishing a meal. Eat your fill.'' Her gaze shifted to roo and Zhis'ta. "All of you eat your fill. Once we enter Shadowkeep the only food we will have is that which we carry in with us.''

"Tut,'' said Norell as he moved over to fill her tankard, "I know that you can pay. A thaladar's word is good enough for me. And what good is ale that lies moldering in its cask? Better it should repose in thirsty bellies.''

"Norell,'' she murmured, "I do believe that you are something of a poet.''

He grinned at her. "Little thaladar, all innkeepers are poets. Most tend to the needs of the soul. I tend to the needs of the body.''

Practor smiled as he chewed something stringy and flavorful. "This is my kind of poetry, friend.''

"Ah, then you must save room for the concluding stanza. Dessert!''

Practor was already full to bursting by the time Norell

rolled out the cart laden with pastries, but their appearance seduced him. Each one contained a different filling, and he was compelled to taste several.

"What do these contain?"

Norell wagged a finger at him. "It's best to leave a chef with some of his secrets, my friend. Besides, I am not sure you really want to know."

That made Practor push a last, half-finished tart aside. "Perhaps you're right, innkeeper. I do believe I've had enough."

"We've all had enough." Maryld pushed her chair back from the edge of the table and rose. Practor hurried to get behind her so he could pull her chair out the rest of the way. She favored him with a slight smile and he felt suddenly warm all over.

"Tomorrow is the day of reckoning. I suggest we all try to get a full night's sleep."

"I agree." Practor turned to Norell. "Do you have three rooms ready?"

"Four," Maryld corrected him sweetly. Wisely, he didn't press the matter.

"Your question is a formality, I assume, little thaladar." Norell nodded toward the stairs at the far end of the dining area. "As you see, my inn is quite empty. One hopes, however, and so you will find that all are ready to receive visitors. Choose what rooms you will and sleep in confidence. There is no variance in price from one to the next. I will tend to your mounts and they will rest as comfortably as their masters. No need for you to worry on that."

"We weren't worried," Maryld told him as she started toward the stairs. "After all, an innkeeper's word is good enough for us." She started up.

Sranul and Hargrod followed, arguing about some obscure point of legend. Practor would have followed save for the massive hand that came down on his shoulder and bid him remain behind.

"Stay a moment, my young friend," Norell asked him. "I have something to show you that might interest you."

"Like what?"

Norell studied his remaining guest. "You four are determined to try Shadowkeep, aren't you?"

Practor nodded. "That's our intention. It's why we're here."

"I asked you earlier. Now I ask again, in all seriousness. Are you certain you have everything you need?"

"You heard what Maryld said."

"Aye, but not even the thaladar can foresee everything." He hesitated a moment longer, then tugged at Practor's arm. "Come with me. It will only take a moment of your time, and if nothing else, I think you'll find what I have to show you interesting."

Practor longed for the sanctuary of a room, for the softness of a real bed, but Norell had taken good care of them so far and he didn't want to offend him. So he allowed himself to be led toward a door behind the counter. He wasn't sure he wanted to go through it alone, but if he feared this huge but very human individual, how could he hope to confront the far more imposing dangers within Shadowkeep?

So he affected an air of confidence and stepped through when Norell opened the door.

They were in a dark room. Norell spoke as he moved along the walls, lighting oil lamps. "I've come by many interesting items, friend. Not every guest can make payment in coin. I have relics of magic, healing potions, fine arms and armor, a great many unusual devices." As the lamps flickered to life, Practor could see a gleam in the innkeeper's eyes, and for an instant he wasn't sure that that hulking body held only the soul of another man.

Fully illuminated, the storeroom was a surprise. Practor expected to see a mundane collection of ordinary goods that had been left behind by hurried travelers. Instead, the board was neatly arrayed on shelves and benches.

A bin held a collection of walking staffs, each one gnarled or twisted in a manner different from the one next to it. On a bench was a box full of large crystals. He bent over them. They were not of gem quality. He knew fine stones because rich customers often had Shone Stelft work them into swords or daggers. But their size and color was intriguing. He was particularly taken with one fist-sized black crystal.

The walls were lined with mounted weapons. There were swords and spears, daggers and stilettos, helmets and breastplates. Golden chain mail dripped from several hooks.

Another bench displayed an assortment of small bottles and boxes. He had no way of knowing what they contained. There was a cushion on which rested a handful of curiously inscribed pendants. His fingers tingled when he reached toward them, and he hastily drew his hand back. Norell watched silently. His expression was unreadable.

Finally he picked up one small amethyst bottle and uncorked it. A look of pure bliss came over his face as he passed it gently beneath his nose. Practor got a whiff of something indescribably delicate and sensuous.

The innkeeper restoppered the bottle, set it back among the others. "Any of this can be yours, traveler, if you have the money." His expression turned conspiratorial and he beckoned Practor over.

From his belt the innkeeper produced a ring full of keys. Selecting one, he used it to unlock a table drawer. Inside the drawer was a shallow box which responded to another key.

Inside was a gold ring. The gold was not what took Practor's breath away: it was the workmanship. As a smith he could fully appreciate the skill which had gone into the making of the ring. It was all filigree work, the designs and motifs rendered and built up through the painstaking use of wire gold. Some of the patterns were so minuscule that even when he held the ring right up next to his eye, he couldn't make out all the details.

"Ten thousand," Norell told him softly, hovering close to Practor's shoulder. "Does it interest you?"

Practor reluctantly handed it back to the innkeeper. "Of course it interests me. I'm not made of stone. It's exquisite, the finest workmanship I've ever seen." He thought of how it would look on Rysancy's finger. "But I don't have a hundred goldens, let alone ten thousand."

Norell shrugged as though it made no difference and carefully placed the ring back in its box. "One never knows. I learned early in life never to judge anyone by their looks."

"Maybe Maryld would like it."

"The thaladar?" He locked the drawer, put the key ring back on its hook at his waist. "They part with their money most reluctantly." He turned to look around the storeroom. "For you then, perhaps something less expensive?"

Practor shook his head, eyed the door leading back to the dining area longingly. "I don't think so. This is all very interesting and I'm not denying its value, but I'm afraid it's not for me. I'd like to buy everything, so I'd best buy nothing and conserve what little money I have left to me."'

"What for? You'll have no use for it in Shadowkeep. Why take it with you? Or do you think you can bribe a demon?"

"As a matter of fact, I've heard tell that can be done. Where evil thrives, so does greed. Demons are not immune to the lure of gold. Who is to say what is possible and what is not inside the castle?"

"Not I, certainly," Norell admitted, realizing that his sales pitch had failed. "Ah well, perhaps one or two of you will come out again. There is a first time for everything, they say. If you bring out any treasure, maybe we can work a trade for something you value highly." He tapped the drawer meaningfully.

"Maybe." He turned toward the door. Norell accepted the cue and carefully extinguished each of the oil lamps in turn before leading his guest back to the main room. There he bid him a good night's rest.

But despite his exhaustion it was difficult for Practor to fall asleep. The gleam of the filigree ring was a bright light in his brain. Where had it come from? What sort of creature had the skill and the tiny fingers necessary to produce such incredibly fine work? He lay on the bed and wondered and marveled at the memory of it.

And eventually fell asleep.

Norell was waiting for them the next morning with a breakfast of eggs fixed many ways, sausages, rolls and muffins in abundance. They ate more out of politeness than desire, since all four of them were still full from the previous night's feast. Maryld in particular was adamant that they be on their way.

"We will sit here and grow fat on this man's cooking," she told them. She looked over at Norell. "Your food is too good and our time too short. We must be about our business."

Norell looked resigned. "I understand. Listen, all of you. I was, well, a bit skeptical of you all when you arrived here last night. I am still skeptical of what you're about to attempt, but not of you. You are fine folk and I want to wish you well before you leave here. Despite knowing better, I hope you succeed. The thought of Shadowkeep swallowing you up forever is not one that pleases me."

"It pleassess uss even less," Hargrod told him.

"Don't try to confront the demon king," Norell urged them. "Go in if you must, find the treasure, and hurry out with whatever you can carry."

"I'm sorry," Practor told him. "We appreciate your concern, but we must try. Whatever treasure we may find is incidental to our purpose."

Norell looked resigned. "My conscience is clear. I've done all I can to dissuade you."

"You will care for our mounts until we return?"

Norell's expression showed clearly what he thought of her last words, but he nodded nonetheless.

"They will continue to receive the best of care. I promise you that I will never sell them. They will always be here waiting for your return. They say time itself plays tricks inside Shadowkeep."

"Then there's nothing more to be done. We're ready." Sranul and Hargrod nodded at him and Maryld smiled.

The fog off the marsh was as thick as it had been when they'd ridden up to the inn the previous night, but the sun shafted cleanly through the drifting clouds and they were able to see quite well.

They approached the castle four abreast. No one challenged them when they stepped onto the causeway and began advancing toward the gate, though Practor found himself eyeing the murky water on either side of the roadbed uneasily. Guards could be placed beneath the waters as well as above them. He contented himself with Maryld's assurances that Dal'brad would concentrate any defenses inside the castle. Be they natural or otherworldly, guards were expensive. Shadowkeep's reputation was enough to keep away all but the most foolish, and demons were notoriously stingy.

Besides, the demon king would feel completely at ease

in his lair deep within the castle and would be concentrating his energies on his planned assault on the outer world.

As they neared the gate, the true vastness of the fortress impressed itself on each of them for the first time. It occurred to Practor that Shadowkeep's very size could constitute their greatest problem. He told Maryld so.

"Gorwyther could be imprisoned anywhere within there. Even if we never encounter a single trap or guard, we could wander around inside for weeks, months, without finding him."

"Never fear, we'll find him," Maryld assured him, "just as we will encounter guards and traps. Even if I knew how to go directly to him, we could not do so for fear of drawing attention to ourselves. We must approach the wizard circumspectly, without displaying too much of our own abilities, or we will draw the attention of the demon king much too soon. Even if he is made aware of our intrusion, we do not want him to guess our true purpose in coming here. Let him think we are just another group of foolhearty treasure hunters.

"We will deal with whatever obstacles are put in our path patiently, one at a time, and without making it appear too easy. In this fashion we may be fortunate enough to locate Gorwyther before the demon king realizes what we are up to."

The gate was not especially massive, but it did not yield to their efforts. Even Hargrod's strength was insufficient to force the doorway. Its composition likely had something to do with the difficulty. The door was fashioned of solid rock.

"Going to be tough to break through that," Sranul observed aloud. He looked to right and left. "Looks like this is the only way in, too."

"We're not going to break in." Maryld stepped past the roo. She touched the door lightly with the three middle fingers of her left hand, ran them over the polished stone surface in several crisscrossing patterns. Then she stepped back.

"I have done what I can." She looked over at Practor. "Hit it three times."

"Hit it?" The roo gaped at her. "You don't think he's going to knock a hole in that?"

"Nothing of the kind." She nodded encouragingly at Practor. "Go on. Three times, as though you were knocking on the door of a friend's house."

Practor stepped forward and did as he'd been directed. The voice that responded came from the stone itself, not from behind the door, and made him jump.

"SPEAK THE WORD AND ENTER."

"This is a first," Sranul commented. "I've never been given orders by a door before."

Hargrod had moved right up next to the stone and was working his snout along the barrier. "I ssmell no sspeaker here."

"That's because there is none, Hargrod. The door itself speaks though the spell that has been laid upon it." Maryld took his place and whispered something Practor and the others did not hear.

Whatever it was proved effective. The door ground back on unseen hinges, allowing them entry.

"How did you know the right word?" he asked her as they stepped through.

"Isn't it obvious? Give it some thought. You must learn to puzzle such things out yourself, Practor."

Once inside, the door shut slowly behind them. They were in a high hallway lit with softly burning lamps. Still nothing leapt from the shadows to challenge them. There was an air, not of abandonment, but of indifferent maintenance to the place, as though it were kept clean and lit only occasionally.

The hall opened on a large domed room. The ceiling was covered with mosaics of a disturbing appearance, though whether the designs were the work of Gorwyther or Dal'brad no one could say. Not that knowing who had rendered them would have made them any less unpleasant to look upon. They were not meant for the eyes of decent folk.

Curved benches had been set out on the floor in neat rows, facing the altar that dominated the far wall. As altars went it wasn't especially large, but it was quite impressive nonetheless.

Sranul's eyes widened as he stared at it. "Would you have a look at that!" Bounding toward it, he cleared the first four rows of benches in a single leap. It wasn't surprising that the roo should find it a source of inspiration.

The altar was solid silver.

Sranul stood in front of it, luxuriating in the bright silvery glow. Someone, or something, had polished it recently and it burned with reflected light. It was as if a supernally gifted metalsmith had taken his hammer to a piece of full moon.

"Well," said the roo gleefully, "a short expedition but a happy one. We've got what we came for. Let's unbolt this and get out of here."

Practor spoke as he worked his way through the benches toward the altar. "Open your eyes, Sranul! Or maybe you should close them. Have you forgotten why we're here?"

"I haven't forgotten why *I'm* here," the roo replied. "See how it shines, even in this bad light? Think what it will look like out in the sunshine!"

"There's not going to be any sunshine ever again unless we do something about it," Practor told him.

The roo hardly heard him. "If that was melted down and cast into coin, it would take half a dray wagon just to haul it. A wagonload of silver." He started toward the altar again, but by now Practor was close enough to put out a hand to hold the roo back.

"Wait a minute, Sranul. You're not thinking. There could be danger here."

The roo frowned at him. "What danger? We came in through a door, walked down a hall and into this room. We haven't been in here five minutes. No one knows we're here or there'd have been some kind of reaction by now. The only danger I see is that you're not going to help me drag this lovely little piece of furniture out of here. That's okay. I'll do it myself if need be. But danger? There's no danger here."

"What about that?"

"What about what?"

Practor pointed toward the intricate bas-relief that dominated the wall above the altar.

The roo shrugged. "A decorative bit of carving. So what?"

"This isn't a playhouse, Sranul. Everything in here likely has a purpose, none of it inclined toward the good. That includes the decorations on the walls and the ceiling above us." He nodded toward the bas-relief. "I'm no mage but even I can see that that's a rune of power."

Sranul squinted at the wall. "Looks just like some stone carving to me."

"I'm telling you, it's a rune. I've done enough reading to know a rune when I see one."

"Rune, ruin, what's the difference?" The roo cleared him in a single leap and commenced a close inspection of the altar. "Got to be attached to the wall somehow," he muttered as he tried to see behind it. "I can see cracks in the rock but no bolts or welds. Maybe it's not attached. That'd make it even easier." He grabbed one end of the altar and tugged.

There was a brilliant flash of white light and a loud

crackling. Sranul lit up like a torch. Then there was a sharp ripping sound in the air and something threw him halfway across the domed chamber. He knocked over a couple of benches, rolled over once, and came to a halt on his back as his friends rushed to his side.

"Foolish," Maryld muttered. "Foolish and stupid."

"Then why didn't you stop him?" Practor was bending anxiously over the motionless form.

"Stop him how? With words? Mine would've been no more effective than your own." She turned her gaze on the roo. "Some individuals cannot be talked to. They have to be shown."

"Yes," Practor agreed, "but must the example be fatal?"

Maryld snorted. "He's not dead. Stunned, but not dead."

"That's good. I'd hate to think we'd lost one of our party only a few minutes after entering." He put a hand under the roo's shoulder, lifted him off the floor. "Come on, Sranul. Maryld says you're not dead. Prove it. Say something."

The roo's eyelids moved, the long lashes fluttered. "Ouch."

Disgusted, Practor removed his supporting hand and stood. "Get up, idiot. Hargrod, give him a hand."

The Zhis'ta nodded and all but yanked the dazed roo to his feet.

"What . . . what happened? Who hit me?"

"No one hit you." Practor jerked his head toward the gleaming silver altar. "I told you there was a rune watching over that. You wouldn't listen. Not know-it-all Sranul, oh no."

The roo couldn't meet his eyes. "Sorry. I really thought it was just a wall carving."

"All you saw was the silver. You got off easy. A cheap lesson."

Sranul rubbed the back of his neck, stretched painfully. "It didn't feel cheap."

"A rune of power it is," Maryld agreed, eyeing Practor curiously. "I didn't know you were so well versed in magic."

He shrugged. "Like I told Sranul, I've done a lot of reading. Then too, we had many customers who visited us in the company of their own personal mages. Under their supervision, my teacher Shone Stelft would set many such symbols of power in metal. I saw enough of them worked into swords and shields to recognize one when I see it." He nodded toward the bas-relief. "At least, I can recognize them when they're not complex, and that one's pretty straightforward."

"Indeed it is." She turned to confront Sranul. "Avaricious roo, take this as a warning. The wealth of Shadowkeep is not free for the taking. Next time your greed may kill you."

On that solemn note she led them onward, past the domed chamber into the hall-like room beyond.

Its purpose was clear: it had been either an armory or a junk heap. It was full of weapons, but most of them were broken, shattered, or otherwise severely damaged. Despite the fact that many clearly were designed for hands other than human, the sight made Practor homesick.

There were a couple of anvils, hammers and saws and chisels: all the familiar paraphernalia of a well-equipped smithy. There was even a forge. Practor walked over and put his hands on it, wondering how it vented to the outside. The firestone was as cold as the floor.

"Nobody's worked in here in a long time," he told his companions. He left the forge and moved to the nearest anvil. It had been set up atop a huge old millstone instead of being bolted directly into the floor. A heavy hammer lay atop it. He picked it up, enjoying the familiar heft of it in his hand. Many was the time he'd used similar hammers to work hot, pliable metal. Although the forge was cold, the business end of the hammer was scored and scarred from frequent use.

"You know, I was working with such tools until just a few weeks ago," he said to no one in particular.

Hargrod's tone was impatient. He was surveying the way ahead. "We have all the weaponss we need." He kicked aside half a dozen broken sword blades. "What iss here iss usseless anyway."

Sranul stood at his shoulder and peered past him. "Anything moving?"

"Nothing. Sso far our pressence here goes undetected."

But Practor wasn't through inspecting the old armory. He knelt next to the anvil. It was heavily marked on both sides, and not by incidental blows of a hammer.

"See here," he murmured. "More runes."

"You look at them," said Sranul. "I've had enough of runes for one morning."

Practor was thinking hard as he picked up the hammer. "I wonder what would happen if . . . ?"

A slim hand came down on his wrist.

"Don't," Maryld told him.

"But it's not valuable, like Sranul's silver altar. It's just an old anvil."

"Marked with old runes. Think a moment, Practor. Why would anyone go to the trouble of rune-marking something so valueless—unless it's not as valueless as it seems. Or as harmless."

He held on to the hammer as he turned this over in his mind. "The runes: do you know their meaning?"

"No, just as I could not decipher the meaning of the carving above the altar. But this I do know: if you do not

137

know the meaning of magical signs, it is safer to leave them alone.''

Practor hesitated. The hammer was comfortable in his grip. It felt natural, not threatening. ''It might work something to our advantage. Might help to show us the way to Gorwyther's prison.''

''Or it might create a new prison, for us. Set it down carefully, Practor Fime. Back where you found it.''

Practor did so, but reluctantly. What harm could result from striking an anvil with a hammer? What harm could there be in touching a silver altar? Sranul's experience was still fresh in his mind. Sure, the action he proposed might be harmless, but mightn't it also blow him across the room? And what point was there in having a thaladar along if he refused to take her advice?

He put down the hammer. As he did so he thought the anvil quivered slightly. More likely it was his own nerves, teasing him.

Hargrod and Sranul had already left the armory behind. He could hear them banging around in the next room.

''What do you suppose those two have gotten themselves into?''

''No telling,'' Maryld replied evenly, ''but at least we don't have to worry about Sranul trying to carry off the next item of value he finds.''

''Don't count on that. Roos have short memories.''

The next room was an extension of the armory in both purpose and appearance. Practor's nose wrinkled at the lingering odors of inhuman sweat and garbage.

Beds of varying size and shape lined one wall. Several were broken and decorated with cobwebs. Broken pots and bottles, worn-out leather, piles of parchment full of unrecognizable writing, and heaps of lesser items covered the floor.

"It'ss ssome kind of barrackss," Hargrod surmised, "but not for the demon king'ss guardss."

"I agree." Maryld eyed the mess distastefully. "Not that demons have a fetish for cleanliness. Quite the opposite. But this, like the armory behind us, has not been used in a long time."

Sranul was poking through a pile of rubbish as tall as he was.

"What are you ssearching for there?" Hargrod asked him.

"Anything useful, my cold-blooded friend."

Hargrod made a face. "It sstrikess me that whoever abandoned thiss end of the fortress would have taken any usseful thingss with them when they left."

"Not necessarily," Sranul argued, throwing garbage in all directions as he plowed through the last of the first pile and started in on the one next to it. "Depends why they left and at what speed. Never know what you might find in living quarters hastily abandoned."

"It doesn't matter," Practor told him. "We didn't come here to go rummaging through trash. Besides, Hargrod's right. You're not going to find anything in this garbage."

"Oh no?" Triumphantly, Sranul emerged from the pile holding three small metal disks. They were thick and heavy with grime and grease. While the fastidious Maryld looked away, the roo used his long tongue to clean them.

"Not find anything, eh? What do you call these? Three goldens, just lying there for the taking." He slipped them into a waist pouch and resumed his digging, using feet and tail as well as his hands.

"It would take days to go through all of this," Practor told him, "and there's no assurance there's anything else to find. So you got lucky and found a couple of pieces of gold."

"You talk like I'd found a few cloves of garlic," Sranul shot back as he continued to send dust and mold flying.

Practor turned away. "Come on. *Now*." It wasn't the roo's reluctance to follow that made him turn back again, however. He looked toward the back of the room. "Maryld? Don't tell me you agree with him?"

"No." She beckoned him over.

She was standing by the back wall, beyond the broken beds and piles of trash. "What do you make of this?"

She had one hand resting on a small podium. Practor eyed it carefully. At first he thought it had been cut from the trunk of a single tree, but close inspection revealed that it was not made of wood at all. It had a shine to it no wood could match, no matter how frequently polished. It was cool and hard to the touch, but hard in a way wood was not. There was no give to it at all.

In the center of the flat top was a diamond-shaped depression. A silver wheel gleamed on the side.

"I don't know," he finally told her. "I've never seen anything quite like it. It's interesting, but not particularly impressive. Although . . ."

Maryld searched his face. "It reminds you of something."

"Maybe—I'm not sure, Maryld. Last night, after the rest of you had gone upstairs, Norell took me into a back room. A storeroom. He had quite an assortment of stuff back there. Weapons, armor, a handsome little ring I wouldn't mind having, potions and the like, all of it valuable, worthwhile, and expensive. Too expensive for me.

"There were also some crystals. Not gem quality, but of unusual size and color." He ran his fingers over the diamond-shaped depression in the top of the podium. "I was just thinking that some of them might fit in this."

Maryld's fingers met his inside the depression. She was thinking hard. "I don't know what to make of what you say, or of this device, for device I am certain it is. It does not look important, but I was taught at a very young age to be warier of nothing that looks like something rather than something that looks like nothing. Still, without one of those crystals there is nothing we can do but speculate as to the purpose of this device."

"Do you think if we had some of the crystals to try this thing might help us?"

"I don't know, Practor. I will think on it further."

"SShey!" They both turned in the direction of the excited cry. "I found the sstairss."

"About time," Maryld muttered.

They followed the sound of Hargrod's voice. After a final, desultory poke at a massive mound of garbage, Sranul joined them.

The wooden stairwell wound its way upward. Hargrod held his spear at the ready as he stared at the uppermost steps. "We go up?"

"It could be a trap, designed to lure unwary intruders, but I think we have no choice," Maryld replied. "Dal'brad would not imprison Gorwyther close by the main entrance to Shadowkeep where any casual passerby might stroll in and free him. We will find the wizard on one of the fortress's upper levels."

"Yes, but which one?" Sranul asked.

By way of reply Maryld closed her eyes and seemed to fall instantly into a deep, soundless sleep. Her three companions waited respectfully until she emerged from the self-induced trance.

"It's no use," she said sadly. "I cannot tell what lies directly above us. There have been so many spells cast and so many magics worked in this place that I cannot sense a clear path toward Gorwyther, the demon king, or anyone else. We will just have to go up and search the place floor by floor, room by room."

141

"All of Shadowkeep?" Sranul groaned.

"What did you think?" Practor struggled not to sneer. The roo was a good soul. He was just a bit naive. "That we would just walk in, help ourselves to the treasure with one hand and free Gorwyther with the other?"

Sranul wasn't in the least perturbed by the human's tone. "Sure, why not? Hope for the easiest."

"Oh, come on," snapped Practor, thoroughly frustrated by the roo's cavalier attitude. He started up the stairwell.

Four corridors led away from the stairs on the second floor. All were empty. At least there was none of the trash they'd encountered below. Which implied that someone had been keeping this part of the fortress clean.

"Nothing," he told his companions. "There are more stairs nearby, leading upward." He stepped clear of the stairwell and started toward them, followed by his companions.

They were halfway to the first step when the spiked club bounced off the rock and fell to the floor. Practor had heard it whistle when it passed close by his skull.

Chapter VIII

"Hurry!" Maryld yelled, "run for the next level!"

Sranul turned toward the dark advancing shapes. Eyes glowed in the dim light and soft, ominous mutterings sounded. "Listen, we're not here to cause trouble. We haven't . . ." he ducked barely in time to avoid a spear. It slid across the floor behind him.

Hargrod emerged from the stairwell. "You two go ahead. We'll hold them off until you've reached the top."

"We will?" Sranul squeaked. He pulled spears from his back quiver as Practor and Maryld began to climb.

Their attackers were not demons, but neither did they belong to any known race. Their movements were slow and deliberate, but there were many of them. Standing and fighting was out of the question. Hargrod kept them from reaching the stairwell to pursue man and thaladar while Sranul picked them off one at a time with his spears.

Practor and Maryld reached the third floor, found themselves standing in a deserted six-sided room. There were tables and sideboards lining the walls. Without hesitating he rushed to the heaviest piece and began wrestling it toward the stairwell. The wood was old and heavy, but need gave strength to his arms. Maryld tried to help, but the massive furniture was too much for her slight thaladar muscles. She rushed to peer down the stairs.

Sranul and Hargrod were being forced upward. Practor pushed the sideboard into position, turned, and began tugging on a huge table. As soon as Hargrod and Sranul stepped out onto the floor, he turned the table on its side, let it crash down on the head of the nearest of their assailants.

While Hargrod used his ax to keep what remained of the opening clear, Sranul hurried to help Practor. Together they shoved several more pieces of furniture over the stairwell opening. Hargrod put his ax aside then, and in short order every table and cabinet in the room had been piled over the gap.

Something began pounding on the tables from below. It went on for several minutes, then ceased.

"Too much weight for them," Practor declared, panting hard.

"Are they gone, then?" Sranul asked.

"I should think so or they would have broken through by now." Maryld, too, was breathing with difficulty.

"What were they?" the roo asked her. "I know I stuck at least four of them, but they didn't even bleed."

"Servants of Dal'brad, surely. Less than demons but more than men."

"I would have sworn that the floor below uss was deserted," said Hargrod. "They appeared ass if from nowhere."

"That may be exactly where they appeared from, my good Zhis'ta," she told him. She moved to stand next to the pile of furniture, staring at the blocked stairwell. "I do not think they will chase us further. I don't believe they have the intelligence to mount a concerted pursuit. Strictly lower-grade servants of the dark forces, suitable for eliminating most intruders. I fear that from now on we will have to be prepared to deal with more sophisticated defenders. Besides, demons dislike repeating themselves. They feel that if one ploy fails, there is nothing to be gained by repeating it. We must be on our guard now more than ever.''

''In any casse, it would ssem that our coursse iss clear.'' Hargrod nodded toward the stairwell. ''We cannot go back now.''

''Why not?'' wondered Sranul. ''If those down there are as stupid as Maryld says, won't they get bored after a while and leave?''

''No,'' she told him. ''They know we are up here. They will wait for us to return, for the stairs to be unblocked, or for directions from elsewhere. But they will not leave.''

''Then we're trapped up here.''

''It does not matter. We will leave with Gorwyther's aid or not at all.'' She turned her attention to the room in which they found themselves, checking the corners, inspecting the draperies and remaining furnishings. ''This way.''

They followed her down the hallway leading off to the left.

''What are we looking for?'' Sranul asked her.

''I don't know. A sign, a marker, perhaps a clue Gorwyther might have had time to leave before he was imprisoned. We will know it when we find it.''

''Suits me,'' said the roo. ''I'm always willing to search.'' He patted the pouch holding the three goldens he'd found below.

''Looks like we're not the first ones to come searching in here.'' Practor pulled aside a curtain to reveal a pile of old bones. ''Whoever this was didn't find what he was looking for.'' He kicked at the pile.

Several of the bones went flying, bounced off the wall. The single skull rolled over a few times, steadied itself, rose slowly into the air and stared straight back at Practor.

Sranul jumped backward. Hargrod hissed, while Practor quickly drew his sword.

"Maryld—I think I may have found the sign you were looking for."

The skull did not rush at him, jaws agape. No lightning lanced from its mouth, no poison, not even a threat. It simply continued to hover before him, as if waiting to see what he would do next. Maryld moved to stand next to him.

Seeing that there was no immediate danger, Sranul and Hargrod came forward. "My, my, would you look at that," the roo whispered in awe.

"What iss?" Hargrod asked her.

"A litch," she told them. "A guard, a watch-thing."

"Guard for what?" Practor wondered. "It's just floating there." He stepped to his right, then walked around to his left until he was stopped by the wall. The skull pivoted to follow his movements with empty sockets, but did nothing to hinder him.

"See? It's not trying to stop me."

"Because you're not threatening whatever it was set here to guard," Maryld told him. "A litch is charged with protecting or watching over a specific thing. Not like those fortress guards we encountered below." She knelt and searched the bones which Practor's kick had failed to disturb. "There, see?" She pointed.

Sure enough, buried within the bone pile was a suggestion of white: a book bound in cream vellum.

"It must be important," she murmured, "else this litch would not have been placed here to watch over it. It may be useful." She glanced to her right. "Sranul?"

"No thanks," said the roo, taking a step backward. "I'm not that desperate for something to read."

But Practor was already edging his way closer to the pile. When Maryld had knelt, the skull had shifted to watch her. But as soon as he'd begun to move, it turned to focus on him.

"Maybe it's only designed to scare," Practor murmured as he reached out with his left hand. "Maybe it's harmless."

His fingers were inches from the book when the empty eyes of the skull flared. Practor yelped and clutched at his arm as he fell backward. At the same time Hargrod's arm moved forward faster than anyone could have believed possible. The massive battle-ax shot toward the skull, which tried to dodge. But the litch had been preoccupied with Practor and it failed to turn in time. The ax split it cleanly in half before burying itself in the wall beyond.

Hargrod permitted himself a satisfied grunt, stepped forward, and nudged the shattered skull with his right foot. The fragments of bone showed no sign of life.

"Sso much for magic," the Zhis'ta commented quietly.

"No human could have done that," said Practor. He was holding his left arm.

"Nor thaladar," agreed Maryld, "but do not dismiss magic so quickly. It is not an opponent to be taken lightly."

"I take no opponent lightly," Hargrod assured her. Suddenly he frowned and squatted before the remnants of the skull, staring. "What could thiss be?" He removed something from the fragments.

Meanwhile Maryld was examining Practor's injured arm. It had turned pink and tingled steadily, but the damage was not serious.

"An instant sunburn," she told him, rising. "You'll be all right." She looked across to Hargrod. "What is it, what have you found?"

"I do not know." He straightened, gazing at something in his hand as he moved to join them. "It was insside the sskull."

147

It was a beautiful little jewel, bright yellow and exquisitely faceted.

"The life-force of the litch," Maryld told him. "It's yours, Hargrod. You won it."

"Better perhapss than a couple of goldenss." He slipped it into his pack.

"Maybe," muttered a jealous Sranul.

"Let's not forget this." Practor turned and walked over to extract the vellum-clad book from the bone pile. He flipped through it. Maryld joined him, looking around his shoulder.

"Worthwhile?" he asked her.

"Too soon to say. I can only understand a little of it."

Practor handed it to her. "You take charge of it, study it when you can." He looked back toward the stairwell. "Maybe those things won't try and break through, but I don't want to wait here to find out."

"Wait, wait a moment!" Sranul had been searching the far side of the room.

"Now what?" Practor muttered as they walked over to see what had excited the roo.

"See?" Sranul pointed proudly at his discovery, a long translucent box lying on the floor. "A sword case! Whoever cleaned this place out forgot this one item of value and left it behind." He grinned at Hargrod. "Better still than even a fine gem."

"I don't know." Maryld eyed the box uneasily. "I'd be suspicious of anything lying out in plain sight like this."

"Of course it's out in plain sight," Sranul argued. "Someone was leaving here in a hurry, set it down intending to come back for it, and forgot to. Or wasn't able to. Besides, what else could it be? See, it's even in the shape of a sword. Oh, it's a case, all right, and a fine one. It must be made for an exceptional weapon." Reaching down, he began loosening the latches that lined both sides of the box.

"Maybe it belonged to the wizard himself, or some great warrior of ancient times," Sranul whispered excitedly. "It may be studded with fine jewels. Or perhaps it's only a ceremonial sword, fashioned of solid gold."

Practor watched dubiously. "Don't you think it would be better, Sranul, if first we..."

Too late. The last fastener had been unlatched and the roo was shoving the top half aside.

There was something inside, all right, but it wasn't a sword, ceremonial or otherwise. The bright orange gas that billowed out into Sranul's face was as dangerous as it was colorful. The roo's eyes went wide as he bent over and clutched at his chest.

Having more presence of mind and faster reactions than any of them, Hargrod immediately grabbed the roo under both arms and began carrying him away while holding his own breath. Practor got a whiff of it before he held his own air, and it started him choking. The thick, cloying smoke expanded with frightening rapidity to fill the whole room. Fortunately, its effects diminished the farther one was from the box.

"Which... which way?" Practor gasped.

"Follow me!" Either the gas wasn't affecting Hargrod as severely as the rest of them, or else the Zhis'ta had moved out of its range.

But how could they follow if they couldn't see him?

"Link hands," Maryld said loudly. Fumbling through the orange cloud, he found hers—small, soft, and warm. She began moving purposefully forward, which meant she must have a firm grip on Hargrod. As for the Zhis'ta, Practor didn't doubt he could carry Sranul with one arm while holding gently on to Maryld's hand with the other.

"Can you see anything ahead of us?" he called out to their reptilian guide.

"Very little. Maryld, what sshould we do?"

"I don't know. If we go up another flight of stairs the gas may simply follow."

Suddenly Practor, who was stumbling up against the thaladar, heard a banging and pounding ahead.

"I have found a door," Hargrod announced. Maryld was pulled away from Practor and an instant later he was himself yanked forward.

To find himself standing in a narrow hallway blissfully free of orange fog. Ahead, Hargrod was easing the coughing, wheezing Sranul to the floor. Practor turned and shut the door behind them. A few orange wisps seeped under the door, dissipated in the clean air of the hallway. Practor watched the barrier warily, but nothing tried to force its way through. The orange cloud had been nothing more than an orange cloud, which was quite enough.

He turned to glare down at Sranul. "I think it's time we came to an understanding. From now on, nobody goes poking into anything unless Maryld first gives the word. You stay away from anything you don't recognize."

"Don't recognize?" Sranul coughed, swallowed. "It was just a box, a sword case. It *was* a sword case!"

"Nothing in Shadowkeep is 'just' a box, just as nothing is what it appears to be," Maryld told him. She put a hand over her mouth, coughed delicately. "We owe our lives to Hargrod, and you especially, my large-footed friend."

"Yeah, well," Sranul grumbled, glanced up at the Zhis'ta. "Thanks."

"Do not hope to be ass lucky a ssecond time."

"There won't be any second time. I've learned my lesson." He climbed to his feet, stared down the hall. "Anyway, we're safe now."

"You certainly are, aren't you?"

Practor frowned. "Who said that?" Hargrod began sniffing the air while Sranul shook his head. The voice was too deep to be Maryld's.

"I said it."

Slowly they started down the hall. There was a door leading off to the right, into a room that appeared to be an office or some kind of meeting place. It was not impressive. There were a few cheap furnishings, some peculiar drawings on the walls, and a huge rough-hewn desk.

"I'm glad you came," said the creature behind the desk. "My lunch is late and I was getting hungry."

Practor stared at it with more interest than concern. He'd never seen a real troll before, though he knew what they looked like from the stories he'd overheard in Sasubree's marketplace. They lived underground, away from the upper world of men and thaladar and the other civilized races. But what place could be darker and more isolated than Shadowkeep?

He appeared to be alone, which was fortunate since another of him would have filled the room to bursting. His appearance upheld the trollish legend quite well. He was very big, very strong-looking, and exceedingly ugly. Even so, his true size didn't become apparent until he rose from his chair behind the desk.

Seven feet tall at least, Practor thought, and as heavy as Hargrod and himself together. It started to edge around from behind its desk.

"Look, I'm sorry if you're upset, but we're not the ones responsible for the lateness of your lunch," he told it.

"I did not say that you were. Those who are will suffer for their tardiness." The troll smiled, displaying an impressive array of twisted, broken teeth. "But I *am* hungry. So you will have to be my lunch."

Sranul let out a final, desultory cough as he backed hurriedly toward the doorway. "I know how you feel, sir.

Why, I've been hungry once or twice myself. But I'm nobody's lunch.''

"Listen," Practor said even as he was backing toward the exit, "can't we strike some sort of bargain?''

"You mean a deal?'' asked the advancing monolith. "I do not deal with scum like you.''

"But you eat scum like us? Strange taste you have.''

That finally wiped the smile from the troll's face. Demonstrating unexpected agility, it pulled out its long sword and struck. Practor dove to his left while Sranul leaped six feet straight up. The huge blade cut nothing but air.

At the same time Hargrod parried with his ax. The sound of the two massive weapons connecting was numbing in the enclosed space of the office. Hargrod gave ground beneath the blow, but the sword slid cleanly off his ax, and he was not injured. The Zhis'ta was strong enough to slow the troll but not to defeat it.

"Which way?'' Practor asked Maryld as soon as they were outside in the hallway again. The troll answered the question for her.

"Take them!'' it roared. A horde of smaller trolls appeared behind their master, and others emerged from a door behind the intruders. There was only one uncontested avenue of escape: down the hall. With Hargrod fighting a delaying action all by himself, they began retreating.

While they differed considerably in size and shape, each new troll was uglier and meaner-looking than the last. The assortment of weapons they carried matched their unlovely dispositions. Fortunately, the hall was so narrow only a few were able to press forward at a time, and Hargrod mechanically dropped any who came too close. The bodies began to pile up in the corridor, reducing the maneuvering room of those trolls who came behind still further.

They came to an intersection. Snarls and mumblings

sounded off to their left, and Maryld hurriedly directed them down the right-hand branch. A few trolls appeared ahead of them, but they'd already outdistanced their immediate pursuers and Hargrod was able to turn his attention to this new threat. With the help of Practor's sword, the way ahead was soon clear again.

Behind them the master troll's battle cry of "Lunch, lunch!" continued to echo in their ears, lending energy to their legs.

Another intersection loomed directly ahead, a tripartite branching this time. "Now what?" Practor muttered as he slowed.

"A trap," Maryld whispered. "An undisguised attempt to eliminate the unwary. The first one we've encountered. Not Gorwyther's work. The demon king's."

Sranul bounded from one corridor to another, turned in the last and announced worriedly, "They're dead ends! All three of them!"

Maryld stepped out into the intersection and studied each in turn. The trolls would be on top of them in moments. "Not necessarily," she finally declared. "Listen."

Practor forced himself to concentrate, to shut out the bloodthirsty cries of their pursuers. What was Maryld talking about? There was nothing else to hear in this place. Nothing else . . . except . . . was that a humming noise? He opened his eyes, tried to let his ears direct them. He nodded toward the corridor on the right. "That way?"

She smiled at him. "You are more sensitive, Practor Fime, than you would have others believe." She started running. Practor followed, with Sranul and Hargrod bringing up the rear. The first trolls were almost to the intersection.

The roo was staring at the black stone wall that lay ahead of them, at the end of the corridor. "Looks like a dead end to me," he muttered. "If it is, it won't be the only thing dead in here."

"It's our only hope," Maryld told him. "We have to take this chance. We can't fight the trolls forever."

As they drew near the end of the corridor the humming sound Practor had heard grew louder. Soon even Sranul could see that the corridor did not end in solid stone.

It was black as basalt, but the wall was uneasy on the eyes. It seemed to move, to shift and flicker. As they approached it began to change color, turning blue from black, then back again, then becoming a startling chalk-white, then violet, and back to black again.

"What started that?" the roo wondered as he slowed.

"Our arrival, our presence," Maryld told him. "I thought it looked funny. It sounded odd, too, and I sensed—something—when we entered the intersection."

"I sstill ssee no esscape," Hargrod muttered. He was facing back down the corridor, hefting his bloody ax. "A wall of colorss iss sstill a wall."

"Perhaps, and perhaps not, Zhis'ta," she replied as she studied the changing hues. "It's certainly a mystery, and one never knows what may lie behind a mystery."

He frowned. "Behind?" He gestured at the flickering, unstable colors. "There iss nothing behind that."

A strange expression had come over Maryld's face. "There is, good Hargrod. Yes, there is!"

"What?" asked Sranul.

Her expression fell slightly. "I don't know."

"That's not very encouraging," Hargrod muttered.

"Neither is our present position," Practor told him. The first trolls had appeared in the intersection. They were cautious in their approach, wary of an ambush. Soon they would spot their trapped quarry. Then there would be no time left in which to make a decision. He looked at Maryld.

"Tell us what to do. We're helpless here."

"But if she doesn't know what lies on the other side—assuming there *is* an other side," Sranul protested.

Practor glared at him. "Would you rather stay here and be lunch?" He turned to face the quivering wall. "Do we go through, Maryld?"

She nodded. "We must try. Anything is better than this."

"Even if it leads us right into the demon king's lair?" Sranul demanded to know.

"You can stay here and talk it over with the trolls," Practor told him. He extended an arm. Maryld smiled at his gallantry, accepted his hand, and together they stepped through the wall.

In spite of himself, Practor closed his eyes. Not that he missed anything. It's difficult to be a tourist in a void. A brief, disorienting shudder passed through his body. When he opened his eyes it was pitch-black, but light reappeared an instant later.

They were in another hallway, higher and wider than the last. It was better lit than most. Oil lamps burned furiously high up on the walls, higher than any man could reach. Turning, he found himself staring at an unbroken granite wall. It did not flicker or change color. He reached out and touched it. The surface was hard, unyielding, and stable.

Even as he watched, a body appeared, pushing through. Hargrod stepped out next to them, followed by a distorted-faced roo. Sranul had both eyes screwed shut and was holding his breath. His puffed-out cheeks gave him the appearance of a bloated mouse, and Practor was hard-put, despite the seriousness of their situation, to restrain a laugh. Maryld had even less success, and her giggle hurt the roo's pride far more than Practor's laughter would have.

"I didn't know what to expect," Sranul mumbled. "I've never walked through a wall before."

Maryld coughed delicately into a hand, tried to assume a serious mien. "You're the last one through. How close were they?" As she spoke she was searching through the pouch that hung from her left shoulder.

"Right behind me. I took one with a spear and..."

"Look out!" Practor said warningly as he assumed a defensive stance.

A scaly arm was emerging from the wall, gripping a sword. Hargrod took a step forward but Maryld gestured for him and Practor to move away from the wall. She muttered something under her breath and threw the handful of powder she'd taken from her pouch toward the barrier.

There was a brief flash of light, not too bright, as the powder contacted the stone, followed by a distant, hollow scream of pain. Practor blinked. Lying on the floor next to the wall was a troll arm and hand, neatly severed at the shoulder. As he stared it began to bleed. Moving forward, he touched the wall a second time. Solid, unbroken stone, unchanged in a thousand years. Nothing else came through.

He glanced back at Maryld. "How did you do that?"

"Any gate that can be opened can be closed. We thaladar have our own skills. We're very good with gates." She turned and began to survey their newly won surroundings. "A more important question is, where are we now?"

"Still within Shadowkeep?" offered Sranul meekly.

"Certainly that. It was not a very wide gate." They started down the impressive hallway.

They had no way of knowing on what level they stood, Maryld informed them. Merely because they had encountered and escaped from the trolls on the third did not mean they had passed through onto the same floor. There were no windows to look through. This particularly distressed the space-loving Sranul. He would have given the goldens he'd found for one glimpse of foggy marshland, of real world.

But for now the real world was no more than a memory. Only Shadowkeep existed, only Shadowkeep was real. Shadowkeep, and its dangers.

Pillars lined with carved gargoyles and monsters supported the arching ceiling. Sranul kept his eyes on them as they passed between, keeping in mind Maryld's earlier admonition that nothing within the fortress should be taken at face value. But those stone eyes did not follow their progress, stone talons did not reach out for them. The great pillars were rock and nothing more. It was peculiarly gratifying to encounter something so imposing that was exactly what it appeared to be and nothing more.

"This is no mere hallway," Maryld was murmuring as they walked. "This is a place of power, designed to facilitate the dispensing of power. An audience chamber, perhaps, or some sort of important meeting place." Her gaze went to the far end of the hall. "There. The power I feel emanates from there."

As they neared the end of the corridor Practor saw the throne. It wasn't especially impressive to look upon, despite the minute inlay work. Sranul rushed forward in search of gold or gems, only to be disappointed. Maryld assured the roo the throne represented far more than it displayed.

"Seat's not built for a roo, that's for sure," he told them. He tapped the backrest. "No tail slot." He moved round to inspect one of the armrests. "Now this ivory-looking white stuff set into the wood here, this looks like *grahu* bone. Not very well fashioned, either." He ran his hand over the smooth surface.

Maryld sighed in exasperation. "Have you learned nothing since your encounters with the sword case and the silver altar?"

The roo shrugged. "What's the harm in touching? This is only a simple chair, not the throne of some great king."

He gave the armrest a sharp rap. "See? Nothing worth stealing, nothing worth getting excited over."

As he said "over" a pulse of light flared from the throne. Sranul's leg muscles convulsed and threw him twelve feet sideways.

Practor shook his head sadly. "Close. Too close."

Maryld had moved to examine the throne carefully. "Not necessarily. Sranul might be right—this time. This chair might not be dangerous. It might even be helpful. A wizard's fortress is likely to be filled with useful magics as well as traps. It did not harm Sranul." She glanced back at the roo, who was breathing hard and fast. "Only acknowledged his presence."

"It could have done so a little more politely," the startled Sranul wheezed.

She reached out, grasped both armrests, and ran her fingers gently over the polished wooden surfaces. "Half-right and half-wrong. This throne is not dangerous, but it *is* the seat of a king. A mage king."

Hargrod made a face. "What iss that?"

"A king and ruler of wizards and other practitioners of magic," she told him. "That's the power that still permeates this audience chamber. The mage king is gone, but his strength still lingers here." She tapped the armrest. "Here in this throne. Whoever sits in it may partake of that power. But there is no way to predict how it will react or who it might adhere to." She frowned. "Then too, it is hard to imagine Dal'brad leaving such power unguarded, for underlings or would-be usurpers to make use of. It could be a trap." She exchanged a meaningful glance with each of her companions. "Remember, I said that the demon king's defenses would grow more subtle, more devious, the closer we got to him." She moved away from the throne. "I am tempted, but if this is a trap, this is what

158

it would be designed to do. I will not chance it, for all that it could aid us. Practor?"

"No thanks. I'm feeling powerful enough just now."

"We have not begun to confront Shadowkeep's real dangers. A boost in one's mental abilities could make the difference between success and failure."

"If you're not sitting in it, neither am I."

"Nor I," added Hargrod. "We Zhiss'ta are cautious and do not dabble well in matterss mysstical. I prefer my mind sslow but unfried."

Everyone looked at Sranul.

"Are you kidding?" the roo told them. "Not a chance. I'm beginning to think there isn't a harmless piece of furniture in this whole cursed structure." He turned a slow circle, his gaze traveling from throne to pillars to friends. "There's treasure here, though. I can feel it, I can smell it! I just can't *find* it." He moved toward the far wall. The throne pulsed gently behind him, trying to entice him to enjoy the smooth curve of its seat. All four intruders ignored it.

"A few goldens," the roo muttered. "A pittance. Here we are in a mage king's throne room, and there's nothing of value to be had."

While Sranul grumbled and searched, his companions rested from their fight and flight from the trolls. Practor nodded back toward the now distant end of the hallway.

"You think we'll run into them again?"

Maryld shook her head. "I think they must be far away, in another part of the fortress entirely. We must have traveled a goodly distance, else why put a transfer wall in a place where a simple door would serve as well? On that matter, at least, I think we can now rest easy."

"But you sstill do not know where we are?" Hargod murmured.

"It doesn't matter," Practor said firmly. "All that matters is where we're going. Me, I'm glad we had to pass through that wall. Not only did it save us from the trolls, it would confuse anything else following our tracks." He glanced at Maryld. "Wouldn't it?"

Her reply was noncommittal. "Mayhap. In any case, I do not feel that anything else pursues us. I do not believe the demon king is aware of our presence as yet, or we would have felt his attention by now." She rose. "Come. The most dangerous thing we can do is linger too long in any one place."

They started up the side hallway, following in Sranul's wake. They hadn't gone far when the roo let out an excited yelp.

Practor sighed. "Now what?"

Chapter IX

No false alarm this time, though. The roo had finally found something.

"A skullcap," Practor said, eyeing the roo's find. "I've seen such before. Certain monkish orders are particularly fond of them. But I've never seen one like that."

"I'm not sure there's ever been one like that," Maryld commented.

The cap was fashioned of spun silver, as light and wispy as if it had been made on a spinning wheel instead of a forge. It reminded Practor of the precious gold ring Norell had tried to sell him. It hung on a hook behind a panel or window of some transparent material.

Hesitantly he reached up and ran his fingers over the protective shield, tapped it with his knuckles.

"Glass?" asked Hargrod.

"No," he replied hesitantly. "Tougher than that. A lot tougher. Mica perhaps, but more likely rock crystal." He used his nails on the surface but it refused to peel. "Yes, rock crystal."

"Such a large piece," Sranul murmured. "It could be worth as much as the cap."

"I don't think so," Practor said. "That's no ordinary

cap, and I'm not referring to the fact that it's made of silver. It's too well protected." Experimentally, he reached out and grabbed hold of the bottom of the panel and tried to shove it upward. It wouldn't budge.

"Let me try." He stepped aside to let Hargrod try. Thick muscles bulged in the Zhis'ta's arms. He employed his great strength silently, the only hint of the strain he was undergoing a twitching of the great tendon in his neck.

Finally he let out a long sigh and stepped back. "Certainly there iss more to that cap than ssilver and art. I pusshed hard enough to crack the crysstal—if crysstal only it iss. Ssomething sstronger than bolts holdss it in place."

A tiny hand touched his arm, making him step to one side. "Let me try," said Maryld softly.

"You?" Hargrod almost laughed. Almost. "If neither the human nor I could move it, then how . . . ?"

"There is a time to use brute strength, and a time to use skill," she told him. She approached the panel and examined it thoroughly. Practor was starting to fidget by the time she finally ran her left index finger around the panel's edge, then across the surface, making invisible diagonal lines.

"Ah." She drew her finger back. There was a *click* from an invisible latch, and the panel slid upward as neatly as if pulled by an unseen hand. Hargrod bowed slightly in her direction.

"Well, there it is," she announced.

Practor stepped forward, reached up, and hesitated.

"I think it's safe enough," she assured him. "I don't sense any of the threatening vibrations that clung to the silver altar. You may take it without fear."

"No, I'm not taking it," Practor told her. He stepped back, gestured toward their big-footed companion. "It's not my right. Sranul found it. It belongs to him."

The roo moved forward, grinning. "If this is a sorry

trick by both of you and this blows me through a wall, I swear by all the festivals of the folk that I'll find a way to get even." Gingerly, he reached out and lifted the silver skullcap off its hook. It was gratifyingly heavy.

"Well?" Practor asked him.

"Real silver," the roo replied, turning it over and over in his hands and admiring the workmanship. "Not plate." He tried to put it on his head, but no matter how he adjusted it, he couldn't make it fit. The reason was obvious enough.

"It's your earss," Hargrod told him. "They are too big to fold beneath the cap and it won't fit between them."

"That's just about right." Sranul yanked the cap off his head and shook it, as though by threatening it he could somehow make it work. "That's just about damn right! I finally find a decent bit of treasure, something worthwhile, and it's useless to me."

"Ssilver iss ssilver," Hargrod pointed out. "You could sstill ssell it to ssomeone elsse."

"I don't want to sell it to someone else," Sranul said sadly. "I want something I can adorn myself with." With seeming indifference he tossed it to Practor, who caught it neatly. "This foolish bauble was designed to be worn by some poor creature cursed with a flat head and no hearing. You wear it, friend Practor. Never let it be said that old Sranul wasn't generous to his friends."

Practor forbore pointing out that the roo's generosity was mitigated somewhat by the fact that the cap was no good to him. Instead, he thanked Sranul profusely. This helped somewhat to soothe the roo's feeling of loss and frustration. Using his fingers to hold it spread, Practor unfolded the cap and placed it neatly over his head. It was small, but not unworkably so, and the feeling of the cold metal against the bare skin of his forehead was a pleasing sensation.

Maryld was giving him a funny look. "How do you feel?"

"How should I feel? Like I have a heavy cap on my head."

"That's all?" She sounded disappointed. "Nothing else? Nothing out of the ordinary?"

"Nope." He adjusted the cap slightly. "I think I'm going to wear it from now on. It's cool and the silver offers some protection against a blow to the head, though steel would be better." He glanced over at Hargrod. "What do you think, Zhist'a? Will this turn a sword?" He bent slightly to give the reptilian warrior a better look.

"That dependss, naturally, on the ssize of the ssword, but I should think it would certainly ssend an edge ssliding, if not a two-handed cleave. It iss a great deal better than nothing."

"I'll just have to watch who I fight, then." He looked past the Zhis'ta and his expression changed. "Guess what I see, Sranul?"

"I'd prefer not to." The roo was still miffed at the uselessness of the silver cap.

"Then I'll show you. Come on, everyone."

They followed him down the hall. Where it widened out, someone had turned the multicolored marble stones into a chessboard. The only pieces visible were a white pawn and rook and a black king.

"This is what you saw?" Sranul examined the rook curiously. "What are these statues?"

"Part of a game, though these are larger than normal pieces. A very complicated game."

The roo snorted, moved away from the oversized castle. "I'm not very interested in games."

"I didn't think that you were, but that's not what I brought you here to see. Look over there." He nodded toward a far wall. "Behind the mirror."

Sranul hopped over to the indicated wall. An ornate oval mirror sat there, mounted on wooden wheels. "This is what you saw?"

"No, behind it. Behind the mirror. There's something else." There'd better be, he added silently, or Sranul's going to think me a hairless fool.

He was worrying needlessly. The door he thought he'd glimpsed was there, all right. From a distance it looked just like another section of wall, but Practor had made too many iron hinges in his life not to recognize one of the size that just showed above the upper rim of the mirror. To anyone not well versed in the arts of metallurgy the hinge would have resembled nothing more than another decoration.

Sranul shoved the mirror aside and gaped at the enormous iron door. It was high and wide enough to admit the biggest troll—or even a demon king in battle garb. Bands of iron crisscrossed the door itself, strengthening it further.

"A vault," Sranul whispered. "Dal'brad's treasure must be inside—all the wealth he's gathered from the nether regions to finance his campaign against the outside world, all the booty pillaged by his demonic legions, here for the taking." He took a step toward the vault, stopped, and looked sheepishly back at Practor. "But how do we get inside?"

"My friend, I haven't the slightest idea."

"You found it from across the hall when no one else noticed it. You must have *some* idea how to open it?"

"I recognized a hinge and thought it must attach to some half-concealed door. My knowledge ends there." He studied the imposing metal barrier. "A small fire-breathing dragon might melt a way through."

"Funny, very funny," the roo griped. "I just happen to have one here in my pouch."

"What do you think, Maryld? Maryld?" Practor turned.

Instead of studying the vault, the thaladar was engrossed in a silent examination of the giant chess pieces.

"It makes no sense," she murmured. "Why only three pieces? Why have only three out on the floor? They're only wood, and not valuable in and of themselves."

"You think they may have something to do with opening the vault?"

"They must have something to do with something besides a game. You can't play chess with three pieces."

Sranul hopped over to join them. "Maybe if they're moved about." Reaching out, he tried to push the black king forward.

His hand went right through it.

He yanked it clear, eyes wide. Practor had a moment of fear, but the roo hastened to reassure him. "I'm okay, friend Practor. I am not hurt. Only surprised."

Maryld was nodding to herself. "I'm sure of it now. Moving these pieces in the proper manner somehow keys the vault door."

"Wonderful," mumbled Sranul. "All we have to do to open the vault is move these statues. The trouble is, they're not there. They just *look* like they're there. Who says demons don't have a sense of humor?"

"They're there," Practor insisted. "We just don't know how to make use of them. I suspect Dal'brad himself knows the secret of manipulating them, or perhaps Gorwyther, too. Trolls like treasure as much as any of us, and their loyalty can waver when gold is involved." He indicated the chess pieces standing insubstantially before them. "I suspect this has been designed to keep the treasure out of the hands of Dal'brad's own minions as much as safe from intruders such as us."

Sranul bounded back to stand next to the door, inspected it minutely. There wasn't a handle or knob to be seen. He tapped the iron. It was too thick to ring.

When his companions resumed their march down the long hall, he lingered behind. "Hey, where are you going? We have to try this door, somehow. We *have* to!"

Practor looked back over his shoulder. "My heart is with you, friend Sranul, but my mind says we should be on our way. We don't want to stay too long in any one place. If that vault does hold the demon king's treasure, it's one of the first places he'll check as soon as he's notified of our intrusion. We don't want to be here when he arrives, do we?"

"But the *treasure*," the roo pleaded. "Hargrod, what about you, my scaly friend? The Zhis'ta are a practical people."

"Later perhapss, if we are granted the time," Hargrod replied. "We've more important thingss to do jusst now."

"More important than the treasure?" Sranul stood before the vault, wringing his hands helplessly, more frustrated than he'd ever been in his life. The riches of the ages were within his grasp, and his friends refused to try and obtain it. His eyes shifted from retreating companions to door and back again.

Maryld called back to him as they turned the far corner. "Maybe there is no treasure in there, roo. Maybe that door is designed to keep something in instead of out. Maybe Dal'brad put it there to tempt intruders, concealing it with purposeful subtlety so that treasure-seekers would waste their time breaking in, only to find something dark and dangerous inside. Think on that."

Sranul frowned at this, a thought he hadn't considered. He turned to stare at the silent, massive door. It looked like a vault door, it even felt like a vault door. But what if the thaladar was right? What if it was nothing more than an exceedingly clever trap? What if behind it waited, not unimaginable wealth, but inconceivable horror? Something so monstrous and powerful and deadly it required a door of such dimensions to imprison it—until the curious and greedy came along and persisted in forcing an entrance?

He found himself backing slowly away from the door, walking carefully so as not to disturb—what? He turned and bounded down the hallway.

"Hey, wait for me! You're right—we've more important business to attend to."

"Right," said Practor, "and maybe we can return to try the door again another time."

"Sure." The roo swung in line alongside Maryld and lowered his voice. "You're just trying to frighten me, aren't you? The vault really holds the treasure, doesn't it?"

She smiled enigmatically over at him. "What do you think, roo?"

"Damn you, thaladar! I can deal with swords and even with magic, but fighting with words isn't fair!"

"What happened to your words of a moment ago? 'We've more important business to attend to'?"

He turned away from her. "Thaladar," he grumbled. "Try deliberately to confuse you. Never mean what they say."

"Ah, but we always say what we mean," she told him gently. Sad to say, that did not make the disappointed roo rest any easier in mind.

"Cheer up," Practor urged him. He gestured at the walls of the new corridor they were walking through. "Enjoy the beauty around you."

In truth, this corridor was the loveliest section of Shadowkeep they'd yet encountered. Not overpoweringly spacious, like the hall of the mage king, it was lined with sculptures of flowers and trees, all done in silver by some unknown, sure-fingered artisans.

"Here's your treasure," Practor told him. "All you have to do is find a way to get Shadowkeep into your pouch."

"Bah. What's a little silver compared to what we may have left behind us?"

"Ah, but what of the guards that lie within?" Maryld teased him.

"*May* lie within," he countered. "If we don't try for the treasure, we'll never acquire any. No, don't tell me again the real reason why we're here. I remember, and I agree with it, or I wouldn't be here. But altruism doesn't fill one's purse. I would like to leave this place with more than moral satisfaction in my pockets."

Of course, there were the three goldens he'd found in the trash heap. Hardly an amount worth risking one's life for. What was he doing here, anyway, so far from friends and family and clan? He'd already missed at least one seasonal carnival celebration. The roos were nomads, but that didn't keep him from feeling homesick.

Home: good conversation, food and drink aplenty, laughter and fine times. Better there than here in this dank dungheap of stone full of mysteries and dangers. Shadowkeep stank of evil. Sure, it would be nice to save the world, but what was wrong with wanting to take back a little treasure to remember it by? He found himself staring at the human who'd somehow convinced him to come along on this crazy adventure.

What drove Practor Fime? In his own way the man was more of a puzzle than either Zhis'ta or thaladar. Now, take Hargrod: there was nothing in the least mysterious about him. His soul, his attitudes, his reasoning was laid out undisguised for anyone to see. As for the thaladar woman, it was clear she relished the opportunity to pit her own skills against those of the demon king, and Practor had mentioned something about her family having personal reasons for wanting her here.

But the man—his motives remained indecipherable. The roo shook his head and marched on.

If poor Sranul had been apprised of one simple fact, all would have become clear to him. He didn't know that Practor Fime was deeply in love. That drives men to do the most insane things, things they would never consider doing for money or glory. But Sranul didn't know, and so he didn't understand even as he poked into the occasional corner or peeped behind a piece of furniture in search of discarded gold.

The silver decorations were quite beautiful. Among the flowers and trees there now appeared the figures of young women, also worked in silver. The poses and clothing were different but the face was the same on each figure.

Practor remarked on the similarity to Maryld. "Who is she?"

"I believe they are images of Sildra, a patroness of a society known as the Brothers of Aid. I cannot imagine Dal'brad putting them here, so they must have been installed on Gorwyther's command."

"There must be a reason for so many of them," Practor murmured. "So much metalwork implies a purpose beyond mere decoration."

As sometimes happened, Maryld didn't offer a reply, and Practor didn't press her for one. He'd learned to leave her alone when she was thinking.

A muttered curse came from Sranul. The roo bent to pick up a small piece of wood. "Tripped," he explained tersely, preparing to throw the bit of garbage over his shoulder.

"No, give it here." Maryld held out a hand. Puzzled, the roo handed the stick to her, watched while she turned it over and over in her hands, examining it carefully. Practor joined her.

"Doesn't look like much," he finally commented.

"It probably isn't, but still—see here?" He had to look close to see the tiny markings on the wood.

"Decorations, or the name of the owner of whatever it once was."

"Decorations, perhaps. An inscription, perhaps. What puzzles me is that I don't recognize the writing."

"Doesn't sound very useful, then."

She explained patiently. "Just because you don't recognize something doesn't mean that it's useless, my good Practor."

He refused to back down. "It's just an old stick."

"Old, yes. Just a stick, I'm not so sure."

"It wouldn't even make a good arrow shaft."

"There is plenty of arrow material lying about. This I intend to keep." She looked back down the hallway. "Trolls can be very persistent. The spell I placed on the wall we came through will not last forever."

Sranul jerked around. "I'd forgotten all about our lovely friends." He turned to face her, sniffed. "Maybe I do think too much about treasure, but at least I don't go around collecting garbage." With that he bounded off ahead of them.

She glanced sideways at Practor. "What do you think of that?"

He hesitated, framing his reply carefully. "I think it is just an old stick, *but* I also think that the only way we're going to get out of here alive is by relying on each other's expertise and advice. So—if you say that a piece of wood is worth saving, I guess that we'd best hang on to it."

She smiled. "You and Sranul may be right. This may be nothing more than an old stick, not even suitable for an arrow."

He shrugged. "There's some usefulness in everything. Perhaps one day it will serve to start a fire."

They continued down the winding corridor until a sudden turn caused them to halt abruptly. They had come to another dead end, only this time there was no wall of shifting colors to greet them.

Ahead, the stone vanished. The hallway ended in a wall of night. Onyx black, motionless, it offered a far less inviting egress than had the flowing wall of colors. There were no switches or levers, no stairs, no side passageways. Only the solid, impenetrable blackness.

"We can't go back," Hargrod told them. "I have heard ssoundss for ssome time now but forbore from mentioning it lesst I upsset you needlessly."

Practor strained but could hear nothing. But Sranul could, and nodded confirmation of the Zhis'ta's warning. "They're back there. Far behind us, but coming closer."

"It is as I feared," said Maryld worriedly. "The spell has faded and the trolls have come through after us. We may have little to worry about. Much of what tempted us should pique their primitive curiosity and slow their pursuit. But they will not forget us forever. We must move on."

"On to where?" Practor studied the darkness before them. "Through there?"

"Why not?" she asked. "It's only another doorway, like the wall of colors."

"It doesn't look very inviting."

"I agree, but it's better than waiting here for the trolls to find us."

"How can you be sure it's another doorway?"

"I can't. One cannot be certain of anything in Shadowkeep, as I have said before, but since we arrived through the wall of colors we have encountered nothing resembling a normal doorway, not even stairs. If the only way in was through the wall of light, it seems highly possible that the only way out is through this wall of blackness. Not even the demon king would leave himself only a single escape route from a part of his domain.

"As Hargrod so succinctly says, we cannot go back. Therefore we must go on."

"Fine," said Practor. Taking her hand and forcing himself to move without thinking of possible consequences, he stepped into the darkness.

The subsequent disorientation came as a relief, since it reminded him of the brief passage through the wall of colors. What was not expected was the abrupt drop in temperature and the absence of light. He began to shiver. Was this what the transfer promised: an endless sightless march toward death by freezing?

The ground beneath him remained solid, and the pressure of Maryld's hand in his was reassuring. Presumably Sranul and Hargrod were somewhere close behind.

And eventually the darkness began to dissipate. His eyes adapted to the intensifying but still dim light. They were in some kind of circular chamber that smelled of decaying vegetation. Below the alcove in which they found themselves was a round pool filled to an unknown depth with scummy water. Mats of brown algae drifted lazily on the surface. Slime and moss clung to the walls.

"I don't much like this," Sranul muttered. "I never was much for swimming. Maybe we'd better go back."

"Go back to what?" Maryld whispered. "Back to a dead-end hall to wait for the trolls?"

Practor had been studying the chamber. Now he pointed toward a dark, round opening set high up in the wall on the far side. "I don't see any doors, but that might be a way out."

"It's not very big." Sranul sounded dubious. "And it's out of reach."

"We can get up to it somehow," Practor told him, "and I don't mind crawling."

"You can stand on my shoulders," Hargrod told the roo. "When each of you hass reached the tunnel, or whatever it turnss out to be, one of you can reach back down to give me a hand up.''

Sranul was still reluctant. "Well, if it's the only way out . . .''

"Do you see another?" Practor asked him.

"Nooo." He leaned forward. "Say, what's that funny pole in the middle of the pool?''

Practor saw the stick, shrugged. "Debris. Got wedged in the mud there somehow. Wouldn't make much of a bonfire.''

"I think not." Both of them turned to Maryld. "That is no mere piece of wood.''

"Not again," Sranul said sarcastically.

"You are not looking closely enough," she admonished him. "Don't you see the engravings and inscriptions chiseled on its sides? It's a staff.''

The roo was shaking his head. "Whatever you say, thaladar. I guess you'd like to add it to your collection?''

Practor was determined to be reasonable. "We have to cross the room anyway. There's no harm in taking it with us. If nothing else, it'll make a good walking stick.'' He braced himself on the side of the opening in which they stood and gingerly tested the water. As the tallest of the four it was incumbent on him to see how deep it was.

His right leg went down, finally contacted something but continued to descend through the mud. He let loose of the wall and jumped in with the other foot. Looking down he saw that the murky liquid did not quite come up to his waist.

"How is it?" Maryld asked him.

He moved around carefully but the water grew no deeper. "The bottom feels like it's level, but there's so much mud it's hard to tell. There're probably deep holes and shallow spots. We'll just have to watch our step. It's lukewarm and full of gunk, but no worse than the marsh outside." He reached up to give her a hand down. Hargrod jumped in next to them while Sranul followed more slowly.

"I don't like water," the roo grumbled.

Keeping close together, they sloshed through the muck toward the center of the room. Practor found a couple of deep spots where the bottom fell away sharply, but they were always able to detour around these.

Hargrod nodded toward the wooden pole. "Maybe it'ss jusst a marker of some kind, to indicate the center of the room."

"No, it's more than that," Maryld insisted. "I *know* it is."

Hargrod froze, stood motionless, listening.

Sranul let out a sigh. "What is it this time?"

"Quiet," the Zhis'ta admonished him.

"Don't tell me to be quiet, you hardheaded snake. I'm getting tired of relying on your ears to tell me when to stop and when to jump. I'm getting tired of silver that's unattainable and sword cases full of poison gas. I'm getting tired of—"

"Sshut up," the Zhis'ta said warningly. Sranul glowered at him but kept silent.

"There. There it iss again."

"I don't hear anything." Practor was turning a slow circle, scanning the room carefully.

At last Hargrod straightened. "Perhapss the roo iss right. Perhapss my ssensses are too highly tuned for thiss place. Water can play trickss on you." He resumed his pace.

When they finally reached the center of the room, Practor reached out to grab the staff. He pulled hard, but it refused to come loose.

"Stuck in the bottom mud," he said. He braced himself

and used both hands. The staff seemed to bend slightly but remained fastened to the bottom.

"Here, let me." Hargrod waved him aside, grabbed hold of the staff with both hands, and gave a heave. It came loose easily. Practor was not embarrassed. Hargrod was Zhis'ta.

Together they examined the wood. "There are some kind of markings," Practor murmured as he ran his fingers over their sodden acquisition.

Sranul wasn't impressed. "When it was being bounced around in the water it hit a bunch of rocks. So what?"

Maryld screamed. Only the Zhis'ta's incredible reflexes saved him from being disemboweled as a clawed hand the size of his head ripped upward from below, reaching for the staff. They retreated toward the alcove they'd emerged from as the owner of the clawed hand began to rise from the deepest part of the pool.

A sudden, hollow roaring made them halt. Maryld stared a moment at the tunnel, then began thrashing through the water, trying to circle around the creature that had suddenly appeared in their midst as she tried to make her way toward the hole high up in the far wall.

Something was gathering itself behind them. It seemed to have neither ears nor neck; only a watery, bloated face. It rose higher above the surface of the pool, displaying several lanternlike eyes and a vast cavern of a mouth.

"By the seven precious metals," Practor shouted above the still-intensifying roar that came from their alcove, "what kind of creature is that?"

"A Brollachian," Maryld told him. "Hug the wall and hurry!" Hargrod was holding his ax in both hands while Practor struggled to draw his sword.

The Brollachian spotted them and began to move, throwing its ponderous body toward them in an attempt to cut them off before they could reach the far wall. At the same time the source of the roaring that had convinced Maryld to change course reached the room.

A wall of water exploded from the mouth of the alcove and poured into the chamber. Practor just had time to replace his sword in its sheath and brace himself. Maryld was knocked off her feet. He dove, fumbled through the swirling flood, and dragged her back to the surface, spitting and coughing.

The sudden deluge had also knocked the Brollachian sideways, but that massive mountain of flesh was quickly righting itself.

Hargrod kicked through the water, ax held high. "Hurry to the tunnel! I will delay it."

Practor watched as the Zhis'ta swung the huge ax. It cut deeply into rubbery flesh, but there was no blood. The creature responded with a faintly threatening moan and leaned toward its attacker. Again a clawed hand struck at Hargrod and again he dodged the blow.

How the Zhis'ta managed to wield the heavy ax with one hand while hanging on to the much-maligned staff which apparently had caused all the trouble, Practor didn't know and didn't have the time to figure out. He was too busy trying to save Maryld and himself, half carrying, half wrestling her toward the far wall.

When they finally stood beneath the hoped-for tunnel, they found themselves confronted by another problem.

"How can we stand on Hargrod's shoulders to reach it while he's fighting that thing?" Sranul shouted.

"It wouldn't matter if he were here," Practor replied, staring at the opening which gaped invitingly above them. "It's too high. We'd have to go three-up, and I'm no acrobat."

"Wait, wait!" Maryld spat out moss and algae. "The rising water will lift us up."

"If it keeps coming in," Practor agreed, "and if Hargrod can keep the Brollachian occupied in the meantime."

As the pool rose higher than their heads, they clung to one another and to the wall, trying to stay close while treading water. Practor saw Hargrod vanish beneath the swirling surface only to reappear moments later in another part of the pool while the furious Brollachian tried to pin him to one spot.

"The Zhis'ta are excellent swimmers," Maryld told them. "I just hope Hargrod has enough room to maneuver."

Practor looked toward their alcove, from which water continued to pour in an unceasing torrent. If anything, the flow had increased. He turned his eyes upward. At the rate the room was filling, they'd soon rise within reach of the dark opening.

Once Hargrod disappeared for an unnervingly long stretch and they were certain he'd vanished down the Brollachian's throat, but he reappeared at last, waved to reassure them, and dove again.

Practor reached high and this time his fingers went over the edge of the opening. He pulled himself up, found he was on hands and knees in a narrow tunnel. The bottom was full of damp mud. That wasn't very encouraging. Suppose they crawled halfway down this stone tube only to have water rush in on them from the far end?

They would have to take the chance. There was nowhere else to go.

He turned, reached down, and pulled Maryld up next to him, trying to ignore the way her wet dress clung to her diminutive form. Sranul was next. The roo collapsed inside the tunnel, coughing and spitting, obviously relieved to be out of the water.

"With those feet and that tail I'd have thought you'd be a good swimmer," Maryld said.

"Afraid not. They work better up and down, not back and forth."

Practor wasn't listening. He was staring out into the circular chamber, now full of water. "I don't see Hargrod."

Maryld moved up next to him. There was so much spray and mist that it was hard to see anything.

"How long can a Zhis'ta hold his breath?" Practor asked her.

"I don't know." Her tone was subdued. Together they searched for evidence that their friend might still be alive.

"What was that thing doing in here, anyway?" he muttered.

"The Brollachian?" She shrugged. "One of the demon king's guards, one of Gorwyther's experiments, a pet—who knows?"

"But there's nothing here to guard."

"What about the black gate we came through? It might have been designed to deliver any intruders to this room. A clever trap. Or the staff Hargrod removed, remember that?"

"That old stick. It wasn't worth losing . . ." Something shot from the water and grabbed his shirt, pulling him forward and almost yanking him into the pool. His arms windmilled as he fought for balance. Maryld's hands went around his waist, but he knew that wouldn't be enough to save him.

It didn't matter. His forward momentum slowed as a familiar face emerged from the water.

"Sstop gaping at me out of fissh eyess, man." Hargrod glanced anxiously at the waves rolling behind him. His ax was slung neatly across his back, and in his other hand he held the staff. "I have run it a merry chasse around the bottom of thiss pool, but it will find me ssoon enough."

Sranul joined Practor, and together they pulled the

exhausted Zhis'ta into the tunnel. Their combined strength was needed. The reptilian warrior was solid as iron.

Once safely inside, Hargrod rolled over onto his back and lay still as he sucked air. After a few minutes he sat up and slowly unslung the battle-ax, let it drop to the floor. It was covered with bits of brown meat and green slime. The wooden staff he extended to Maryld, together with a choice understatement.

"Little thaladar, thiss sstick had better be worth ssomething." She accepted it without comment, and he leaned back against the curving wall of the tunnel. "I can't remember how many timess I cut the monsster," he told them. "I might ass well have been hitting it with pebbles. I think it would look on a decapitation as a minor inconvenience."

"The Brollachian's body regenerates itself," Maryld informed them. When Hargrod's expression twisted she explained, "It means that you cannot kill such a creature unless you strike it through the brain."

Hargrod got on his knees. "It issn't alive for lack of my trying. Filthy thing."

Practor crawled past him. "We'd better get moving. If the water in the pool rises any higher, it's going to start filling this tunnel. We want to find the other end before that happens."

"I don't think we'll have to worry about that." Maryld leaned out of the tunnel's mouth for a better look at their distant alcove. "The water's stopped coming in."

She went right over the edge, a pseudopod of brown flesh wrapped around her waist.

Practor dove after her without hesitating, without thinking. His sword was out by the time he hit the water.

It was dark in the pool. The water was full of suspended organic solids. But he could make out the slim form of Maryld being dragged downward. He swam toward her and swung the sword, pulling it back toward him in a sawing motion. The Brollachian flesh parted with surprising ease.

As the pseudopod parted and fell away, he grabbed Maryld under her arms and kicked for the surface. Sranul was there to pull her clear. The water heaved beneath Practor. He reached up, felt Hargrod's powerful fingers wrap around his forearm. He all but flew into the tunnel.

The pool erupted behind him and he turned to find himself staring into the face of the Brollachian. Half crawling, half sliding, they backed away from the tunnel mouth. A long, greenish tongue flicked out of a cavernous mouth, but reached only far enough into the tunnel to lash the bottom of Practor's boot. Another couple of feet and they were safely beyond the monster's reach.

Still it refused to give up. It slammed its bulk against the tunnel opening. The walls quivered and a few pebbles fell from the ceiling, but it held under repeated assaults. When it tried to reach them with another pseudopod and Hargrod chopped it in half, it finally gave up and sank back out of sight below the surface of its pool. Its moans and roars of frustration followed them for a long time as they turned and made their way down the tunnel.

"I hope this doesn't run on forever," Sranul grumbled.

"Just be glad it isn't filled with water." Practor felt a hand on his arm, turned to see Maryld staring up at him in the near blackness.

"You saved my life back there."

He was glad the darkness was there to hide his face. "Just like you said: we're all dependent on each other's abilities. Your directions and advice have saved all of us several times already."

"Giving advice is not the same thing as jumping thoughtlessly into a Brollachian's face. It was an act of utter selflessness, done without concern or regard for your own safety.''

"I didn't stop to think, if that's what you mean. I would have done the same for Hargrod or Sranul.''

"Yes." She considered thoughtfully. "Yes, I suppose that you would. It's the sort of man you are. But that doesn't lessen your gift in my eyes: it enhances it.''

He wished he could see more of her expression. Sranul and Hargrod were fumbling along somewhere ahead of them. "Come on," he whispered, "or we'll lose the others.''

"Are you so anxious to see what lies at the other end of this tunnel?''

Was she teasing him now? He didn't know. "It's bound to be better than what's behind us." He started crawling again.

Chapter X

The tunnel seemed to go on forever. That neither surprised nor upset any of them. It is in the nature of dark tunnels that they seem to go on forever. So they continued crawling patiently, resting only when it was absolutely necessary, and were quietly relieved when light began to appear directly ahead of them.

"Quietly now," Maryld warned her companions. "We've no way of knowing what this opens onto. It might be a drain for the main troll barracks or Dal'brad's sanctuary itself. If we are lucky, it will empty into some abandoned storeroom or hallway."

The circular basin they found themselves staring out into was plastered with a thin coat of mud. On the far side was a small round door. Illumination came from unseen sources overhead.

Maryld put her legs over the side of the tunnel's lip and sighed. "I think we can relax here for a while. This is not a room at all. See . . ." She indicated several smaller holes that formed a neat line just above floor level. "This is the reservoir. Or one of them. Water is pumped from here to fill the Brollachian's pool." She pushed off and found herself standing on a solid stone floor covered by less than an inch of mud. "Our passage through the black gate set things in motion, and we triggered the filling mechanism somehow when we set out across the pool." She held up the staff Hargrod had saved.

"I imagine this had something to do with it."

"You mean we broke something?" Practor was trying to scrape the mud off his boots.

"I am not sure. It may be, since only Hargrod was able to move it. Or it may be more complex than that."

Sranul was leaning gratefully against the wall. "Well I, for one, am ready for a rest." He tried to find the sources of light in the ceiling, failed. "I've completely lost track of time, and I feel like we've been running and fighting in this mausoleum for weeks. We don't even know if it's day or night outside."

"You're absolutely right," Maryld told him.

"Who, *me?*" He grinned at her. "Please, thaladar, I don't think I can take another shock."

She smiled back at him. "Really, now that we have the chance, we should rest and eat."

Practor was studying the empty reservoir warily. "Are you sure this place is safe? Every room we enter seems to be some kind of trap."

"It's hard to make a bowl into a trap, and that's what this place is, Practor: an oversized water bowl. No, I think we can rest easy here. For a little while, at least."

He nodded, found a piece of stonework that projected from the wall. It was wide enough to accommodate all four of them. "Here. A good place to sit. It's damp, but not too dirty." He put both hands on the stone and pushed, setting himself on the edge.

His companions joined him and began to unpack food from their stores. Sranul munched tiredly on several sticks of cane that had been coated with some dried, honeylike substance. His crunching was loud in the empty chamber.

"You know," he told them, "I'm getting to the point

where I don't care if we find the treasure, or this Gorwyther, or stop Dal'brad, or anything else. If we could find our way back to the entrance, I'd be tempted to leave. Let someone else save the world."

"Sorry," Practor said. "The only way out seems to be back the way we've come. That means swimming past the Brollachian, then trying to make the black gateway work in reverse, then . . ."

"All right, all right. I was just talking, that's all." The roo gestured toward the small door on the far side of the reservoir. "I guess if we can get through that I'll have to take my chances with whatever waits for us on the other side."

He went silent. No one else chose to make conversation, which was fine with Practor. He was talked out. It was indescribably relaxing simply to be able to sit quietly and eat.

When talk did resume, it was with a question. "Tell me something, Sranul—" he asked the roo, "what if we did find a great treasure here? Roos are constantly moving about, always living somewhere else from one month to the next. You've no need of a grand castle to live in and the countryside provides amply for your people. I know that roos are fond of good entertainment and gourmet dining, but how much of that can you stand? Of what use to a roo is a great fortune?"

"Well, perhaps I've no need of a *great* fortune." Sranul finished the last of his cane and spoke while licking his fingers. "But even a roo could find employment for a small one. And there's more to it than that."

"Enlighten me, then."

"Gladly." Sranul's eyes gleamed. "It's the *idea*, the thought of acquiring a great fortune that intrigues me. Remember what you said once about we roos being a fun-loving bunch? It's true, and I can't imagine anything

185

more delightful than bathing in a basin filled to overflowing with gems and gold and other beautiful things.''

"Then it's the beauty you're after and not the wealth," Maryld said.

"The beauty, yes, and the excitement of acquiring it." He frowned, looked from human to thaladar as if puzzled by the question. "Why else did you think I wanted the treasure of Shadowkeep?"

"Sranul, I think I owe you an apology. I've been misjudging you." Practor extended a hand.

The roo ignored it, slapped his friend on the back. "Don't worry yourself about it, friend Practor. You can't help but think like a human. Now, knowing something of humans as I do, I have a pretty good idea of what you would do with a share of the treasure."

"I am curious." Maryld leaned toward him. "What would you do with great wealth?"

"Never go near a forge again, for one thing. No, that's not quite true. Never go near a forge again to do someone else's bidding. I've always considered myself an artist. So did my instructor, Shone Stelft, but he never had the time to do just as he wished. He had to provide for his family, and the fine, delicate things he fashioned from metal weren't as much in demand as swords and shields."

"War is always more popular than art," Sranul observed somberly.

"But that's what I'd do, make only what I wanted to make. That, and marry Rysancy, of course." He looked at the slight form of the thaladar seated so close to him. "What about you, Maryld? The thaladar are traders and merchants. Surely you would have a use for wealth?"

She nodded. "We want the same thing, Practor Fime. To be able to purchase our own time, to own our own lives. You to practice your art, I to teach when and what I wished. I've always dreamed of being able to found a school to teach young thaladar about the world outside. It would be a place where our children would be able to learn alongside yours, and the offspring of roo and Zhis'ta as well. The isolation that exists now must be broken down. We must learn to interact with those whom we share the world with. My mother and grandmother would help gladly to design a curriculum for such a school.''

Only the least talkative and most soft-spoken of the party had failed to share his dreams with them.

Hargrod cleared his throat. ''Since you are all sstaring at me, I ssupposse I must ansswer alsso.'' He looked away from them, speaking suddenly as if he were seated beside a Zhis'ta campfire instead of in the forlorn emptiness of the stone reservoir.

''Far to the ssouth lies a country called Jantaria. It endss in a ssheltered bay lined with tall green treess of many kindss. Game sswarmss through the foresst landss that ssurround the bay.'' His voice deepened in the manner of Zhis'ta storytellers.

''But Jantaria iss dominated by humanss, and they are not overfond of Zhiss'ta company.''

''Don't judge all of us by some,'' Practor advised him.

''You are kind, but be honesst with yoursself ass well ass with me.'' Hargrod ventured a slight, reptilian smile. ''You know me becausse we have lived and journeyed and fought together. What if you had never met a Zhiss'ta before but had only heard sstoriess about uss? Would you willingly open your home and heart to a wagon full of Zhiss'ta, ferociouss reputation and all? Would your friendss and neighborss?''

Practor nodded sagely. ''I guess not.''

Hargrod's smile faded. ''There iss truth in that, jusst ass there iss truth in treassure. Treassure sspeakss to all peopless. I would take my sshare of any wealth we found and usse it to buy a fine living place atop a hilsside overlooking thiss

187

bay, where my family and I could resst and live in quiet. A family of poor Zhiss'ta would not be welcome to live in Jantaria, but one that doled out myssterious gemss and ancient gold would be made to feel right at home. We would be welcomed with open armss and palmss.''

"No race is perfect," Maryld observed thoughtfully, "and yet we four seem to get along well enough together. When you are compelled to work with people on an individual basis, you see them as an individual being, little different from yourself or others of your kind. Rumor, innuendo, and superstition tend to fall by the wayside.''

"I don't understand why it's so complicated," said Practor. "I never thought of any of you as anything but a good friend and equal.''

"That marks you as unusual among your own kind," Sranul told him, "but that was apparent to me as soon as we met.''

"He's right," said Maryld, "and the proof of it is that all of us are here because of you.''

Practor found this new image uncomfortable. "No. That's not true at all. Sranul, you came along because you were searching for some fun and excitement. Maryld, you had reasons of your own for wanting to challenge Shadowkeep, and Hargrod came because his family felt obligated to us for helping them against the goblins.''

"All of what you say is true," she countered, "but only in part. You were the motivating force behind our decisions, Practor Fime. But what of your motivations? Why are you risking your life?''

He thought a moment. "Someone had to attempt to stop Dal'brad.''

She nodded. "Exactly. You can claim all you want that you came for a chance at glory or treasure, but those are nothing more than rationalizations for your inherent altruism, Practor. You came because someone had to. You came

188

because others faced danger and you wanted to try and help them. Deny it all you want. You have no idea what an unusual person you are. But the rest of us know." Hargrod and Sranul nodded agreement.

Practor turned away angrily. "Dammit, I am *not* unusual. I was just in the wrong place at the right time—or something like that. Besides, the Spinner who set me on this course didn't come looking for me. He was hoping to engage a real hero, Shone Stelft. When he refused, the Spinner was ready to depart. I had to talk him into letting me try. He did so only out of desperation."

Maryld seemed to be concealing a smile. "Is that so? From what you've told me, this Spinner is a most peculiar individual indeed. How do you know what he really wanted, what his hidden requirements were, and who he most wanted to recruit? Perhaps he was after you all the time. Perhaps in appealing to your master he knew he would refuse and that you would jump in to take his place. How can you be certain of the motives of this stranger?"

"I . . ." Practor didn't know what to say. The idea had never occurred to him before, and his silence showed he didn't know what to make of it. Could Maryld be right? Had the Spinner really come to Sasubree looking for him? If so, then that meant that the Spinner's appeal to Shone Stelft had been nothing more than a sham designed to tempt Practor's interest. But that implied that . . .

"That's crazy," he told her, "crazy."

"Is it?" Maryld was warming to her theory. "The Spinner saw you as less experienced but far more willing and compassionate than your master. He knew that if he approached you directly, you might have hesitated or refused outright. So it made a show of trying to recruit this Stelft person, with the result that he did not have to try to convince you. You ended up working to convince *him* to let you go."

"You're being absurd, Maryld." Actually, the thought of being duped by the Spinner bothered him more than the possibility that the thaladar might be right. In any case, he didn't want to talk about it anymore.

He pushed himself off the outjutting section of stone. "That's enough. It's time we were on our way."

Sranul made a face. "I was just lingering over my dessert, and . . ."

"Come *on,* roo." Realizing he was being unnecessarily sharp to conceal his own unease over Maryld's suppositions, he added in a softer tone, "Remember, the longer we stay in one place the easier it becomes for the demon king to pin us down."

"Yeah?" Sranul grudgingly began to repack the remainder of his food. "Well, I for one wouldn't mind being pinned down here for a while. This is the first place we've found in this above-ground garbage pit where something wasn't trying to bite my tail off every time I turned around." That said, he hopped down to join Practor and the others in slogging across the muddy floor of the empty reservoir.

Though the stone beneath the shallow mud was solid and they had no reason to suspect the footing, they still proceeded cautiously. Maryld went first this time, using the staff to probe the path ahead.

Eventually they found themselves standing on the far side of the chamber, to their considerable surprise and relief. For the first time since they'd entered Shadowkeep, they'd encountered a room that was nothing more than what it appeared to be.

In front of them was the small door they'd spotted as soon as they'd emerged from the tunnel. It was fashioned of brass braced with steel straps. The steel was badly corroded. In place of a handle, a large brass ring was fastened to the left side of the door.

"How do we get through thiss?" Hargrod fingered the haft of his battle-ax. "I could try to cut a way through, but I have no idea how thick the metal iss."

"Thick enough to keep a roomful of water from leaking out." Maryld pushed back her sleeves. "We will open it without muscle, my good Zhis'ta." She raised her hands and muttered an invocation. When she'd concluded she stepped forward, took hold of the brass ring, and pulled. The door groaned and Practor had to give her a hand, but it swung inward easily enough.

"Fine magic," said Hargrod, complimenting her.

"Not really." She smiled at him. "You see, normally this reservoir is full of water, which keeps the door sealed tight since it only opens inwards. That was *my* little show. The door wasn't even locked."

"Oh." Hargrod's expression fell while Sranul roared at the deception and clapped him on the back.

"Who says magic doesn't work? It's a good thing we have a thaladar along to help us with the heavy stuff, eh, Hargrod? And with the occasional joke. Who says thaladar have no sense of humor?"

"And it iss alsso a good thing," the embarrassed Zhis'ta growled, "that you can hop ass far and fasst as you can or I would tie those long earss of yourss in a tight knot."

"Tch, what's this?" said the roo. "A Zhis'ta who can't take a joke? And here I was thinking you had such a bubbly personality."

"All right, that's enough." Practor forced himself to hide his grin. "Come on." He turned and bent to step through the open portal. His companions followed.

The room beyond was not as well lit as the reservoir. One would've thought the reverse would be true, but nothing in Shadowkeep went by the rules of the outside world.

"What do you see?" Practor asked his companions.

Sranul was swatting at the air and brushing at himself. "Bugs." He ducked as something small and super-fast shot past his head to enter the empty reservoir. They could hear it buzzing around in the mud as they moved further into the room.

It was the smallest they'd yet encountered, but contained the familiar assortment of old furniture, most of it in disrepair. There were badly scuffed tables, chairs without legs, torn banners drooping morosely from the ceiling.

"Here's something—maybe." Sranul wasn't going to make any more predictions about his finds. He'd been wrong too many times already.

Practor and the others joined the roo in staring down at the chest he'd found. It was sealed but didn't look particularly sturdy.

"Wonder what's in it," said the roo.

"Your gold and jewelss, no doubt," Hargrod said mockingly.

"Is that so? Well maybe they are, maybe they just are." He reached to open it.

Maryld put a hand on his arm. "Careful, friend. Remember what happened the last time you opened something."

"You mean the sword case?" He nodded at her. "You're right. The rest of you move to the far end of the room."

"You don't have to open it, you know," Practor told him worriedly, eyeing the chest.

"I know, but what if the Zhis'ta's right? I can't take the chance. Maybe I'll find another couple of goldens."

Practor found a thick table, turned it on its side, and crouched down behind it. Maryld joined him, but couldn't keep from peering over the top.

"I have to see," she apologized to him. "If the roo loses his head, there may still be knowledge to gain. I must watch."

Practor shrugged, crouched lower. "It's your head."

Hargrod refused to retreat, taking the suggestion as a personal challenge. If the roo wasn't afraid of the chest, then neither was he. But he held himself ready to run. He was proud, but he wasn't a fool.

Sranul slipped his fingers under the upper edge of the chest, took a deep breath, flipped it up and over, and jumped ten feet straight back. Nothing came out of the chest. There was no flare of light, no all-encompassing flame to incinerate the curious. Practor and Maryld slowly stepped out from behind the protective table.

Cautiously the roo approached the open chest. He leaned forward, straining his neck to see inside without getting any nearer than necessary. Finally he walked right over next to it.

"Nothing," he snapped. "Some worn old armor, sticks and stones, a couple of cheap daggers, and cobwebs." Putting both hands on the lid, he slammed it down. "Where is the treasure!" He whirled, yelling at the silent walls. "I'm tired of tiptoeing my way from one danger to the next for a bunch of old garbage!"

"Would you prefer a bunch of new garbage?" Hargrod taunted him.

"Don't toy with me, Zhis'ta. There's supposed to be treasure in this bedamned fortress, and I damn well expect to *find* treasure. This is Shadowkeep, the most notorious pile of moldy rock in the whole world, and—"

He let out a startled wheeze as Hargrod hit him in the ribs and knocked him sideways. The two of them rolled over and over. Meanwhile Practor had thrown himself on Maryld in an attempt to shield her with his body.

With his back to the chest, Sranul hadn't seen the bulging orange-red blossom of fire which had erupted from the wood to engulf the entire chest in a ball of flame. Practor kept his eyes shut tight. He could feel the intense heat against his back. He thought his skin was burning, then there was a violent explosion. The little room became as bright as midday.

Heat and light dissipated rapidly. He turned and tried to find the chest. It was gone, along with the heat and light. There were no ashes, no blackened cinders, no skeleton of charred wood. The chest had simply *gone*.

Hargrod rolled over and with great dignity disengaged himself from Sranul. The roo sat up and stared dumbly at the place where the chest had been only a moment earlier.

"There was nothing in there," he mumbled in a subdued tone. "Junk. Worn leather, useless weapons."

"And treasure." Maryld dusted herself off, began straightening her hair. She smiled over at Practor. "Thank you, Mister Fime, though in the future it would be nice if your demonstrations of chivalry were tempered with a bit less violence."

"Sorry. All I saw was that growing fireball. I didn't know what it was going to do or how much time I had in which to do something about it."

"I'm not criticizing you. It was a brave and thoughtless gesture, typical of you."

And he'd thought she *was* criticizing him. Would he never figure the thaladar out?

Sranul was examining the floor where the chest had been. He reached out and touched it, quickly drew his fingers back and shook them. The stone was still hot enough to burn, even though it hadn't been blackened. Whatever had destroyed the chest had been no normal fire.

"What do you suppose was really inside?" Practor asked Maryld.

"I've already said: Sranul's treasure."

The roo gave her an indignant look. "What do you mean, treasure? I saw no gold or gems, no pearls or fine woods."

"How do you know what you saw?"

His expression darkened. "Thaladar, are you saying I lied?"

"Of course not. I'm saying you were deceived. You saw only what you were intended to see. Do you not think Dal'brad would take care to disguise his treasure from any who might stumble across it?"

Sranul mouthed the words slowly. "Disguise . . . his . . . treasure?" He blinked, shook his head confidently. "No. That was no treasure. In any case it doesn't matter, because whatever was there is gone."

"What makes you so certain it's gone?"

The roo gaped at her. "You talk in riddles, like all thaladar." He waved his hand through the air where the chest had been. "There's *nothing* here. Nothing!"

Maryld rested her delicate chin in a hand. "Think a moment, roo. A chest full of useless things is opened. You peer inside, ascertain what is there, and then dive for cover as it all vanishes in a most impressive ball of flame. What is that designed to do? To pique your curiosity further? Or to discourage you and send you on your way? No, the trick is neither to become frightened nor frustrated. Remember the vault door we encountered?"

"The big iron door none of you wanted to try and open. Sure I remember it."

"It's not worth trying to open, Sranul, because it's too obvious. It says to any and all who find it, 'Here I am, a barrier concealing something indescribably valuable, priceless, unique!' One who has something to hide, roo, does not advertise its presence by placing it behind a door as big as a house. He secretes it in a small, unimpressive location, disguises it with everyday artifacts, and as a last resort, places deceptions in the path of the curious." She nodded toward the floor where the chest had lain.

"A clever deception, the jewel chest devoid of jewels. But thaladars are trained to see through such deceptions.

195

We are not easily fooled. A good magician occupies the eyes of his audience with busy movements of one hand while quietly preparing his trick with the other. To find the source of the illusion one must learn to look beyond the obvious. The chest was a work of subtlety, but not the flame that followed. That was *too* obvious."

Turning, she strode across the room and halted before the line of torn and battered banners that hung limply from the ceiling. "See, here."

"See what?" Sranul hopped over to join her. The floor around the banners was piled high with broken furniture. "Nothing here but garbage."

"Yes. Too much garbage." She waved at the room. "Not nearly as much as there, or there. The distribution is not even."

"So what does that prove? That they preferred to dump their junk here instead of over there?" Suddenly the roo hesitated, as if seeing clearly for the first time. He started digging at the old chairs and couches, shoving them aside, pulling down the frayed banners. They came apart easily in his hands, shredding in his fingers. Most were rotted through.

When he saw what was hidden behind the banners and woodwork, Practor joined him. It was a vault door, much smaller than the one they had encountered before, careful-ly painted to resemble the rockwork in which it was set.

"Is it real?" Sranul whispered as he stared at it, unable to believe.

"I am not sure. I sense no danger within, but I would not bet your life on my senses. Not in a place as devious as Shadowkeep."

"Sense-shmenses," burbled Sranul, "what are we wait-ing for!" He reached for the handle set in the iron mass.

"Don't touch that!" Maryld said suddenly.

Sranul jerked his hand away. "I thought you said you didn't sense any danger." He sounded hurt.

"I said I didn't sense any danger *within*. With those ears I'd think you'd listen better. Haven't you heard anything I've said about deceptions?"

The roo studied the handle intently. "Looks just like a handle to me."

"Yes, and the chest looked like a simple chest, full of simple junk. Nothing in this place is simple, my big-footed friend." She pointed toward the center of the door. "See? The handle is large and obvious. That little hole in the iron is small and inconspicuous. It has to be a keyhole. Touch the handle without first inserting the proper key and you might find yourself going the way of the chest."

Sranul swallowed. "I understand. But what are we to do?"

"Well, you could still try the handle, but I wouldn't." She pursed her lips and spat toward the door. It wasn't very ladylike, but it was effective.

The saliva struck the handle. The handle looked quite normal, but when her spit struck the black metal, the room was filled with a crisp sizzling sound.

"Suppose you'd grabbed that with both hands?" she asked the roo.

Practor stared at the handle. It looked no hotter than the surrounding metal of the door. "How could you tell? It doesn't even look warm."

"Not to you or to Sranul, perhaps, but thaladar eyes are different from those of human and roo, and Zhis'ta as well. It is hard to describe. To us heat has a color all its own. We can see it, just as you see green or yellow." She nodded at the door. "To me that handle looks red-hot. Just as your cheeks look different when you blush."

He turned away from her. "I don't blush," he growled softly. "Sranul's question still applies. If we can't use the handle and we have no key, how do we get inside? Wrap the handle in something fireproof?'' He searched the room. ''All I see are the shreds of these old banners, and they would burst into flame in an instant.''

''Well, we certainly must try.'' She smiled at the impatient roo. ''We have to do something to assuage poor Sranul's curiosity, or he'll be no good to himself or anyone else until we do. We don't want him thinking of treasure when he should be thinking of saving others.''

''Now just a minute, thaladar . . .'' the roo began, but she put up a hand to forestall his protest.

''Do not trouble yourself, my friend. There is no need for you to apologize for what you are. You are brave and bold and willing, if a bit on the avaricious side.''

Sranul frowned. ''I'm not sure I like the sound of that.''

Hargrod unlimbered his ax. ''What about thiss? The curve of the blade will fit through that handle. I could brace myself on the wall and pry the door open.''

''I fear not, good Hargrod,'' she told him. ''The heat that permeates that handle is not of this world. I am afraid it might melt even the steel of your redoubtable weapon. No, we need something that will not burn. This—'' and she held out the staff that they had taken from the Brollachian's pool.

''That's just wood,'' Sranul protested. ''It'll burn up in a minute.''

Maryld shook her head sadly. ''Have you heard nothing of what I've said? This is not 'just a piece of wood.' I've been saying that ever since we acquired it. Now I will prove it.'' She stepped to the left of the door. ''Hargrod, would you give me a hand, please? Your grip is steadier than mine.''

The Zhis'ta came forward. She handed him the staff. ''Slip it through the slot in the handle,'' she directed him. He did so.

Practor waited for the wood to erupt in flame. It did not. It didn't even smoke. There was a slight odor of charcoal, and that was all.

Maryld let out a sigh of relief. "I thought, but I wasn't certain until now. As for the key we don't have—" She reached into her pouch and produced the tiny stick they had found so long ago, the one that Sranul had almost thrown away but which Maryld had insisted on saving.

"I thought this might be good for something. Have any of you noticed that it fits exactly in that center hole?" She stepped in front of the door and carefully inserted the slim wand into the opening. When it had penetrated nearly all the way, she was rewarded with a sharp *click*.

She moved out of the way and nodded toward Hargrod. "Now. Use the staff, Zhis'ta."

Hargrod strained, putting one foot against the wall to give himself more leverage as he pulled. The wood began to bend and Practor was sure it was going to snap in the Zhis'ta's hands. It did not. Instead, a metallic moan came from the vicinity of the door's hinges, an echo of eons. No knowing how long it had been since that door was last opened.

The sound lent strength to Hargrod's muscles and he pulled again. This time a gap appeared between the thick metal of the door and the wall. It was wide enough for a hand to slip through. Practor sniffed. There was a new smell in the air and it issued from behind the door. A musty smell of air infrequently disturbed.

He moved toward the opening, sniffed cautiously, peered inside. "No light."

Hargrod held onto the staff and pulled again. The gap was now wide enough to step through. "Expect trouble."

Practor nodded and moved back. He searched the room, then selected several broken chair legs. Wrapping them in torn material taken from the ruined banners, he shoved straw stuffing from chair seats between the wooden legs. Then he returned to the door and shoved this makeshift torch against the handle. Wood and straw burst instantly into flame and burned with a satisfying steadiness.

Hargrod and Sranul duplicated his actions. When all was in readiness, Practor held torch in one hand and sword ready in the other as he stepped through the opening. Whatever lay inside, at least they wouldn't be confronting it blindly.

His companions crowded close behind him. "What is it?" Sranul called anxiously to him. "What can you see?"

"Nothing much," Practor told him. But there was a strange lilt to his voice which belied his words. "It's really quite ordinary, if you stop to think about it."

"Stop to think about *what?*" Sranul was about to die of impatience. He forced his way past Hargrod until he was standing alongside Practor.

The vault was awash in flame. But it was a cold flame, a flame different from the kind that had incinerated the old chest. The fire stabbed at the roo's eyes, making them water. Still he refused to turn away from the brightness. The brightness of his torch thrown back at him from millions of pieces of gold. There were familiar goldens as well as tiny coins the size of a fingernail which were alien to both man and roo. Jeweled crowns and bowls set with diamonds splintered the spectrum, while atop a richly inlaid table of silver were six table settings all done in platinum and rubies. In front of each plate was a glass. As they moved nearer, Practor saw that each glass had been cut from a single ruby. They looked like they were filled with crystalized blood.

"Now, isn't that grand?" Sranul murmured. Hargrod and Maryld had joined them.

"Thiss iss not wealth." The Zhis'ta stared dumbly at the hoard. It filled the vault completely, reaching almost to the ceiling where it was stacked against the back wall. "Thiss iss beyond wealth. I do not have a word for it."

"I do." Maryld knelt and picked up a golden flute, studded with tourmalines and topaz. "It's beautiful. There is great art here."

"Art, yes." Sranul handed Hargrod his torch, took a single bound, and landed atop the nearest hill of gold. Grabbing his toes, he tucked his tail underneath his backside and slid down the pile of coins as smoothly as a kid on a snowbank. He tossed coins in the air and watched as they twinkled in the torchlight.

"Think, Zhis'ta," he said to Hargrod without looking over at him, "what your share of this will buy for your family. You want a piece of land for them on the shores of the southern sea? You can *buy* the southern sea. Humans there giving you trouble? Buy the whole country and move them somewhere else."

Practor wanted to join in the celebration but couldn't. Not yet. "We're not on our way home with saddlebags full of gold yet, my friend." Was he unnecessarily concerned? If opening the vault had triggered some kind of demonic alarm, it sure was a quiet one. Sranul toyed with the riches of the ages and still nothing appeared to challenge them.

"Worried?" Maryld had moved to stand close to him. He nodded. "You know what I am thinking, Practor Fime? I'm thinking that this vault may in itself be a distraction. The ultimate distraction. What matters a little treasure to one who plans to conquer the world? Perhaps Dal'brad senses that anyone clever enough to get this deep into Shadowkeep could represent a real danger to him. So he plants his treasure here to buy off a clever intruder's good intentions. How many adventurers, chancing upon this hoard, would fill their packs and return home, leaving the demon king in peace to continue his scheming?"

"There is more to it than that," he muttered. "I've seen

men blinded by gold. It changes more than just their intentions. And a blind man makes a poor fighter.''

"We agree, then?"

"Yes. We have to get away from here, and quickly, before the treasure seduces us. If we succeed in our ultimate aim, we can return to load ourselves down with gems. If not, it will not matter. There will be no rich men in a world ruled by Dal'brad." He raised his voice. "Come on, Sranul. We're leaving. Now. We can come back for this later."

"Later? What do you mean, later?" A dozen necklaces, each different in size and composition and each worth a king's ransom, hung from his neck.

"You know what I mean." He started for the exit. "We have a job to do here in Shadowkeep. We have been assigned a mission. We cannot take the time to think of ourselves until we have accomplished what we came for, until we have addressed the problem of the demon king."

"You want to address him? Send him a letter! Mission? It's your mission. No sneaker through the infinite appeared before me." He leaned back against the gold. "Me, I've accomplished what I came for."

Practor stared at the roo for a long moment, then nodded. "That's right. You're under no obligation to follow me, Sranul. None at all." He switched his attention to the mountain of gold, surprised by the indifference he felt. Norell's precious gold ring would be nothing alongside this; a mere bauble, a trinket. Maybe he was as unmoved as he was because there was too much of it to comprehend.

As a child he'd been fond of fruit ices. Once he'd eaten too much and had lain in bed sick for three days afterward. From that moment on he'd never felt the desire for fruit ice again. Was this the same? Could you overdose on wealth as readily as on food?

Not that it didn't tempt him. It did. But there was more at stake here than mere wealth. Much more. Maryld too recognized the hoard for what it really was: a gigantic bribe. It wasn't hard to turn away from it if you realized that. Besides, to one who'd been poor all his life, so much wealth in one place was almost obscene.

"Come," he said softly to Maryld, "let's be about our business."

"Lead on," she replied, and for the first time he had the feeling that she was speaking to him as an equal. He walked a little taller as he slipped past the vault door.

Sranul, who by now had buried himself in gold and jewels, gazed after them in disbelief. "Crazy. They're both crazy. Hargrod, you'll help me carry the choicest gems back to the inn, won't you? We can come back in after those two later. You remember your dream, the land for your family. What about their future?"

"They will have no future if Dal'brad iss not sstopped." He let out a reptilian sniff. "One can alwayss find wealth if one sseekss it long enough. But there is something more valuable one cannot alwayss find."

"More valuable than this?" Sranul rooted through the pile over his belly and produced an exquisitely inscribed dagger carved from a single deep tangerine sapphire. The handle was inlaid with a profusion of small, flawless diamonds.

"Yess. More valuable than that." The Zhis'ta turned to follow Practor and Maryld back out into the hallway.

"Well, I don't see it," Sranul snapped angrily. "Come on, show it to me!"

"I cannot." Hargrod paused in the doorway, turned back to look at the roo. "It iss a worthy causse." He disappeared.

Sranul was alone in the vault. His torch burned steadily

next to him, its light illuminating the wealth of continents. He was rich, richer than even emperors dream of being.

So why did he feel so uncomfortable? Why the queasy feeling in his stomach? It was all that Practor's fault! Sure, that was it. The human had professed indifference to Sranul's chosen course, but he'd magicked the poor innocent roo on his way out.

Well, he wasn't going to get away with it! He wasn't going to go off and leave Sranul behind feeling sick and guilty for claiming what was rightfully his. Not Sranul he wasn't.

"Wait, wait a minute!" The roo struggled to kick his way free. Gold and brightly hued rings went flying in all directions. "You're not getting away that easy. Wait for me!"

He was clear of the hoard and hopping for the exit when a sudden thought made him turn and rush back to the pile. Hurriedly he stuffed a couple of handfuls of rings into his pack and shoved the sapphire dagger into his belt. Then he raced out to find his friends.

Chapter XI

The empty hall sickened him further, but he soon tracked them down. They had turned a far corner and were walking up a side corridor. Practor didn't turn to look at him.

"Guilt can be a powerful stimulant, Sranul."

"Guilt? What guilt? I don't feel the least bit guilty." The roo groomed his long ears. "Besides, the treasure will be there for the taking once we've defeated the demon king." He looked around and frowned. "What happened to the thaladar?"

"She's up ahead," Practor told him, nodding down the corridor.

A pair of wooden doors gaped at the far end of the hall. Maryld stood in the opening beneath the stone archway. "Hurry," she called to them, "I've found a treasure greater than any we've yet seen."

Sranul's eyes bulged. "More treasure? It can't be. There can't be so much wealth in one world." He increased his stride, bounding on ahead of his companions.

Hargrod's voice was subdued. "I fear our long-legged friend'ss affinity for gold may kill him ssomeday."

"I share your concern. We'll both have to keep a close watch on him."

Their immediate fears were unfounded. Sranul's enthusiasm slumped considerably the moment he entered the room that lay beyond the double doors.

"What is this?" He glanced briefly at Maryld, then scanned the room a second time. "There's no treasure here."

· "It is your perception which is poor, my good roo, and not the contents of this chamber. There is ten times the wealth here than in the vault you just abandoned." She waved a hand at the tall shelves which lined each wall. "I believe we have found Gorwyther's library."

Practor had never seen so many books, not even in Sasubree's highly respected university (where he had once gone with Shone Stelft to repair some water pipes). Not only did the books fill every shelf all the way to the ceiling, there were more stacked on the floor and piled haphazardly on reading tables. Some were so big it would've taken two men to carry them.

Others lay open on reading stands and were marked with strips of fine leather. He and his companions wandered through the room and tried to make sense of so much knowledge. Many of the tomes were printed in obscure script. Practor examined an occasional volume in a familiar language but found the contents no less incomprehensible for all that they appeared in a recognizable alphabet.

Some of the contents he was able to divine from interpreting the accompanying pictures. There were books on metallurgy and books on plants, books on sculpture and books full of pictures of monstrous things that no doubt existed only in the author's imagination. Nightmarish concoctions that, for Practor's peace of mind, he *had* to believe did not exist. There were volumes on war, on architecture, on law and child-rearing, and of course, an endless series on magic. Some were printed on vellum, some on parchment or papyrus. There were inscriptions on thin sheets of metal and stone tablets laboriously chiseled. There were even books whose words came and went before your eyes as you tried to make sense of them.

There were books that contained only pictures and next to them on the same shelves, tomes filled with print too small to have been written by any known hand.

"Treasure beyond compare," Maryld murmured. She was seated behind a heavy wooden table that itself stood on a raised platform. A pile of books sat by her right hand. She was perusing the one that lay open on the table before her.

The light in the room came from two towering brass candlesticks that flanked her. The candles they supported burned steadily without melting. Painted globes served as table legs. Practor did not recognize the lands they depicted.

But Hargrod went immediately to one and turned it slowly until he'd located one particular place. He pointed to it and looked pleased.

"There iss the bay that I have sspoken of, the place where I would buy land for my family."

Practor bent to study the globe. "Where are we now on this thing?"

"I am not ssure. The bay I know only becausse it wass once sshown to me by a Zhiss'ta of much learning." He studied the globe closely and hesitantly put a finger on a dark place far to the north of his dreamland. "SSomewhere up here, I think."

"Gorwyther would know." Practor glanced back up at Maryld. "This must be his place of study."

"It doesn't appear to have been disturbed," she decided. "Dal'brad hasn't had the time to spend in here yet, which means Gorwyther's knowledge is still safe. We're not too late. No doubt with Gorwyther safely out of the way, the demon king feels he has plenty of time in which to drain this library of its knowledge.'' She shut the book before her.

''So much wisdom at our very fingertips, and all of it useless without the wizard to interpret it for us.'' She sighed, then dropped to the floor and began scanning the parquet tiles.

''What are you looking for?'' Sranul asked her.

''A journal or diary of some kind. Not a record of experiments or work. Something personal written in Gorwyther's own hand. The sort of notepad he might have kept close at hand. If there was such a thing, he might have had a chance to jot down a warning or plea for any who might come looking for him.''

''Something that might be of use in freeing him, I see,'' said the roo excitedly. He and his friends immediately fanned out around the table and joined in the hunt.

''What would this diary or whatever look like?'' Practor asked her.

''I don't think it would be very bulky. It would be something he could carry with him everywhere. Not larger than pocket-sized, surely.'' She bent to check under a seat cushion. ''The spine might not be imprinted, or there might be nothing more than a date.''

''Wouldn't the wizard keep something that personal in a place of concealment?''

''He might not have had the chance to hide it before he was taken. The very fact that he's imprisoned suggests that the demon king surprised him. He might have had only a moment or two in which to make a note and quickly slip the book out of sight of his attackers. If he placed it somewhere in hopes of possible rescuers finding it, it should be somewhere obvious.''

Hargrod lifted a massive tome on crustaceans, withdrew a small brown tome leaved in gold from beneath. ''Might thiss be it?''

The others crowded around as he handed it to Maryld. She opened it and her face lit up with excitement. "His daily diary, yes! Written in his own hand." While she turned the pages and read, Practor found himself glancing uneasily around the library. They had penetrated farther into Shadowkeep than anyone except demons, helped along by a fortuitous mix of skill and luck. Their skills remained sharp, but their luck couldn't last forever.

Maryld turned another page and her expression fell. She flipped through the rest quickly, without enthusiam.

"What's wrong?" Sranul asked.

"Blank. The rest of the pages are blank." She held the book up to the light and flipped the empty pages backward. "Or are they? We've found similarly 'empty' volumes. Maybe they're full of insightful inscriptions that Gorwyther has disguised." She lowered the book and concentrated on one blank page for a long while, finally gave up and rubbed at her eyes.

"It's no use. I see only blank paper."

"Let me see." She handed it to Practor. As she did so, something fell from between the front pages. He knelt and picked it up.

"What iss it?" Hargrod asked.

"Looks like a very thin piece of glass."

"It's just the bookmark," said the discouraged Maryld.

Practor studied it and frowned, wondering to himself. Why would anyone, least of all a wizard of Gorwyther's stature, use a bookmark in a small daily diary? "A magnifying lens," he suggested.

"We don't know that Gorwyther had poor eyesight," Maryld argued, "but it could be." She shrugged. "Keep it. It may prove useful later."

"For what?" Sranul wondered. "Reading blank paper?" Practor shoved it into a pocket.

"No, my long-eared complainer. It belonged to the

wizard. Who knows what it might do in his presence, or if we pass near to him? It might be nothing more than what it appears to be, or it might be a key. Perhaps Gorwyther left no message for Dal'brad's minions to find and erase. Perhaps he left only that.''

''That's what bothers me about this place,'' the roo groused. ''Too many perhapses.''

''Let uss ssearch a while longer,'' Hargrod suggested. ''We may yet find ssomething usseful.''

They made a thorough search of the library but encountered nothing else of promise. Finally they reassembled in the middle of the room.

''Now what?'' Sranul demanded to know.

There were two doors opening into the library. One they had entered through. The other barred the far end of the room. Practor shrugged, nodded toward the closed portal.

''We know what's behind us. I'd rather head on. Maybe it opens into the same hallway, but we might as well find out. A step back the way we've come is a step into the arms of any pursuers.''

They left the candesticks burning behind them. Practor put a hand on the door at the far end of the library and pushed. It opened easily at his touch.

Beyond lay a much smaller room, as empty as the library was full. There were no bookshelves, no tables, nothing at all except naked stone and at the far end of the chamber, a single statue of grotesque appearance.

''Our firsst demon,'' Hargrod observed, ''and it cannot harm uss. A good omen.''

''You and your omens.'' Sranul hopped toward it, the others following.

The statue was no taller than the roo. Its clawed hands were extended, palms upward, as if in supplication. Behind the statue was a large, curved mirror.

"Dead end," said the roo brusquely. "Seems we go back out through the library after all."

"Not necessarily." Maryld made a circuit of the statue, which was carved of some smooth, polished stone, inspecting it minutely. When she'd completed this study, she turned her attention to the mirror behind it. Her eyes shifted continually back and forth from mirror to statue.

"Let us consider, my friends. This room seemingly has no use. It is too barren to be a place of worship, and there is nothing stored here except this statue and mirror. Yet no one constructs a room to no purpose. The door from the library appears to be the only way in or out."

"The last room we saw that was this empty," Sranul said uneasily, "held the Brollachian." He found himself looking for vents or outlets in the ceiling. It was solid rock, but he still couldn't relax.

"It musst be a private temple of ssome kind." Hargrod approached the statue. "An asscetic might usse ssuch a bare place for meditation. He would not want such disstractionss as decorationss might provide." He indicated the upturned palms of the graven image. "Ssee, it iss ass if thesse wait for ssome kind of offering."

"How do you explain the mirror?" Sranul asked him.

"Designed to reflect the gaze of the ssupplicant back at himsself, sso that he may conssider hiss own unworthiness in the pressence of whatever god or deity thiss sstatue repressents."

"We didn't come here to pray to the demon king's gods," said Practor decisively. "We'll have to go back out through the library and find another way."

Maryld stood there shaking her head as her male companions turned to depart. "Forgetful. So forgetful."

"Of what?" asked Sranul challengingly.

"Of deceptions. Have you forgotten so quickly? The false vault below, the containers which held everything but

211

treasure? Did you not hear what I said a moment ago? No one constructs a room for no purpose. Hargrod, your guess was good, but, I believe, wrong. This is not a private temple, though it is carefully designed to look like one. Previous attempts have been made to distract us with something. Here the idea is to distract with nothing.''

"It's succeeded in that," said Sranul. "If there's more than nothing here, then where is it?"

She turned. "I don't know—yet. But it must have something to do with this statue, or mirror, or both."

"Souse-weed," the roo muttered, hopping forward. "This mirror, for example, is intended to do just what Hargrod said it was intended to do. It's just an ordinary mirror. See?" He put his hand on the smooth surface.

It went right through.

Sranul let out a yelp and jerked his hand back, was immensely relieved when he saw he still possessed this usual number of fingers.

"There iss much to be ssaid for the cautiouss, analytical approach," observed Hargrod sagely, "but directness hass itss virtues ass well."

"You okay?" Practor asked him, stepping forward to examine the roo's hand.

Sranul nodded. "It tingles a little, but that's all."

"Could you feel anything on the other side?" Maryld asked him.

"No. The air was cooler, I think."

Practor reached forward and felt nothing as his hand passed through the solid glass. He bent his hand back toward himself. "Stone wall on the other side, just like here. It's another gate, like the wall of colors and the wall of blackness. Another doorway."

"Sure, but a doorway to where?" Sranul mumbled.

"Does it matter? It leads onward, and that's where we want to go."

"I'd prefer a more precisely defined destination," the roo objected.

"You went without quesstion through a wall of changing colorss," Hargrod reminded him. "Why hessitate at the thought of doing likewisse through a mirror?"

"I went through a wall of colors because the father of all trolls and his unlovely helpers were chasing me," the roo said. "No one's chasing me now."

"You are still not thinking, my good roo," Maryld told him. "There is no need to set up such an elaborate deception unless you have something to hide. You do not make traps difficult to find, you make them obvious and appealing. You don't conceal them in mirrors. You hide them in things like sword cases."

Sranul let the remembrance pass. "All right, I'll go through—but only if Practor goes first."

"Don't I always?" Practor murmured. There was no hint of sarcasm in his voice. It would've been inappropriate. He was, after all, the leader. Maryld might be more knowledgeable, Hargrod might be stronger, Sranul quicker, but they all deferred to him when it came time to make an irreversible move. "It's decided, then. We go through the mirror."

He considered the reflective surface. It was plenty big enough to admit him. If it *would* admit him. The passage of a hand was no guarantee of anything. There were no guarantees in Shadowkeep.

Suppose it turned solid when he was halfway through? Became a real mirror hanging on a real wall? Would half of him fall through to the other side and his back half tumble at the feet of his stunned friends?

As usual, there was only one way of finding out. He took a deep breath and stepped through.

For an instant he seemed to slow and it was as if he were walking through gelatin. Then there was air around him again. Turning, he saw a mirror hanging innocently on a wall. He tried to reach through it, struck unyielding glass.

He'd been half right. His passage *had* turned the wall solid again, but only after he'd gone through. Now he was cut off from his companions, perhaps forever.

Then a hand came through, a small hand, feminine and petite. He grasped it and the fingers curled tightly in his as he helped Maryld through.

"That wasn't so bad," she said. "An unpleasant, greasy sensation, but not an intolerable one."

More hands and a long snout appeared as Sranul followed close on the thaladar's heels. Hargrod brought up the rear.

"We can't go back," Practor informed them. To demonstrate, he rapped his knuckles on the now solid glass. "The gate is one-way."

"Maybe," Sranul murmured nervously, "it's designed not to keep others out, but to keep something in."

They turned and began to inspect the room the mirror had deposited them in. The walls made a sharp turn to the right. Beyond lay brighter light.

Practor led them around the bend. "Something back here," he told them.

Something indeed. The corridor opened onto a large, domed chamber. In its center was a carved stone platform and atop the platform an enormous crystal globe of milky white. The light in the room came from within the crystal itself.

There was nothing else in the chamber. Not a stick of furniture, not a bas-relief on the wall: nothing. Maryld bent to examine the inscriptions that had been chiseled into the stone platform. They were unlike any she had ever seen.

Sranul circled the platform warily, checking the other

walls. "No mirrors. No walls of light or blackness to step through. This really is a dead end this time."

Hargrod was using the handle of his ax to tap the rockwork. "Not necessarily, my friend. We have become sso ussed to looking for magical wayss of entering and leaving placess that we might eassily overlook something ass ssimple as a concealed door."

"Let's not be in such a rush to leave. There may be something here of value to us." Suddenly he leaned forward, until his face was almost pressing against the crystal. "I'll be damned. There's someone inside!"

His friends hurried to join him in probing the crystal's depths.

"Sure is." Sranul reached out and touched it. The surface was slick and unexpectedly warm.

"What do you think, Maryld? Is it Gorwyther?"

She stared silently at the softly glowing globe. "I can't tell. It's hard to see very deep. It *could* be. I wish I could have read some of that book we found."

Sranul had his face pressed sideways against the crystal. "It doesn't look much like a wizard to me."

"How would you know what a wizard lookss like, long-nosse?" Hargrod taunted him.

"I've been around. I'm an educated person," Sranul shot back. "And I say that's no wizard in there." He looked again, out of his other eye. "It doesn't look like a demon, either."

"I do not conssider you an expert on either."

"None of us is," Practor put in. He turned his attention back to the crystal. "Whoever or whatever it is, someone's gone to a lot of trouble to make sure it can't move freely about."

"It can't be a demon," Maryld said. "Dal'brad can control his underlings, and as a punishment it's far too elaborate. Rebellious minions can be restrained without

215

having to go to the trouble of imprisoning them in crystal.'' She ran her fingernails along the perfect curve of the sphere. ''You only go to this much trouble to hamper the movements of an enemy, not an ally.''

''Then it *could* be Gorwyther,'' Practor said.

She nodded. ''It could. Or it could be someone else.''

Hargrod hefted his massive ax. ''Let uss find out.''

''No, Hargrod.'' She stepped between him and the sphere. ''Not that way. Your ax will not penetrate. Even if you could cut the crystal away piece by piece it would take too long.'' She glanced significantly toward the mirror. ''We may not have much time left.''

''Very well. Where magic iss concerned I defer to you.'' The Zhis'ta shouldered his ax and stepped back. ''How will you free the trapped one?''

She turned to regard the sphere. ''I don't know. But there must be a way. No prison is invulnerable. I wish I knew what magic to use.''

''There was the wand-key,'' Sranul pointed out, ''but it's still stuck in the vault door.''

''And we still have the staff that Hargrod retrieved from the Brollachian's pool,'' she said. Hargrod had removed it from the vault handle when they'd departed. Now she extended both hands and he passed it over to her.

She assumed a strong stance in front of the crystal. ''Move clear. I don't know what's going to happen when I try this.''

Practor took a step toward her. ''Let me. I'm quicker than you and can take a heavier blow. Besides, if something goes dangerously wrong, you'll be able to puzzle it out better than I will.''

She hesitated for a long moment, their eyes locked. Then she nodded reluctantly and handed the staff over.

''Never let anyone say that you lacked courage, Practor Fime.''

He shrugged it off. "Just being sensible. If this . . . doesn't work out, then you must go on with Sranul and Hargrod. Promise me that."

She nodded once again. Then the three of them retreated to take cover behind the turn in the corridor.

Practor hefted the staff, holding it firmly in both hands. He could hear the thaladar muttering strange words behind him. He raised the staff over his head and brought it down sharply. It made a ringing sound when it struck the crystal.

Nothing happened. He hit it a second time. His wrists tingled from the shock of the impact, but the crystal did not react. Turning, he gazed helplessly back at his companions. They started to rejoin him.

As they did so, the glow from the sphere began to intensify. They ran for cover again and Practor went with them. He held the staff out in front of him as if it might afford them some protection.

The glow increased until they had to shield their eyes to look toward the platform. The ringing echo of Practor's blow grew louder and louder, repeating itself down the corridors of time.

Practor had to shout to make himself heard above the noise. "If that's some kind of alarm we're going to have visitors soon!"

"It may not be," Maryld yelled back at him. "Be on guard but don't panic."

As they stared, the light gradually began to fade from the crystal. It retreated back into the substance of the sphere, leaving ghost-spots dancing before their eyes.

There was a sharp crash. Practor and the others instinctively jerked back behind the protection of the corridor wall as the sphere shattered, sending crystal shards flying in all directions. Then there was silence.

Practor peeked around the bend, frowned. He started

back toward the platform, accompanied by his equally speechless companions.

Standing and swaying slightly in the middle of the stone stage was a little old man, stooped forward at the shoulders. A few days' growth of beard formed a dirty stubble on his chin and cheeks. His white hair was cut short, in a manner new to Practor. His clothing consisted of long brown pants and a green shirt beneath a leather vest, and simple leather sandals. He was rubbing circulation back into his upper arms as he watched them approach. He was considerably heavier but no taller than Maryld.

"Free," he muttered, "free at last. And it's about time, too." He eyed each of them in turn. "What kept you?"

Practor found himself apologizing without knowing why. "For one thing, we didn't know we were coming."

The little man leaned forward and squinted at them. "Say, you're not the Knights of the Legion of the Sacramental League, are you?"

"Uh, no," Practor admitted readily.

"Hmph. Have to have a word with that bunch. Well, free is free, I suppose."

"Are you . . . ?" Sranul started to ask. The man cut him off curtly.

"Yeah, I'm Gorwyther." He stepped down off the platform, demonstrating a spryness that belied his age. "Frozen in crystal, hah?" He was nodding to himself. "I'll give this much to old Dal'brad—he don't take no chances." Ignoring his openmouthed rescuers, he dropped to all fours and began scrabbling among the crystal fragments that littered the floor.

Several minutes passed. Practor exchanged a glance with Maryld, then moved forward. "You *are* Gorwyther, the great wizard? The one who raised up Shadowkeep?"

"Yes, yes. Please don't bother me, young man." He

continued pawing through the rubble like a dog searching for a favorite bone.

"Well, you don't look much like a wizard to me," Sranul snorted. "I said it when you were stuck inside the crystal and I say it now that you're out."

The little old man perked up at that, stared straight at the roo. "Oh, I don't, eh? And how do you expect a wizard to look, long-ears?"

Sranul was momentarily taken aback but recovered quickly. "Well, you ought to be wearing a hat. Yes, a tall hat inscribed with mystic symbols. And you should be, uh, taller, and, uh, more impressive-looking."

" 'Uh,' you don't say. Typical rooish observations. As if height had anything to do with power or size anything to do with achievement. As for my attire, I'm sorry I didn't have time to change into something more impressive before I was imprisoned, but I just hadn't planned on being locked in crystal for a few hundred years. If I'd known, I would've dressed for the occasion. Of course, my sarcasm is wasted here. Unless I guess wrong and your brains are as big as your feet."

"Now, hold on a minute." Sranul took a single belligerent hop forward.

The man ignored him. He was crawling around the base of the stone pedestal now. "Hold on a minute? Hold on a minute? My long-tailed friend, I've been holding on for a damn sight longer than that, and I can't be bothered with silliness now." He glanced up at the roo, then over at Practor, Hargrod, and Maryld. Bushy white eyebrows drew together and he seemed to see them for the first time.

"Say, you are a funny-looking collection, aren't you?"

Sranul muttered under his breath. "He thinks *we're* funny-looking."

"A human, a thaladar, a roo, and a Zhis'ta. What brought the four of you together?"

"Circumstance and necessity," Practor told him.

Hargrod put a hand on his friend's shoulder. "It was thiss man who did it, wizard. It wass he who insstigated thiss journey and motivated uss and hass kept uss together desspite dissagreement and argument."

"You don't say? Well, well, the world is ever full of surprises." With that, he turned away from them again and resumed his search as though he'd never spoken to them.

Practor let more minutes pass before finally moving close. "What are you looking for, sir? If you could give us a moment of your time, we were kind of hoping you might tell us how to defeat the demon king. Then maybe we could help you look for whatever it is that you're looking for."

"Ah, Dal'brad." Gorwyther sat back on his haunches. "That lying, deceiving, meretricious, smelly imp! Tricked me, he did, or I wouldn't have been stuck fuming to myself in that blasted sphere for the last couple of hundred years. Well, it was my own fault." He looked up at Practor. "Take some advice, young man. Never turn your back on a smiling demon."

"You're free now," Practor reminded him. "Why not help us and take your revenge on Dal'brad at the same time?"

"Yes, and then we can be on our way," Sranul added. The memory of the overflowing vault they had left behind was still strong in the roo's mind.

"Oh, I couldn't do that." The wizard returned to his search. "I can't do anything to Dal'brad now. See, I'm dead."

Practor blinked. "Dead? Pardon me, sir, but you look very much alive."

"Appearances can be deceiving. Oh, it's not a bad echo, I suppose. I'm only alive on another plane of existence." The "echo" picked up another piece of broken crystal, studied it a moment before tossing it disgustedly over a shoulder. "Very much alive there. How else do you think I've managed to retain consciousness these past years, trapped in that crystal with nothing to eat or drink, much less anything to breathe? I am 'here,' yes, but only for a little while. I'm retaining myself on this plane by sheer force of will, you know. Really be much easier on me when I let go. Better to be alive on another plane than dead on this one."

"But what about the demon king! Something's got to be done about him before he can break out of Shadowkeep and wreak havoc on the rest of the world."

Gorwyther sat back and sighed. "Yes, I suppose so. Shouldn't have demon kings running amuck, destroying worlds at their whim and all that, should we? People would begin to talk. But I'm afraid I can't do anything about it now. I'm dead, remember? No, you'll have to handle that yourselves, my friends."

Practor swallowed. "That's what we came here to do, but we were hoping you might be able to help us. We did free you, you know."

"Yes, and I am trying to find something that will aid you. I just can't assist you in person, is all. What do you think I'm doing down here on my hands and knees, anyway?"

"I already asked you that, sir."

"Hmph. So you did. I'm looking for a special piece of crystal. It's the key to reconstituting a certain gem. A special gem. I thought I had the piece with me, but I seem to have lost it."

Maryld sounded suddenly interested. "Had it with you? What does it look like?"

"Like a piece of crystal, young thaladar. Why do you think I'm having so much difficulty finding it?" He gestured at the floor, which was coated with crystalline fragments. "It could take weeks to find it, and I don't have weeks."

From his pocket Practor pulled the small shard that had fallen from the little book. "Could this be it, sir?"

Gorwyther stood and took it, turned it over in his fingers. His hands did not shake as he examined it closely. For the first time he broke out in a wide grin.

"You are very observant, young man. How much training have you had in matters arcane?"

"None, sir. It fell out of a book in your library."

"Ah. So you were just lucky, then. A fortunate fool."

"Fortunate he is, but he's no fool," snapped Maryld, moving close. "He has an instinctive feel for what is right. He knows just when to proceed cautiously and when to plunge boldly on ahead."

"And when to pick up and open the right book, eh?" Gorwyther chuckled, leered at Maryld. "A fine compliment from one so pretty." He glanced up at the silent Practor. "All right then, perhaps not a fool, but not a scholar either. Something in between. Yes, that is best. A fool would end up as amusement for Dal'brad, whereas a scholar would not know when to commit himself. Maybe you do possess the right combination of ingredients to get you and your friends out of Shadowkeep alive. Now be kind enough to give me some room. New magic can sometimes burn the unwary."

Practor and his friends stepped out of the way. Gorwyther held up the fragment of crystal and fluttered the fingers of his right hand above it, all the while muttering to himself. As the incantation speeded up, a faint, eerie red light appeared. It emanated not from the piece of crystal but from the wizard's eyes, and suddenly even Sranul had to admit that the old man now looked very much more like the great wizard of legend.

The room began to tremble, the floor to shake ever so

222

slightly underfoot. Now the transparent shard Gorwyther clutched between thumb and forefinger also began to glow. Practor found he had to look away from that pulsing radiance. It didn't seem to affect the wizard. He concluded his incantation on a rising note, waved his hand three times over the crystal. The light went away.

"You can look now."

They rejoined him, admired the extraordinarily transparent jewel that rested on his palm. Only the facets indicated there was anything in his hand at all. It was round and big as a plum, with the most peculiar compensating internal index of refraction, for no matter at what angle you looked through it, there was no distortion of whatever lay beyond.

"I've never seen anything like it," Practor said reverently. "It's beautiful. What do you call it?"

"The key to Dal'brad's destruction—in the hands of one who will use it effectively." He extended his arm. "Take it, young man."

Gingerly, Practor took the gemstone. It twitched once in his hand and he almost dropped it. There was an aliveness to it, a suggestion that something besides mere mineral rested in his palm. He was sure he could feel it moving, a tight little bundle of crystalline agitation waiting for something to happen. The stone was anxious, expectant. It was ready for him to do something with it. But what?

"I can't help you anymore," Gowyther declared. "You must find the demon king. Find him and destroy him. The evil that inhabits these halls can be annihilated with one decisive blow. You have the means to strike that blow. You must cleanse Shadowkeep. Cleanse it of the disease that stains it and threatens to spread to the world beyond these walls. I know you are capable of doing this. In any case, you have come too far to turn back."

"We've no intention of turning back," Practor told him quietly.

"Spoken like a true hero." Gorwyther clapped him affectionately on the back. "You have fortitude, young man, and sound companions to help you."

Maryld moved to stand close to Practor. "We won't fail. I have no fear for the future."

"If you can survive the rest of this day, then you may have a future. That's more than you can say for me, on this plane, at least."

"Look." Hargrod stared in awe. "He iss beginning to dissappear."

"Not disappear." Gorwyther looked down at his fading self with interest. "Just leave this plane of existence. I told you it was hard to maintain my presence here once I was dead."

"How is being dead?" Maryld was unable to restrain her curiosity.

"Not too bad. The only real drawback is that there's no future in it. Don't worry about me. I'm looking forward to a long and full existence in the elsewhere." He took a last long look around and waxed nostalgic. "You know, I am going to miss this place, though. Quite a pile of rubble, ain't it? Even with sorcerous powers and magical forces to do the dirty work, it took quite a while to build." He grimaced.

"And now that rotten relic from the underworld, Dal'brad, is about to inherit all of it."

"Not if we can help it," Practor assured him.

"That's the spirit, young man!" By now even his voice was growing faint.

"There's just one problem." Practor tried to hurry his words lest the wizard vanish forever before the question could be asked. "How do we find the demon king before he finds us?"

"Yes, it would help if you could surprise him, wouldn't

224

it? Might even be your only chance.'' The wispy wizard beckoned Maryld closer.

She put an ear close to his thinning lips. They seemed to linger a little longer than the rest of his disintegrating face. She listened intently. Practor strained to overhear but could not make sense of the weak whispering.

Finally Maryld pulled away and nodded solemnly to the wizard's shade.

"You understand how this is to be done?"

"I do."

"You understand also that once you commit yourselves you will not be able to retreat or turn back? Once you have presented your challenge it will be you or Dal'brad who prevails, good or evil?"

"We understand that,'' she told him softly. "We've known it ever since we entered Shadowkeep.''

"Good." All that was left of the great Gorwyther were a pair of disembodied lips drifting in the air before them. "I wish you all the good luck in existence and elsewhere. You're going to need it." A pause, then, "The other elsewhere draws me and I must leave you now. I wish you could see it. It's a beautiful dimension—though I'm told they have trouble with the plumbing from time to time.

"Farewell and good-bye to you all, and most especially to you, young Practor Fime. You've already exceeded your fondest expectations for yourself. Press on but a little farther and you may gain the world." With those final words of encouragement, the lips of Gorwyther vanished.

The four adventurers were alone in the domed chamber.

Chapter XII

Hargrod leaned back, balancing himself on his thick tail. "That ssounded pretty final to me."

"Not as final as it was for him," Sranul pointed out. "For a dead wizard he sure was talkative."

"Fortunately for us." Practor gazed down at the thoughtful Maryld. "What instructions did he give you?"

"There is a way. A way to approach and confront Dal'brad before he can prepare." She was looking around the room. "A way that only the one who designed and built Shadowkeep would know of." She looked up at him. "You heard what he said. Once we enter the presence of the demon king there can be no retreat, no escape. We must defeat him, and defeat him quickly before he has a chance to marshal all his forces, or we will be lost."

Practor put a hand in his pocket and felt the gently quivering jewel that lay within. "The gem that Gorwyther gave me: what's it supposed to do?"

"He didn't tell me that. We can only hope that it will do enough."

Hargrod unlimbered his battle-ax, held it in front of him. "I am ready, and I will place my trusst in thiss, ass I alwayss have. It hass not let me down yet. Incantations and mysstic meanderingss I leave to you two. But if they fail, perhapss a straightforward attack will ssucceed.''

Maryld nodded, then knelt and began searching the floor.

"What are you looking for now?" Practor asked her.

"A few choice splinters of the wizard's crystal. Ah, here's one the right size." She slipped the fragment into her pouch. "And here's another."

"Can I help?"

"No, that's all right." She chose several more fragments, then straightened. "I have enough."

"Something to help us defeat the demon prince?" Sranul asked her.

"Not exactly, my good roo. These are to help us find and surprise him and then, should we succeed, to escape the attentions of his servants." She studied the floor. "Perhaps just one more. For luck."

Practor watched as she picked at the pieces of the wizard's shattered sphere, but try as he might, he could see no difference between the fragments she saved and those she tossed aside. Of course, Gorwyther had instructed her, not him.

His hand strayed to the hilt of his sword. That and a small gemstone didn't seem like enough to challenge a demon king with, but it was all he had. Hargrod might be right. In the coming fight their weapons might prove as useful as their wits. He was prepared to do battle with both.

"Are we ready, then?" Maryld nodded. So did Hargrod, while Sranul waved a spear wildly about more to inspire himself than any of his companions.

"Since I can't convince any of you to return to the vault with me, which would be the sensible thing to do," the roo said, "I guess we might as well get it over with. Let's see if this king of pests is all he's cracked up to be. I'll bet he isn't so tough!''

Practor glanced at Maryld. "Which way?"

She led them to the back of the room. Hidden in a tiny niche in the wall was a waist-high stone pillar. They hadn't noticed it before because it looked exactly like the stone-work that enclosed it. There was a neat depression in the bowl-shaped top and a small silver wheel concealed near the back.

"Hey, I've seen that before," Sranul murmured.

"One like it," Maryld corrected him. "In another room far behind us."

Hargrod eyed the tiny wheel dubiously. "That doess not look big enough to open a section of wall."

Maryld only smiled at him. "You should know by now, my good Zhis'ta, that the world is full of strange gateways, and that size and effect are not always proportional." She reached out with both arms. "We must join hands."

Sranul was the last one to step forward, completing the semicircle of friends surrounding the pillar. "It's not even carnival time," he muttered.

"Be ready," she warned them. "Gorwyther warned me, as he warned us all, that once we are committed there will be no time for second thoughts. Any who wish to back out can still do so. Hargrod?"

The Zhis'ta smiled. "I have been waiting for thiss for ssome time."

Her gaze traveled to the next in line. "Sranul?"

He shrugged. "I suppose we have to take care of this Dal'brad before I'll be allowed to enjoy my share of the treasure in peace."

She did not have to put the question to Practor. "Very well, then." Reaching into her pouch, she withdrew one of the broken pieces of crystal she'd gathered, murmured some strange words, and set it neatly in the center of the depression atop the pillar.

The fragment began to hiss and to glow a deep blue. An intense blue cloud began to coalesce around them. It reminded Practor of something previously encountered, but he was too tense and preoccupied to remember what. Then Maryld spun the small silver wheel once, twice, thrice. The room began to spin. Practor half stumbled, worked to steady himself. He felt like a child rolling wildly down a grassy slope. Sranul's hand almost pulled free of his own, but he tightened his grip, steadying the unseen roo.

Eventually the rolling and spinning ceased. The blue cloud evaporated. They were standing together in a room, but it was not the room where the wizard had been imprisoned. For one thing it was far larger. Enormous, cavernous, awesome: these were the descriptive terms that flooded Practor's mind as he gazed about.

The ceiling was so far overhead he was sure clouds could form beneath it. For the first time since they'd entered Shadowkeep, he saw windows, but they were fashioned of black glass and each was taller than the tallest buildings in Sasubree. The walls were curved, indicating they were in some kind of tower, but a tower constructed on an inhuman scale.

The far wall was dominated by a mountainous carving of some hideous otherworldly monstrosity. The sculpture towered above the floor. It squatted on six hind legs separated by a bloated stone belly. A hand rested on each of the six knees. The distorted face was full of tusks and fangs. There were no eyes: only six slits that rose in a line from the flaring nostrils toward the forehead.

Resting at the base of this obscene idol was a throne fashioned of black enamel set with dark garnets the size of skulls. Lounging on the throne was a bipedal figure eight feet tall.

It had the general shape and proportions of a man, but the penetrating reptilian stare of a Zhis'ta. At their appearance it seemed to come alive, leaning forward and trying unsuccessfully to conceal its surprise.

"Oh well, now where did you come from?"

"Come on." Practor led his companions toward the throne.

As they approached, large, rat-shapes began to emerge from behind it. These loathsome apparitions were armed with a disturbing, ragged assortment of weapons. They hopped and squirmed off to left and right, forming a line in front of their master.

Practor halted a few feet in front of the first creature and eyed the thing on the throne. "Are you Dal'brad?" He was surprised at how calm he sounded, now that the ultimate moment had arrived. He might as well have been talking to a street vendor back in Sasubree. But Sasubree was very far away now.

The giant stayed slumped on the throne, rapping long fingers on one enameled arm. "I'm certainly not your Uncle Tavehl. I wouldn't think my identity would be in doubt—whereas yours is a matter of some minor interest." He smiled and they had a brief glimpse of teeth filed to sharp points. "Who are you trespassers?"

"I am Practor Fime, of Sasubree. These are my friends." He introduced each of his companions in turn. "And if there are trespassers in Shadowkeep, we both know who they are."

"How did you get in here?" the giant asked, ignoring Practor's not-so-subtle accusation, "and how did you get into this tower? Outsiders are not allowed into the tower."

"That's funny," said Sranul. "*You're* here."

"It doesn't matter." A hand waved indifferently in their

direction. "You will be departing soon, and quietly. Very quietly. This discussion is at an end."

Practor took a belligerent step forward. "Someone's going out quietly, all right, but it isn't us. This isn't your fortress. Shadowkeep wasn't built by you and you don't belong in it. We've come to make sure you don't take anything else that doesn't belong to you."

"Really? Tell me, voluble man, who does it belong to?"

"The wizard Gorwyther."

The nasty smile returned. "Gorwyther is dead. Dead and entombed forever. His interest in Shadowkeep is of no consequence to anyone anymore."

Practor was about to reply when Maryld stepped forward and put a quieting hand on his arm. "You must go from this place," she told the giant. "We know what you plan and we will not allow it to happen."

"You don't say? *You* won't allow it to happen?"

"No," said Hargrod quietly, "we will not."

Unholy eyes shifted to the speaker, narrowing as they did so. "What's this? A Zhis'ta interested in something besides his family? And one who can put together a sentence of more than two words. Novelty piled upon novelty!" He shifted his position on the throne. "Yet I regret that I have no more time to continue this amusement. I have much to do. Great plans are about to come to fruition. My reach is about to extend beyond Shadowkeep."

Practor drew his sword. "Your reach stops here."

The giant sighed. "So much confidence born of such small success, though I suppose you can congratulate yourselves on having come this far. A hollow victory." He slumped back in the throne, looking bored. "This conversation grows stale." A hand waved at them, casual and curt. "Take them."

A small army of servants now surrounded the intruders.

At the signal they threw themselves forward, howling and barking, mewling and whining.

"Form a triangle!" Hargrod snapped.

The three warriors arranged themselves elbow to elbow, with the vulnerable Maryld in the center of the triangle. Besides protecting her, there were two guarding a third's back at all times.

They were heavily outnumbered, but Sranul could leap over the highest swing to bring a spear down with tremendous force. Practor put to use everything he'd ever learned about combat at the hands of Shone Stelft, while Hargrod cleared the floor in front of him with great horizontal swings of his double-bladed ax.

The demons yelled and howled ferociously, but they were unable to penetrate their prey's defense. Their origin might have been unnatural, but they died just as messily and easily as any natural creatures.

The giant observed all this from his throne. Both his humor and indifference began to leave him as he saw his servants cut down in droves.

"Enough of this play," he finally growled. He drew a large scimitar from a sheath attached to the underside of the throne and rushed to the attack.

Sranul saw the first sweeping blow coming toward his head and jumped to avoid the blade. He brought his spear down with the intention of driving it through the demon king's skull.

The point passed completely through its intended target as though the roo had struck at smoke.

Laughing, the giant stabbed with his sword. Sranul looked surprised as the point caught him beneath the sternum and emerged from the middle of his back. Practor cried a warning, but much too late. Most of the lesser demons had been cut down and he tried to go to the roo's aid as the giant pulled his blade clear.

Sranul looked down at the blood that was pouring out of the hole in his chest and said to no one in particular, "And all I ever wanted was a little treasure." Then, very slowly, he dropped to his knees.

With an incoherent scream, Practor charged the demon king. His target stood and smiled at him through pointed teeth. Practor feinted high, cut low, and was astonished to see his blade pass completely through the giant's thighs.

The scimitar sliced down at him and he barely managed to parry it. The force of the blow knocked Practor to the ground. Immediately the giant raised the huge weapon for a killing blow, but this too was parried as another figure stepped between the curved blade and its intended victim.

After blocking the blow cleanly, Hargrod moved in close, slicing repeatedly at the giant's legs. Three such swings struck nothing but smoke, but did force the demon king to turn his attention to the irritatingly persistent Zhis'ta and away from Practor. Only Hargrod's prodigious strength enabled him to defend himself against the attack. The sound of scimitar against ax echoed thunderously through the tower.

Maryld helped Practor to his feet. He spared a sorrowful glance for the form lying motionless nearby. "Poor Sranul."

"Come on," she urged him, "we have to help Hargrod."

"Maryld, wait!" He ran after her. She had drawn her ladylike rapier and was stabbing repeatedly at the back of the giant's legs. Her thrusts had no more effect than Hargrod's ax.

The demon king took notice of her, however. She barely dove beneath a backhand swing. Then Practor was at her side, adding his own futile strokes to those of Hargrod's. A scimitar stroke came his way again and he blocked it without being knocked down this time, but the shock of the contact numbed his wrists. Another such blow and either his sword or his wrist would break.

Maryld was at Hargrod's side, whispering to him. The Zhis'ta hesitated, uncertain, then gritted his teeth and threw the battle-ax. It passed directly through the demon king's head. The giant frowned for a moment, then turned away from Practor and back toward his reptilian opponent. The ax struck the base of the statue and clattered to the floor.

"Foolish snake-legs," the giant growled. "Did you think letting loose of your weapon would make it more effective? Haven't you learned by now that you cannot touch me? It is time to end this charade. I have no more time to spend on such diversions, however amusing." The scimitar went up and Practor could see that the demon king intended to decapitate Hargrod with one blow.

Except that Hargrod wasn't retreating, he was moving in to the attack with something he'd drawn from across his back. Something familiar. Practor immediately recognized the staff they'd taken from the Brollachian's pool. It had helped to open the vault door, had been used to shatter Gorwyther's prison, and now they would see once and for all just what kind of power it contained.

Hargrod slammed it into the giant's chest. It passed halfway through the insubstantial form of the demon king and stopped as though striking something solid. A look of utter bafflement came over the giant's face. The scimitar fell to the floor as he grabbed at his heart. Hargrod released his grip on the staff and stepped back, but the wood remained locked in the middle of its target. The demon king stood staring off into space, trembling violently.

A voice shocked Practor back to the present. Maryld was screaming at him. "Now, Practor, now!" He covered the distance between himself and the giant in two bounds and struck, his sword penetrating deeply into the undefended back. Not the blow a hero might strike, perhaps, but there was much more at stake here than outmoded concepts of chivalry in battle.

He could feel the resistance as the sword bit deep, and not into smoke this time. The demon king spun around, wrenching the sword from Practor's fingers and sending him flying. As the giant stumbled toward him, reaching for his tormentor with one hand while grabbing futilely for the sword stuck in his back with the other, Practor scrambled out of the way. With each step, the demon king moved a little more slowly, had to fight a little harder to retain his balance. Real blood was spilling from the huge body. It hissed where it struck the floor.

"How?" the giant moaned. "How?"

It swung at him but he was able to dodge easily. Arm followed hand and body followed arm as the demon king collapsed and sprawled motionless on the floor in front of Practor. He stared at it, moved close and kicked at the head. It did not react.

Hargrod and Maryld came over to join him in staring at the corpse. The Zhis'ta indicated the sword which still protruded from the center of the giant's back. "Good ssteel." The demon king's left hand was still twisted up behind his back, reaching even in death for the sword that had pierced his spine.

"I forged it myself," Practor murmured. "I never thought I would use it for anything besides practice."

Maryld shuddered and sat down suddenly. Practor bent over her. "You all right?"

She nodded. "Just exhaustion." She sounded puzzled. "I didn't think it would be this easy, this simple."

Practor nodded toward the nearby body of Sranul. "Don't try to tell him this was easy."

Something let out a deep, ponderous groan. The tower trembled and a wind sprang up that seemed to come from nowhere.

"It's not going to be that easy," said a voice like distant thunder. They turned toward it.

Creaks and groans, heavy rafters squeaking, the sound of stone in motion.

"Wisdom protect us," Maryld whispered.

The statue was moving. Slowly, ponderously, the great head arched forward and down. Rock crumbled to powder as the body pulled away from the back wall of the tower. The facial slits parted to permit a dozen glowing green eyes to glare down at the minuscule creatures frozen on the floor below.

"But—the demon king is dead," Practor stammered aloud.

"Yes, that thing is dead," said the creature, which by itself weighed more than all the people and buildings of Sasubree, "but *I* am alive! I, Dal'brad, king of the demons. That thing was the demon prince. An underling. A slave. *I* am king here! *I* rule in Shadowkeep—as I will soon rule everywhere." The clawed fingers of half a dozen hands began to twitch expectantly.

"I am angry, very angry, awesomely angry." The voice boomed through the hollow tower, reverberated from the walls. It was the voice of death itself. "I was pleased to maintain my anonymity, my silence, and now you have forced me to move. I despise movement. It is a crutch for the unthinking. I use others to move for me, like that insect." He pointed with a gnarled hand the size of a house toward the corpse of the servant Practor had slain.

"You will die now," it told them, "but you will die honorably. Only those of great resourcefulness can force me to life. I will honor you with the most exquisite torments I can devise. You will perish slowly, painfully, yet always aware of what is happening. I will make certain of it. I owe it to you."

Large enough to admit a six-horse team, the vast cavern

of a mouth dipped toward them. Three hands reached down. They had been toyed with, played with, but now the game was over. Death was close, and very real.

Practor thought only of the gem which Gorwyther had pressed into his palm prior to vanishing. It seemed so tiny, so feeble a thing to throw against this incarnation of evil, and yet it was all they had left.

He reached into his pocket and brought it out, feeling it quiver against his palm. There was no time to think how best to use it, no time to ask Maryld's advice. He flung it into that gaping mouth.

A hand was upon him, ready to crush him to jelly. The fingers did not contract. The gem went down Dal'brad's throat and the monster's attention shifted for just an instant to what it had swallowed.

The explosion blew Practor head over heels, sent him skidding across the stone floor. Bubbles of light filled the tower, rising toward the distant ceiling. He rolled over several times before coming to a stop. His right shoulder throbbed painfully.

And still the volcano of light gushed ceilingward from the far side of the room. There was a roaring in his head as if he were standing next to a waterfall in spring flood. The bubbles grew more infrequent and the light began to fade.

When he could see and hear again he pushed himself up on his elbows. The light-geyser became smaller and weaker, imploding back on itself. Then it was gone entirely. Silence reigned once again within the tower.

Dal'brad was gone.

The corpses of his servants remained, as did the body of the demon prince. Practor's sword, a small link with the real world, was still imbedded in the giant's back.

He felt fingers on his shoulders, rubbing reassuringly. Looking up and back he saw that it was Maryld. Her face was bruised but nothing was broken.

"I'm okay—I think." He ventured a hesitant smile and she responded as he climbed painfully to his feet.

"Hargrod?"

She nodded. "Over there." Practor turned and saw that the Zhis'ta was kneeling next to the body of the unlucky roo.

"Gone," Practor muttered. "It's gone. We did it." The far wall of the tower where the statue that had been Dal'brad had once stood had been burned black.

"Gorwyther gave you the *cithque,* the demon gem," Maryld told him. "I could sense its power, but I had no idea . . ."

"Neither did Dal'brad," he said grimly. He winced, felt as though he'd just swum two leagues of rapids. Everything worked, though. He was skinned and scraped and bruised, but unbroken.

They walked slowly over to join Hargrod. "It's done," Maryld assured the Zhis'ta, "over with. Finished." She looked around the empty tower. "Can't you feel it? Even the air has lightened in this place. Shadowkeep is cleansed." She gazed up at Practor. "The evil that was here is dead. You slew it. You did the right thing at just the right moment, just as I told Gorwyther you would."

As always he had no idea how to respond to a compliment. "I didn't know what else to do, so I threw it. If I'd had anything else in my pocket I probably would've thrown it, too."

She was nodding sagely. "Gorwyther knew that's what you'd do. He knew you'd react instinctively. So he didn't try to confuse you with instructions."

"If only we had known ssoner." Hargrod lifted the roo's head gently. "Ssranul died insstantly. No one could ssurvive a blow like that, not even mysself."

"We'll take him back," Practor muttered. "Back to his clan so that he can be properly remembered and honored."

He could feel the tears starting at the corners of his eyes. Sranul had been loud and boastful and argumentative, but always ready to help and, when it came down to it, utterly fearless. He was going to miss the roo a great deal.

Hargrod saw his distress and added, "I too am ssaddened."

Maryld held off joining in the terse chorus of despair. She was thinking. "There may yet be a way. May yet, may yet."

"What are you talking about, female?" said Hargrod. "He iss dead. One doessn't have to be a sscholar to ssee that."

"I know he's dead," she admitted, "but so was Gorwyther. Yet he talked to us and helped us."

"Gorwyther was a great wizard." Hargrod glanced down at his dead friend. "Sranul wass only a roo."

Her gaze shifted from Zhis'ta to man. "Both of you forget where we are. This is Shadowkeep, the fortress of wonders. Both of its masters, good and evil, have fled from here, but the wonders remain."

Practor stared at her. "What are you getting at, Maryld?"

"Maybe nothing. Maybe foolishness. But we owe it to Sranul and to ourselves to find out. Bring him." She turned and started across the floor. Man and Zhis'ta exchanged a glance. Then the reptile shrugged and easily hoisted the body onto his shoulders. Together they followed the thaladar across the pile of demon corpses.

A familiar object awaited them in a distant corner. To anyone else it would have looked like a broken section of wall, but Practor recognized the central depression and soon located the silver wheel.

"Gorwyther told me how to make use of these," she explained. "If only we'd known when we'd first entered Shadowkeep."

"What good doess it do Ssranul?" Hargrod asked her.

"Of itself, nothing. Do not condemn my efforts until I

have failed, good Zhis'ta. Come and join hands around the pillar, as we did before.''

They did as she requested, watched as she placed another fragment of broken crystal in the central hollow and spun the wheel. Once more Practor felt himself spinning helplessly, swaying as though the ground beneath him had given way. Once more the firm grasp of his friend's hands assured him he wasn't being whirled off into oblivion.

The tower was gone. They were in a torchlit corridor. Practor staggered a moment, then recognized their surroundings. "We've been here before."

"I remember it alsso." Hargrod readjusted the weight on his shoulders.

They had returned to the hall of silver bas-reliefs. Saintly faces and flowers shone all around them.

"What do we here?" Hargrod asked her.

"Remember that I told you these were representations of Sildra, patroness of the Brothers of Aid. The Brothers are a very ancient and powerful order, not completely understood." She started down the corridor. "We must find a certain one."

They followed, wondering what the thaladar had in mind, until she halted before a particularly fine sculpture. It was almost a full figure instead of the more common portrait.

"Now we must make a proper offering. Something that would appeal to Sildra herself." She searched the floor until she found a silver flower that had been callously jarred loose from its location, perhaps by passing trolls. This she placed in the cupped hands of the patroness.

"Now what?" Practor wondered why he was whispering.

"Now—we will see," she told him, taking a step back.

As they stared, the cupped hands of the statue began to glow. It was not a cold, distant light this time. They could feel the gentle warmth emanating from the bright metal.

The voice that sounded in their minds was equally warming. "You have done well. Your offering pleases me. May I in turn please you?"

The pleasant soothing sensation faded from Practor's thoughts just as the silver lost its glow. He blinked, turned to Maryld.

"That's it? That's all?"

"I don't know." She was chewing her lower lip. "Maybe the books were wrong. Perhaps I didn't study the right passages." She slumped. "It was worth trying, anyway."

"What was worth trying?" said a new voice. "Hey, what's going on here? Put me down, you great scaly assassin!"

A startled Hargrod dropped Sranul. The roo struck the floor hard, bounced once, and rolled into a standing position. He rubbed his forehead. "What's the big idea?" He looked around. "This isn't the tower where we were fighting. What happened, anyway? Did I miss something?"

Practor tried not to laugh. It wasn't hard. He was too tired. "Not much. Just the fight to the death with Dal'brad himself. We won, by the way."

"Dal'brad? You mean the oversized human-looking thing with the funny eyes and the badly tailored suit?"

"No, that was just the demon prince. He was supposed to kill us. We were never supposed to see Dal'brad himself."

"Do you remember the statue behind the throne?" Maryld asked him. "*That* was the real Dal'brad. That was what we had to deal with after you were killed."

Sranul eyed her uncertainly. "You had to fight that stone mountain?" She nodded. "And I missed it? I missed it because . . ." he hesitated, "I was killed? I was—dead?"

"Very dead, my friend." Hargrod gave him a hearty clap on the back. "Run through by the demon prince'ss ssword. You hipped when you sshould have hopped."

"Now that you mention it . . ." Sranul rubbed his chest and gazed down at himself. "I do have this uncomfortable memory. It was like fighting an evil cloud."

Maryld nodded again. "Hargrod paralyzed reality with the staff, and Practor slew him. Then he finished Dal'brad himself with the demon gem which Gorwyther had given to him."

"The gem," Sranul murmured, "I remember that. But nothing else. And if I was dead . . ."

She indicated the silent statue before them. "Sildra brought you back. The evil of Shadowkeep has gone, but its wonders remain. Though we should still beware of trolls and Brollachians and their ilk. They still haunt these halls."

"For some reason they don't worry me much anymore." Practor was grinning at her. He looked both ways, then nodded to his left. "If I remember right, this will be the way out."

Maryld put a hand on his arm. "Wait. Isn't there something you're forgetting, my good Practor?"

"Forgetting?" He frowned at her. "What could I be forgetting? We've done what we came to do. The Spinner should be pleased, wherever he is. I don't think there's anything left undone."

"Just one thing, perhaps."

She led them into a room and over to the by-now familiar pillar with its tiny wheel. For the third time she placed a bit of carefully selected crystal in its center. Disorientation, spinning, and then he was reminded of what they'd left unfinished.

Rysancy, he thought. Rysancy, you're going to be a queen. I'm going to buy you a kingdom. Hargrod will have his bay and Sranul a lifetime of fun. Maryld will build her school for children of all the races.

The transport pillar had returned them to another familiar part of Shadowkeep, another room where they'd been before. In the flush of victory over Dal'brad he'd forgotten all about it. Now they could enjoy it and no one could stop them.

How had he managed to forget the treasure, the wealth of the eons? It seemed impossible for anyone to do so, but that was the kind of person Practor Fime was.

He'd had his mind set on more important things.